Seidman

and Son

by

ELICK MOLL

SEIDMAN AND SON is a heartwarming novel of manners and character—a story told by a dress manufacturer who has a factory and wholesale business on Seventh Avenue and a lively interest in all human situations.

The charm of this novel is in its telling, in Mr. Seidman's colorful and forceful idiom, his irrepressible love of life, his good-naturedly sharp tongue, his warm and expansive heart.

Not long after Morris Seidman introduces himself and his way of life, his son, Harold, returns from Korea with plans of his own that are strange and disturbing to his father. Harold has a great need to reform the world and remain independent of his family. While Seidman is having trouble with his son, his partner and lifelong friend develops an unseemly interest in a pretty model. Then Seidman himself encourages gossip by taking an interest in the problems of his designer, Miss Youssem.

(continued on back flap)

Seidman and Son

ELICK MOLL

Seidman and Son

G. P. Putnam's Sons   New York

Library of Congress Catalog Card Number: 58-8062

PRINTED IN THE UNITED STATES OF AMERICA BY
KINGSPORT PRESS, INC., KINGSPORT, TENNESSEE

Reality has many forms, and I would not presume to tell any reader of this tale that it is fiction. One man's fantasy is another man's back yard. If anyone thinks he recognizes himself in these pages, I would remind him that all men are brothers. I should be happy to think that anything I wrote helped, even a mite, to reaffirm that truth.

E. M.

Seidman and Son

one

Excuse me. You don't mind if I share this bench with you for a couple minutes? Got to rest a little from this dog. You wonder sometimes how could such a small creature hold so much energy. So much emotion. *Sit down already, Sam. Sit. Give me a chance to catch my breath at least.*

You're sure we don't disturb you? I mean some people are getting nervous from dogs. My sister Bessie only got to look at him, she starts sneezing. Yes, he's a nice little feller, very friendly, so long as you're not a milkman. I'm sorry you're not seeing him at his best, he made himself these bald spots from scratching. I had him to the doctor this morning, he put on some medicine, it's such a hideous color, like a couple black eyes in the wrong place. *All right, Sam, don't get insulted. On you it looks good.*

9

Excuse me, I didn't make the introductions. My name is Morris Seidman, I'm in the dress business, wholesale, I got a factory on Seventh Avenue. This is Sam, short for Samson, fox hunter, retired. Only every time I take him for a walk here in Central Park you would think he's back in business. The name? Well, it's a long story but I could make it short. A St. Bernard he's not, like you see. But when he was a puppy you could hide him in your pocket and there would be room for your gloves besides. Only put him down, he would stand so fine, proud, with the chest out, like a little gladiator. So the first time my boy Harold saw him he says, "Hello, Samson." And that was the name.

Thank you, I'm not much for cigarettes. Could I offer you a cigar. No, I'm not going in to the shop today. For one day my business could run itself. What is your line, may I ask? You run a little adjective factory? You mean you're a writer? Is that so? I'm very honored to make your acquaintance. No, seriously, I got a big respect for writers. To me it's a wonderful thing, talent. Listen, I'll ask you something, if you wouldn't laugh. It's often in my mind to ask a writer. From where does it come, the idea for a story, or a book?

Well, I suppose it's a foolish question. But actually—somebody should start out with nothing, an empty page, and pretty soon there's a story, people living through things, experiencing—well, it's kind of a magic, no? I mean, creating. Like you would be, in a small way, God. You said it, this is a big responsibility. These days especially. It's lucky when it's only pages, not a world. Pages you could throw away, and start over.

Excuse me. *Sam, you got to stop scratching yourself. You'll make yourself a disaster there. Stop it now. You want Harold should come back, see you like this?* So what kind of writing do you do? Books? Stories mostly? Movies too? My goodness, you're a celebrity altogether. Never mind, if Shakespeare was alive today he would maybe write for the movies too.

Tell me, you live in Beverly Hills, I suppose. It's beautiful there, the climate, everything. You're here for a visit? Yes, I could understand. Got to take a vacation sometimes, even from sunshine. Believe me, you came to the right place. Where could you find four seasons all in one day—not counting slack?

Look how he's chewing himself to pieces there. Just look. Isn't it terrible? I don't know what to do any more. The doctor put a collar on him for a while but I had to take it off, I couldn't stand it. We tried everything already, shots, vitamins, salve. Doesn't help. I'll tell you the truth, I'm getting worried. Another time, if something would happen, I would maybe take it philosophical. But now I got a special responsibility. You know, belongs to my boy, the dog, and before he went away he said to me, "Pop, I want you to see nothing happens to Sam while I'm gone." And if I got to tell him now the dog got sick and, I don't know, we maybe got to put him away or what—

No, I didn't burn myself. You'll excuse me, I'm a little upset myself. Breaks your heart, you know, to see a creature like this, depends on you for everything and you can't do anything for it. I got, anyway, a little bit of a guilty feeling toward the little feller. You see, in the beginning, I got to confess I was against the whole idea, to have a dog in the house. I figured, a city apartment, who needs it, it could only be a nuisance, with the training, the feeding, the pills, hair on everything, running up and down six times a day and it's not even fair to the animal, it's got no place to move around, cooped up the whole day. Now we got a house, in Great Neck, with a yard, it's a different story, but in those days we were living on the 14th floor, in the Majestic Towers, it's right there, you could see, 72nd Street. My boy Harold practically grew up together with the dog here in Central Park. I got in the neighborhood a vet, on 84th Street, the dog is used to him and vice versa, I don't like to change now, you understand, he is anyway so nervous, the least little thing he starts chewing himself, like the devil would be grabbing his behind there. So I bring him in from Great Neck. The automobile ride, some peculiar reason, he likes. Relaxes a little. And lately the doctor is giving him a bad time with the medicine, it stings, so I give him a little reward. I take him for a stroll in the Park. Well you should see. From two blocks away he's already shaking himself to pieces with excitement. Who knows what he remembers, in his little dog's head? Expeditions. Safaris. Fox hunts with Harold, in those rocks there.

Why did I change my mind? You mean to get the dog? This is kind of a long story. You got time? Me, I got plenty of time. Mrs. Seidman is visiting this afternoon, my daughter Jenny is at her club. If I go back to the house there's only the television. And I'll tell you the truth, lately I haven't got the patience to sit and watch.

Well, you want to hear, I got to go back a few years. I

don't know if you remember six, seven years ago, there was starting up a whole business with psychology. I mean, maybe it started before, but in our neighborhood, our friends, got to be an epidemic about that time. Lectures, courses, child psychologists, aptitude tests, Rohrschach tests, people were running to the analyst, it was a whole commotion. You would go in the evening visiting, no more bridge, canasta, music, politics, only big discussions about who's having analysis, who is ambivalent about whom, what is the latest theory, you should let the children suck their thumbs or not. It's still going on, you know, plenty, and I'm not saying anything against it. Only, seems to me people are going to extremes. But anyway, those days, if you wanted to be in the swim you had to learn a whole new language, transference, repression, inhibition, libido, you should excuse the expression—I'm telling you it was a regular circus. So my wife Sophie, God bless her, she doesn't want to be left in the lurch, she starts going to lectures and *shlepping* home books and pretty soon we got an expert on psychology in the house.

One morning, breakfast, after the children are going away to school, she says to me, "Morris, did you notice how shiny Harold looked this morning? His hair? His shoes? Do you know he's wearing a stocking cap on his head now when he goes to sleep?"

Did I notice! You think there's something about my Harold I never noticed? How he is sleeping, stocking or no stocking, with his hand under his chin, like a baby, how he's got to have always the cover tucked in real tight, how he is making with his mouth when he reads a book—

believe me, I got it all in my mind, word by word, from when he was a minute old.

"And he's polishing his shoes every day," Sophie says, "and there's phone calls coming in from girls I never even heard of them. I'm afraid, Morris," she says, "we got on our hands an adolescent boy."

"What do you mean you're afraid," I said. "What do you want to have on your hands, an adolescent man? Or a middle-aged boy?"

"Never mind," she says, "it's a problem. We've got to think about it. I think we should get him a dog," she says.

Well, you know, it's not such a bad idea, for a growing boy a dog, but I'll tell you the truth, I got such an earful of the psychology business, everything is a big problem, I'm getting a little irritated. It's like I would be some kind of an ignoramus, I don't know anything about raising a son. Common sense isn't good enough.

"A dog?" I say. "Where does it stand written an adolescent boy needs a dog? Why not a horse? Or a cow?"

"Because," she says, "in the first place a horse or a cow will not fit in the apartment."

"Sure," I say. "On account of *I* take up too much room." It's a little silly, I admit, but I made up my mind, this argument she's not going to win.

"Morris," she says, "don't be stubborn. A boy Harold's age, it's not good his head should be filled up with nonsense, girls and Vaseline on the hair. With a dog he can care for it and run with it after school and be occupied."

"I'll tell you," I say, "I got a better idea. I picked out for him a bicycle for his birthday. English model. He can care for it and run with it and be occupied. And I won't have to pay every six months for new rugs and new furniture from a dog."

Well, this is just the beginning. We are meeting, about this time, a certain Dr. Thalberg, a dentist. A D.D.S. Now I don't want you should misunderstand me. I got the greatest respect for the professions, I was always hoping myself Harold would study to be a doctor. But this Thalberg—well, I better not talk about him, I'll only raise my blood pressure. The main thing, he is such a fancy feller, with social connections, Union League Club and I don't know what, that if he's got a dog it's got to be a special kind, nobody else in the country has got one like it.

So one evening we are invited to his home—I suppose a dentist, he figures people like Sophie and me, it's sooner or later with the dentures, anyway we're getting to meet Rudolph. You know who Rudolph is? A wire-haired dachshund. Did you ever hear of such a dog?

Well, maybe. Me, I never heard of it before. And I'll tell you the truth, to me this is an animal for which there is absolutely no reason. A plain dachshund is already bad enough, its stomach drags on the ground and the whole mechanism walks like a duck, but this one has got besides gray hair and a beard and when you come into the house it lays down on its back on the rug with its feet in the air, you should only scratch its stomach. Would you tolerate such a thing from your own child even? But it's doing, besides, tricks. And the big celebration is when Thalberg says to the dog, "Rudy, go in the bedroom and bring me out my slippers." So Rudy goes in the bedroom and comes dragging out half of a pajama and my Sophie practically loses her mind, the dog is so cute.

15

"Morris," she says, "I don't care what, we've got to have a dog like Rudy. I never saw anything so darling in my whole life."

Darling. To me this is not such a valuable asset in a dog. I like better that a dog should have about himself a little dignity. But can you say this to a woman? With them, if something is *darling*, a dress or a hat or a dog or a dentist, it's the greatest thing in the world.

"David knows where we can get a puppy from the same family," she says to me the next day.

"Who's David, all of a sudden?" I ask her.

"Dr. Thalberg," she says. "They're only three hundred dollars."

"Three hundred dollars," I holler. "Are you crazy? It would be cheaper to build a machine to bring you half a pajama from the bedroom."

But my Sophie, God bless her, when she makes up her mind to a thing, sarcasm is like spitting in a tornado. So she tells me now a story, how in the movies she saw somebody, Jimmy Cagney, Robert Taylor, I don't remember, anyway he was a gangster. So why is such a good-looking feller growing up to be a gangster. You know why? In the picture it was because he was an orphan and he didn't have a dog when he was growing up. So this is now a crisis for our family. If we don't get a dog for Harold, just like Rudy, then Harold will become, I don't know, maybe a gangster too.

Can you imagine? My Harold a gangster? If he saw you drop a cent from a Rolls-Royce automobile he would run five miles after you to give it back. Well, I don't want you to think my wife is a dope. She's an intelligent woman.

Only when it comes to dogs and dentists people are sometimes losing their judgment altogether. I know.

Starts up now a campaign between my Sophie and Thalberg. Harold has got to have his teeth cleaned and, naturally, he goes to Dr. Thalberg and he is introduced to Rudy. Well, you can imagine. A boy, thirteen years old. Pretty soon he is dropping in after school to play a little with Rudy, take him for a walk, give him a bath, teach him new tricks. You know how it is with a boy and a dog and my Harold is anyway the kind of a kid who would carry around a beetle in his pocket to keep it warm. Such a gentle heart you never saw in a boy. And don't think he is a sissy, neither. Let anybody start up something—well, I'm talking too much about Harold. I want to tell you about this little creature, Sam. You sure you got time? Maybe you got something else to do?

All right, so I was telling you about this Thalberg, how he's making with Sophie a business, like a regular conspiracy, Harold should fall in love with Rudy. This is, you know, a foregone conclusion. This boy would fall in love with a mouse if it came three times in a row in the house. So it's finished, homework, library, games, everything. Only Rudy. Rudy can sit up and beg. Rudy can count up to four. Rudy is from a royal family of dogs, Thalberg told him, he's got the papers to prove it, the king of Italy owned the grandfather and Ribbentrop owned the grandmother. Can you imagine? If I was a dog and somebody gave me such a recommendation I would hang myself.

But that's how it goes. Once upon a time in our house, in the evening, you could hear sometimes a word of cul-

ture, literature, a child was practising the piano sometimes. Now it's a business with blue ribbons and wirehairs
and smoothhairs and schnauzers and cockers, you should
excuse me, and pretty soon I'm up to here with it already,
I can't stand it any more.

"Listen," I say, "I got enough already. What is this, a
house or a kennel? Look at you," I say to Harold, "you're
even beginning to *look* like Rudy. I don't want any more
dog talk in this house. Finished."

You think it's finished? Maybe you're a family man too,
you know how it is. . . . But this is only the beginning.
Harold is getting upset, nervous, he can't do his homework, he's getting bad marks in school.

"Look what you're doing to the boy," my wife says.

"I'm doing?" I say. "Harold was an average boy, like
other boys. All he wanted was a new bicycle for his birthday. Now all of a sudden he's an adolescent, with problems, the only thing that will help him is a dog for three
hundred dollars. You and your psychology," I say.

Well, it's no use. You heard already the saying, a prophet
is without honor in his own country. This is me, Seidman,
Apt. 5C Majestic Towers. A couple days later, Thalberg
calls me up on the phone, he wants to have lunch with me.
All right. I meet him at Manny's Pastrami Heaven and right
away he starts.

"Seidman," he says, "you ought to be ashamed of yourself."

"All right, I'm ashamed of myself," I say. "You want
appetizer or soup?"

"That's a wonderful boy you've got," he says. "What's
three hundred dollars?"

"Well, I'll tell you. Since you are asking," I say. "I got a bill from you for two hundred and seventy-five dollars for inlays, acrylics, I don't know what. Three hundred dollars is twenty-five dollars more."

"I'm surprised at you," he says. "A man in your position, measuring money against a fine boy like Harold."

"Listen," I say, "why are you so busy selling me my own son? I know he's a fine boy. I spent thirteen years bringing him up and all of a sudden you're adopting him."

"All right," he says. "*I'll* get him the dog."

"Over my dead body," I yell out, so the waiter runs over to see is anything the matter with the soup. But it's making me a little excited, you know, the nerve of this dentist, a perfect stranger, first he makes my boy crazy with his wire-haired dachshund, then he's going to do me a big favor and buy him a dog. You think it's the three hundred dollars? I would spend ten times three hundred dollars to give my boy a little happiness. It's the principle. I don't like a man should be pushed around in his own house. Psychology, shmology, a head of a house is entitled to a little respect, people don't have to go running to their dentist to tell them what to do.

But I see finally it's no use. I got no alternative. So I come home and I give in. All right, I say, get the dog. You think maybe now I'm a hero in the house? On the contrary. I'm still a monster—only a little reformed. Right away Harold's got to call up Thalberg to tell him, like they won against me. Thalberg is the hero, not me. That's how my Sophie is fixing me up with a situation, God bless her.

But I don't care. It's true, I'm a little hurt, but the main thing, Harold is in seventh heaven, jumping around, he's going to own a wire-haired dachshund, one of maybe twenty in the whole country. I don't even care if Thalberg is blowing himself up like a frog, he's a big man, he'll call up the kennel, make all the arrangements, pick out the dog, everything. All I got to do is just sign the check and be a monster.

So I'm a monster but Harold is happy. Except now steps into the story, like in a regular story in a book, Fate. Maybe you would think what does Fate want to bother with such a local situation. But I'm telling you something, lately I got the feeling Fate doesn't look on your business card to see if you're living in a palace or a flat, if it says Prince of Wales or just plain Seidman.

What's happening, this kennel, it's some kind of a penthouse for dogs, I guess, and you can't go right away to pick out a member of royalty, you've got to make an appointment. There's altogether three puppies. These dogs, you understand, are so fancy, they're not even born in bunches like regular dogs. One at a time, like an antelope or something. So finally, finally, there's an appointment made for Saturday, Harold should come and the dogs will look him over.

Well, like I said, on Friday night comes along Fate, or somebody, with a match, the whole place burns down to the ground, pedigrees and all. A very tragic thing. It shouldn't happen to a dog, believe me.

So now I really got a situation on my hands. And all of a sudden, Thalberg isn't there. Before, to make a mishmash, he was Johnny on the spot. Now I got to call him three times before I can talk to him on the phone.

"Listen," I say to him, "you know what happened. The boy is heartbroken. You got to do something."

"Don't worry," he says. "Tell Harold not to worry. Leave everything to me. I'll get him a dog."

A week goes by, Harold is so worked up he don't eat, he don't sleep and he's got such a look on his face I can't sleep from it neither. I ring up Thalberg again. "How about it," I say. "In two weeks it's Harold's birthday. You got to get him a dog. I don't care what it costs."

"Leave it to me," he says. "I'm working on it right now. I'll get him a dog, don't worry."

Again a few days. Nothing. I call up Thalberg. It's a business with messages, his nurse, the exchange, he's consulting, he's operating, I don't know what. Finally he's on the phone.

"Mr. Seidman," he says, "I'm very fond of your boy. But I'm a busy man. I've got a practice to attend to."

"Why didn't you attend to it in the first place?" I ask him. "Who asked you to mix in in my family? I was going to get the boy a bicycle, he was happy——"

"What would you like me to do," he says, "manufacture him a dog?"

I'm holding myself in. What I would like him to do, he would have to be an acrobat. "I would like you should get him a dog," I say. "A wire-haired dachshund. A grandson of the king of Italy. This was your idea in the first place, no?"

"Look, Seidman," he says, "in the first place I didn't set fire to that litter. In the second place——"

"In the second place," I'm shouting now, "the trouble is that somebody didn't set fire to you in the first place. I don't want my boy to grieve, he should get sick. You hear me?"

"Don't get excited," he says. "I told you, I'm working on it. Relax. Leave it to me."

So it's another two days. Nothing. Again I call up Thalberg. His nurse is on the wire. Dr. Thalberg is out of town. He went to Florida for a month. For a rest. I'm telling you. If I could have got my hands on him just then, he would have had a rest, permanent.

So what should I do? I know as much about dogs as you know about Greek. Excuse me, maybe you know something about Greek. But anyway, one thing I know. In my business, when I want something I don't run around like a chicken with my head cut off. I put an ad in the paper, let them come to me. So I write up an advertisement in the Sunday *Times* and they're starting to come to me. Such letters I never got in my life. From the Society for Prevention of Cruelty to Animals, would I like to make a donation. From the Ellen Speyer Home for Old Dogs, would I like to become a member. From people they want to sell me dog biscuits, cocker spaniels, harnesses, veterinary service, everything in the world—but from wire-haired dachshunds not a single, solitary word. Seems like just because I want a wire-haired dachshund there isn't one for sale in the whole country.

Well, I'm getting a little desperate. I don't want to have on my hands a boy with a nervous breakdown. So finally, on a Saturday, I take him out for a walk and I talk to him, like a man.

"Harold," I say, "I know with young people nowadays it's a theory that if you want a foolish answer, you only got to ask your father a question. What I want to say to you is only one thing. Supposing some day you are falling in love with a girl, a beauty, the most wonderful girl in the world, she looks just like a wire-haired dachshund. Something happens. She moves away. Or she likes somebody else better. So what are you going to do in such a case? Kill yourself? You got to have a sense of proportion in life. You're getting to be a young man. There's other dogs in the world. Let's go take a look at least. Maybe you'll find one you'll like just as good."

Well, my Harold, when he's not got standing over him a fancy dentist to make him crazy, is really a fine, sensible boy, so he says, "All right, Pop, let's go take a look," and he smiles and then he gives such a sigh from the bottom of his shoes I would like to take an X-ray machine and hit Thalberg in the head with it.

Anyway, to make a long story short. Starts now a business with pet shops and kennels and more pet shops, you wouldn't believe it. How many. Westchester, Long Island, New Jersey, Brooklyn, it's swimming already in front of my eyes, black dogs, brown dogs, red dogs, spaniels, Scotties, setters, and such a racket going on all the time, I got a permanent headache from it. But it's no use. Harold's got in his head this fixed idea of a wire-haired dachshund and he can't see anything else.

So I get a call now from my sister Bessie, in Flushing. She is the Helpful Hannah in our family. She talks to Sophie and she's got a solution to the whole problem. What is it? Her neighbor, Mrs. Feldman, has a cat, it just had kittens, she doesn't want to keep them, so we can have them, all six.

23

"Thank you very much," I say. "A boy wants a dog, you want to give him instead six kittens?"

"Why not?" she says. "A pet is a pet. You don't have to spoil this boy with fancy dogs, Morris, for three hundred dollars. Just because you are making now a little money."

"Bessie," I say, "don't start up now with how much money I'm making. This has got nothing to do with the case. I promised the boy a dog——"

"So he'll have a cat. My Sidney never had anything but a cat and it didn't stop him from growing up."

No. Didn't stop him from being a dope neither. But I wouldn't tell her this.

"All right, Bessie," I say. "I'll talk it over with the boy. I'll let you know."

Well, I wouldn't even say anything to Harold, naturally. I got nothing against cats but there's cat people and dog people, and if it was up to me I would never have a cat in the house. Selfish, inconsiderate animals, they only give you an inferiority complex. Anyway, I should have known, if my sister Bessie comes up with a solution to a problem, it will fit like a girdle on an elephant. So I'm at the end of my wits already, I'm ready to give up, go to a sanatorium myself or something, steps in again Fate. One day we are passing a pet shop, right in our own neighborhood, we passed it a hundred times, we never went in, looked so poor, you know. So I say, "Harold, let's try here, we got already flat feet, what can we lose?" We go in, and it's the same story. Cages with bulldogs, with poodles, with Scotties, jumping and yelling and, you should excuse the expression, not smelling so wonderful, and Harold is

24

standing, looking, with his sad face, it hurts me just to look at him.

Well, I'm ready to turn around and go out when again, like I said, Fate. In a cage, in back, like they would be hiding it, are standing four puppies, fox terriers, the lowest kind of a dog, I mean from a money point of view. They haven't got pedigrees, most of the pet shops wouldn't even handle this type of dog. So three of the puppies are jumping around, barking, making themselves crazy like all the rest. But in back of the cage is a fourth one, a little number, standing by himself, with one ear up and the other falling down and honest to God, it looks just like he would be saying, "You want to make fools of yourselves, go ahead. Me, I got more important things to think about."

I'm starting in to laugh, looking at him, it's so funny, he's such a little feller, and I call over Harold he should take a look. So he looks and at first it's nothing, like always, he's still looking for a small Rudy. You know, like in the opera, *Tristan?* Like he would have drunk a love potion. But all of a sudden, a miracle. I see a smile is coming on his face and he goes closer to the cage. I quick call over the man from the shop.

"What are you calling these dogs?" I say. "They got a name, or they're just dogs?"

"They're mostly fox terrier," he says. "They're not pedigreed."

"Who cares, pedigreed," I say. "What am I buying, a piece of jewelry? We got to live with the animal, that's the important thing."

"Sure, sure," he says. "I agree with you. But you were

25

talking about wire-haired dachshunds, I thought you were interested in a more expensive breed."

So he opens the cage and he takes out one of the dogs and holds him out to Harold. "Not that one," I tell him. "The one in back."

He gives me a look. "That's the runt of the litter," he says.

"No insults," I say. "I'm not so tall myself. Just introduce us."

So he takes out the little feller and puts him on the floor and he stands there looking up, not excited, not jumping, so much dignity, I'm telling you, I don't know what to say. And Harold, I see how he don't want to give in but he can't help himself. He kneels down and he picks up the little number and holds him in his two hands, big as a minute.

"Hello, Samson," he says and I know it's no more a problem about a dog in our family.

Excuse me. Every time I'm thinking about the little feller—ach, I'm getting to be an old fool. Well, you know, there's things in this life you can't explain so easy. Feelings. To me, when I'm reading in a book about horses or dogs, you know some people are writing about them like they would be better than people, but I say such a writer is not thinking very good. Sure, I'm getting disgusted with people myself sometimes, they got a beautiful world and look what they are doing with it. More bathrooms, more plastics, more inventions, and more they are killing each other. So what am I going to do, retire from the human race? Go live with horses and dogs? You think they're not selfish and cruel too? Try sometimes, with a bone. I'm not this much of an animal lover, I'm willing to say it's a mistake, the whole evolution. You know, there's people they talk like this, a tiger is a beautiful thing, doesn't know from civilization, animals are not spoiled, they're like in the beginning, innocent, noble. You think in the beginning was noble? In the beginning was gas and scum. This is nonsense, such talk. In the whole world, there wouldn't be such a thing as noble if people didn't invent it. Yeah, the same people who made the gas chambers, brainwashing, all the wonderful modern inventions. It could make you a little crazy, you know, thinking. But what are you going to do? Noble shmoble, show me a dog that's making an institution where other sick dogs can go.

Maybe I'm not explaining myself so good. What I mean, I'm not a fanatic from animals. But with this little person, this Sam, it's something funny. From the minute he came into the house it's like there would be another member of the family. In the middle of the day, I'm having lunch, or I'm in the showroom talking to a customer, all of a sudden falls into my head a picture of that creature standing, with his little face like somebody dropped some ink on it, and his chest sticking out, so manly, and it's giving me a twist inside, I got to run to the telephone, find out how is he, did he have his cod-liver oil—I'm telling you, like there would be a baby in the house. Even my Sophie is laughing about it already.

"Listen," she says, "who is the adolescent in this family, you or Harold?" But don't worry, she's not immune herself. Three, four times a night she's sneaking into Harold's room to see is Sam warm, does he want water, is he maybe lonesome, she's cooking him Farina, she heard somewhere it's good for him, you could tell he doesn't even like it but he's such a polite little animal, she made it for him, he eats it. Even our Jenny, she is what my wife calls an extrovert, I call it only fresh, she's taking the time to make him a little sweater, in her sewing class in school.

And with Harold, well this is altogether a wonderful thing. You want to see sometimes between a boy and a dog something noble? You look on the boy, not the dog.

Just to show you how it is, I'm getting one day a letter from a man in Dubuque, Iowa, he just woke up, he's got a wire-haired dachshund he wants to sell me. I bring the letter home and show Harold. He gives a look, like it's a notice from the gas company, then he picks up Sam and he says, "We've got all the dogs we need in this family."

I don't know, maybe I'm prejudiced. But take, for instance, the bathroom business. You know, this is always a big problem with a dog, no? But Sam, maybe five times we showed him, you know, about the newspaper, and finished, the whole business. Did you ever hear something like it? Tell the truth?

Yes, it's like a dream, how the years are going by. I'm talking about this like it would be yesterday. It's already six years Samson isn't a puppy. And my Harold—one day he's a boy thirteen and it's a big tragedy with a dog, a wire-haired dachshund he can't get, and you turn around for a minute and he's a man, a soldier in a uniform, he's got to go away to war. So this time they're not calling it war. Police action. It's still shooting, killing . . .

Yes, he was going to get anyway a notice from the draft, so he enlisted. I don't know was it a good idea, not a good idea. All I know is my boy is in Korea, another world.

His mother nearly died, I'm telling you. And the dog, you know when he started up this scratching business? Maybe you will think I'm not so good in the head, imagining things, but honest to God, it was on a Saturday, three weeks ago, I'm home from the office and I see the dog is acting somehow funny, I don't know what, restless, something, he's jumping up every few minutes, going to the door, looking, like he's expecting the bell to ring and when finally it's the Western Union boy standing there you maybe wouldn't believe it but the little feller is starting to shiver and he makes a noise in the throat, like he is trying not to cry, and I can't look at my wife, I know already what kind of telegram this is, from the War Office.

Hah? Yes, sure, we got yet hope. The commander, he wrote us a very fine letter. He says when they are missing it's always hope. But it's a little hard, you know, you are wondering all the time where, how, is he cold, sick, maybe they took him prisoner, those crazy fanatics, what they do to people. If only I would be sure he's got something to eat, decent, he was never fussy but in the house my wife was always careful with the meals, you know—balanced, vegetables and whole wheat and so on.

Well, you must excuse me, I suppose you got your own troubles. When you got nothing to do but wait and wait you're sometimes talking too much.

Come on, Sam, we got to go home. Got to put on some more medicine. Maybe will give you a little relief. Can you imagine how an old fool is carrying on about a dog? It's like a child would get sick in the family, honest to God.

two

   Well, my writer friend, you are just in time. I am going to buy you the finest lunch in the city of New York. First you'll have with me a drink, yes? I got wonderful news to tell you. You remember what you wrote me in your letter—I shouldn't give up hope, sometimes God writes happy endings too, not only Hollywood? Well, I wouldn't keep you in suspense. We got word from our boy. He is in a hospital in Pusan. He wrote the letter himself. Sure I'll show you. Here. But why should you strain your eyes? I could quote you, word by word. He says he is not even wounded but the doctor put down for him shock and exposure and he insisted Harold should have a rest a couple weeks in the hospital.

  You see here what he says? "Some racket, Pop. Vacation with pay." Well, this is Harold. I suppose when he will tell the whole story finally what happened, it will be like he went for a walk, or to wash out his socks in the Yalu and he lost his way. Looks a little shaky, his handwriting, no? But still and all if he could sit up and write must be he's okay. Don't you think so?

So you can imagine how we're feeling here. I wouldn't try to describe it. Mrs. Seidman and I were up the whole night talking. The silliest things. When did he lose his first milk tooth? How many words did he have in his vocabulary when he was nine months old? Incidentally, it was a remarkable thing, thirty-two words. Well, you know parents.

No, don't worry about my business. Today I am too excited to pay attention to business. You remember you said in your letter you were breaking your head to think of a Christmas story? Tell me, the studio still wants you to write one? Because happens I got for you a Christmas story. I don't think you could use it for a scenario. But maybe you could get from it an idea. You know, turn it around some way. The way we're doing here in the shop with patterns, materials. Sometimes, we're working around to save a little goods, or improve a little the fit of a garment, comes an idea for a different kind of a style entirely. I remember one season, it was '47, I think, I got this way the biggest leader in our whole line. I suppose you writers are doing the same thing. There's tricks in every trade.

So, anyway, I had a partner in my business one time, Max Birnbaum. He is retired now, living in Florida with his wife, she had all the time a problem with her health and it's better for her, the climate in Florida. The last few years I lost a little the contact, you know it's hard to keep up with people you only see them every couple years. But for quite a few years we were inseparable. This experience I want to tell you happened also wartime, 1945. Don't think I'm telling it because it makes me out to be a hero. Just the opposite. But we're talking about Christmas, it fits for the season.

You'll let me be for a minute a little philosophical, yes? I've been working since I was thirteen years old. I made quite a good success in business. I'm not denying there's a satisfaction. And the money is good to have too. Still and all, it's not the whole story. I'm getting sometimes a feeling like I'm in a prison. True, it's not a prison like Sing Sing. It's got lots of conveniences, steam heat, linen drapes, built-in bar, I could go home nights, in the summertime Loon Lake, in the wintertime sometimes Florida, or California, or even a Mediterranean cruise— all the same it's a prison. Seventh Avenue, Long Island, Long Island, Seventh Avenue.

I'm not complaining, you understand. I got things a king couldn't have, couple hundred years ago. Only sometimes there's this feeling, how should I explain it? I'm thinking like this. Here I'm living in the greatest city in the world, a city like an Arabian Nights, and what do I know about it? What do I know what's going on here? It could be, I don't know, Podunk. Things are happening every minute, sad things, funny things, crazy things, even Shakespeare couldn't think of them so fast. And me, I'm living like in a tunnel, with steam heat. Styles, orders, materials, orders, styles—you know what I mean?

I'm standing sometimes in my office where I got a window, you can see the river, and I'm looking at the boats down there and thinking: Even on the Staten Island Ferry I'm a stranger. It's a tragic thing. Do I ever stop in the street to say hello to a truck driver, a sailor, a loafer, to ask him how is he doing, is he living or dying, is he happy, sad, is he saving money, is he planning a revolution—what's going on with him? What is he thinking? Seven million people, maybe more, I didn't count them lately, God knows what's going on in their heads. One sure thing, I don't.

It's not so simple, what I'm talking about. For instance, Sunday I'm opening the paper and I see there's an exhibit, a collection of wonderful old masterpieces, the Nazis had them hidden away in a salt mine during the war. And now they're discovered and they're at the Metropolitan. Rembrandt, Rubens, Titian—a roll call from the Ages. So am I rushing down to the Museum to take a look? Lift up my spirits a little? No. I'm taking off my shoes and turning, in the paper, to the financial page.

Can you understand it? What I'm saying? Well, it's a kind of feeling, it don't make much sense, but when you got it, you got a hunger to talk to somebody. You don't want to sit down with the same old bunch, with a pinochle deck and say three sixty, three seventy, hundred aces, pay the kitty. So whom should I talk to? My wife? Right away she gives me a look and I'm sitting with a thermometer in my mouth and a teaspoonful of cascara. My daughter Jenny? She would say, "Come on, Pop, turn the record over. This side's gruesome." Even Harold, I would feel embarrassed. You understand, they're fine kids, both of them, but this is the way with the young people today. No philosophy. Two and two makes four, action, reaction, start up the motor, let's go, period. Mystery, thoughts, what is it all about, life—nothing. I don't know. Maybe it's the war, science, or what.

So who? My designer maybe? I'm only too happy I can stay out of her way, she shouldn't turn on me the temperament. My customers, they would think I'm crazy altogether? To my salesmen, they would get out their little black books, fix me up with a number? My models? My silk man, my button man, my embroidery man? They would run back to their office and one, two, three, chop off the credit. Seidman is going broke, they would say, he's making with the double talk.

You see what I mean? All right, I got friends too. Pinochle friends. Poker friends. Friends who got daughters and they think maybe it could be something with my Harold. Friends who got sons and my wife thinks it could be something for our Jenny in a few years. Friends who think I got more money in the bank than I got. You know —all kinds of friends. But to talk to, from the heart—you look around and there's nobody.

So, one day I'm looking out of the window in my shop and I got this feeling. I got other feelings too. This was depression time, business was very bad. So what should I do? Write to my Congressman? I go down to Solowey's Dairy Restaurant, I'm sitting having a cup of coffee, gloomy like I said, comes in and sits down at my table a man, big, maybe six feet, with a thick head of hair, gray, like chopped-up ice in a skating rink. He looks like he would be maybe a poet, a philosopher, a Disraeli. So who is he? He's Max Birnbaum, Sally Simpson Stylish Stouts. But this I don't know yet. He sits with his cup of coffee and he

34

takes out of his pocket one of those little blue books, you don't see them around any more. Haldeman-Julius. You know what I mean? The little ones? They cost a nickel. I got an education from them.

Well, I'm getting sideways a look at the cover, it says, *The Maxims of Epictetus*. Ah ha, I say to myself. Eureka, like that Greek in the bathroom. You know who I'm talking about? Here is a man who is maybe talking my language. So to make it short, I start up with him a conversation, thank God it's not about styles, or the union, or the depression, pretty soon I'm quoting him a piece of poetry from *The Prisoner of Chillon*, Byron's, and he is conversing with me from Spinoza and Pushkin and we are having, I'm telling you, a time, you could almost forget the bills that are laying on the desk upstairs and the operators complaining they haven't got enough work to make a decent day's pay, and you got to wonder every morning you're coming in the place, could you go on or will you have to close up.

So a funny thing, how life works. Where does this man live, he's like a lifesaver to me? Turns out, a block away from me in Parkside Towers. Can you imagine? Sunday, I take a walk over there with my wife, we should get acquainted. I don't want you should misunderstand me but I'm falling in love with Molly Birnbaum in one second net. Such a face she's got, so sweet, such a voice, like a pigeon. And such a tenderness between these two people. Like in a book. They got a lovely apartment, a daughter, a lovely girl, Naomi, there's a wonderful atmosphere in the house, you could feel it when people love each other, got respect for each other. You know how it says in the

Bible: Better a meal of herbs in a house where there is love than a roast ox and hatred with it? Well, just think how fine it is if you could have the love *and* the roast beef too. We're sitting in the parlor, drinking tea, talking, and every minute Max jumps up and he says, "Molly, you want a pillow? Maybe you'd like better a rocker?" And so on.

You can imagine, when we're going home, my Sophie says to me, "What's the matter you can't bring me a rocker sometimes?" And I'm saying, "What's the matter you don't look at me like I was Sir Lancelot Seidman?" You understand, I'm just making a joke. We understand each other very fine, my Sophie and me.

Well, to make a long story short, pretty soon I'm having lunch with Max every day, and three times a week we're at his house in the evening and four times a week they're at our house and one day I get an idea. "Max," I say, "we're spending so much time together, maybe we should make it unanimous? You got a business, I got a business, it's both lousy now, maybe if we put them together we could figure out something. Mergers are only for the Gentiles? What have we got to lose?"

So now you'll say, ah ha, here is the end of a beautiful friendship. But that's where you are wrong. Eleven years, nearly twelve, we were partners, depression, wartime, good times, not a single hard word, not a single argument. All right, sometimes we're yelling a little about business things, expenses, or when we got to change the line, everybody has got his own ideas, there's a little electricity in the air, so could be sometimes a little thunder. Don't mean anything. Between us, the feeling, like brothers. Not a murmur. I'm telling you, such an atmosphere we had in the place, even the union delegates were taking off their hats when they came in and putting their ashes in the ash trays instead of on the rug. So you can imagine. And with all this we're making money, too. We made a big success those years. Of course, it was the conditions too. Wasn't hard to make money then. Terrible thing to think about, how war is good for business. Sometimes, lately, you know when my Harold was missing, I would open up the mail in the morning, see the orders coming in, my accountant would come in to tell me how much money we made that month, I would get such a feeling— well, I don't even want to think about it. So if I throw away my business, am I going to change things? This will stop the Communists? Bring the boys back from Korea?

So, anyway, I'm describing to you the situation between me and Max. This was a kind of friendship comes to a person once in a lifetime. I had for him respect, you see, besides everything else. I looked up to him, his mentality, his character—you know, man is supposed to be a creature of God, you figure He must have some hopes for them, like parents for their children. Well, sometimes, you're meeting a person, you think God must get from him for a change a little satisfaction. Not very often in this world. But sometimes.

Well, you know how in the Bible, in Paradise, came in one day the serpent? Only in the Bible it's a he and he's selling apples. This is a girl, with a refined accent, maybe twenty-three, four, she wants to be a model. Patricia O'Donel, and speaking without prejudice, she was a fine-looking girl, no question. Blue eyes, very dark hair, good

37

figure, slim, very full in the bust. Happens we're putting out a more expensive line that season, we remodeled the showroom a little fancier and we decided to put on a couple more models. So we had an ad in the paper and we're interviewing, with the designer, some girls. I don't know if you know the fashion business, maybe you think any girl, she's a little pretty, could be a model. But it's not so. It's a profession. Like to be an actor, or a singer. Doesn't take so much talent but you still got to have the right measurements, and you got to have a certain style, and you got to have also some experience. And I see right away this girl don't qualify. She don't carry herself like she would understand how to show a dress. I ask her where did she work before, she tells me she never worked before, she had once in the summer a job in a music store while she was going to school, before the war. She comes from Ohio somewhere, she's in New York a couple months and she decided she wants to be a model.

Well, I take her name, she shouldn't feel too bad, but in my mind I already got her crossed off the list. The designer agrees with me. But Max thinks different. He wants to give her the job. Why? Because she looks like she needs it.

"Did you see the coat she was wearing?" he asks me. Well, this is Max all over. I'm looking to see can the girl show a dress, make an impression on a customer, he's only thinking does she need the job.

"Listen, Max," I say, "a coat is a coat and a model is a model. We got a business here, after all, not a social service. This girl don't know how to walk even."

"She could learn," he says. "And the way business is

38

now, anyway, she could be a lamppost and we would still sell out the line."

"Max," I say, "is this an approach for a businessman? Why are we putting ads in the paper and talking to people? If all we need is a lamppost, let's put up a lamppost in the showroom and be done with it. Will be cheaper in the long run. And I wouldn't have twice a week an argument with some hall-room boy with an expense account, he wants to have a date with the lamppost."

"Morris," he says, "do me a favor. I want to hire this girl. Give her a chance. I just got a feeling. Please."

"Okay," I say. "Why should I fight with you? You want to give her the job, give her the job."

So goes by a couple weeks, I don't pay any more attention, sales is anyway not too much my department. I left it in those days for Max to take care of the customers. I like better the production end of the business. And, what I hear, there's no complaints about the new girl. The designer says Patricia is very nice, she learns fast, my shop foreman, Sam Rosenzweig, says she is very willing and she's got a nice disposition, and the salesmen are happy with her bust measurement, so fine. Business is rolling in and I got all I could do to get out the orders, get in the materials and so on.

On a Saturday, it's maybe a month after the girl came to work for us, I'm in my office checking over some figures, Max comes in. "How does it look?" he says.

"Depends on who's asking," I say. "If it's the union delegate, the payroll is too high. You, I'll tell the truth. Keeps up like this, the government is going to get rich."

So he says, "I'm glad to hear it. The government

39

wouldn't mind then I told the bookkeeper to give Pat a ten-dollar raise."

"That's a pretty fast raise, Max," I say. "The girl's only been here a couple weeks——"

"Almost a month, Morris."

"All right, a month. We're going to raise her salary every month?"

"She can use the money."

"And what's with our other two models? They can use it too?"

"It's different with them," he says, "They know how to get along. This is a very reserved girl, she's not going out for dinner every night with somebody else. She's got a small child, she's got to keep up a flat——"

"How is it you know so much already?" I ask him. "In just a few weeks? If she's so reserved, especially? The big one, Marcia, is here a year, you're still calling her Martha, I'll bet you couldn't tell me does she live in a flat or a trailer or under a table at Manny's Pastrami Heaven?"

"There's something about this girl," he says. "The eyes. There is a sadness in them, Morris. Squeezes my heart. Didn't you notice?"

"Frankly, no," I say. "I didn't do any research in this department. I got a lot of other things to notice around the place. Did *you* notice, for instance, how many returns we got in from the Bon Ton this month? I think we got to have an understanding with them, once and for all. Order what they need and keep it. Or else cut them off altogether. We can't run for them a consignment business."

"Morris," he says, "don't be so tough. It's an old account, the Bon Ton. They've been pretty loyal to us. Don't

40

forget, it's not so long ago we were very glad to have their business."

"Max," I say, "the trouble with you is you are always mixing up business with sentiment. Would be fine if the banks and the silk mills and the union felt the same way. Then we could afford to indulge ourselves. But they are waiting for us with hatchets. You know this. We had plenty experience. Save the sentiment for where it's appreciated. After hours. For the family."

He gives me now a smile, with that wonderful face like one of the old-time prophets. "Look who's talking about sentiment," he says. "You are always trying to persuade yourself what a tough customer you are. But you're not fooling me, Morris." And he says to me, in Hebrew, from the Bible, "As a man thinks in his heart, so is he."

And I answer him back, also in Hebrew, "Do you see a man diligent in his business? He shall stand before kings."

So he laughs and he goes away, shaking his head. Well, I'm certainly not going to make an issue. My partner tells me a girl has got sad eyes, he wants to give her a ten-dollar raise, the two don't go together exactly, but okay, if this is what he wants I'm not going to have a big argument with him about it. It's not the ten dollars anyway, you understand. I don't have to tell you, we were giving away plenty that time, for the refugees and so on. Maybe half the profits. But when you got an organization, couple hundred people, you got to have some system, you can't treat one different than the other. Starts up jealousies, and so on, with this you could make a whole mishmash of your business.

Well, I'm trying to give you an idea, as good as I can

41

remember, how it's building up, the frame of mind, little by little. I remember one time we were in the showroom, it was after closing time, we were waiting to discuss with the designer, a customer gave us an idea for a certain change in one of our styles. So this girl, Patricia, puts her head in the door, she says, "Will you be wanting me for anything else?"

"No," I say, "you done your day's work. It's after quitting time."

"I'll be glad to stay," she says, "if you want to see the dress on again."

"No, we know already the problem," I say. "We only got to figure out, with the material. Thank you very much. Good night."

"Good night," she says to me, and then she looks at Max and she says again, "Good night," the same words but it's like it would be a different language, and she gives him a smile, private, just for him, and she goes out.

Well, maybe it's only in my own head, this idea. You know, when you're looking back on a situation, could be you're putting into it something you know now, wasn't there at the time. But I'm trying to explain you exactly how it was happening, not only from the outside, actually, but my own reactions. A little thing like this. Like a leaf falling on your head. You know what I mean?

Another time we had in the place photographs made, we're running an ad in *Women's Wear*. So we're looking at the prints, to pick out which of the dresses we want to feature in the ad, and I see Max is looking at one of the pictures like he would be hypnotized. I look over his shoulder, I see it's a picture of Patricia in an evening

42

dress, number 614, was one of our big numbers that season. To me, for my taste, the girl is too thin. But I got to admit, with the dress, she looks very chic. Looks stunning, the whole thing.

Max is sitting, looking, shaking his head. "What's the matter," I say. "You don't like it?"

He looks up at me, like his eyes would be made from glass. "You're shaking your head," I say, "like there would be something wrong."

"I was just thinking," he says. "You didn't know Molly in those days. But Patricia reminds me of her so much. I couldn't tell you."

I give him a look like he would be crazy. Granted, this is a very pretty girl, Miss O'Donel, I wouldn't say no. But she looks as much like Molly as I look like Mickey Rooney. Completely Gentile, the appearance, you know? I don't say better or worse, it's not a question of a beauty contest. But different. Like night and day. But, again, I'm not going to argue with him. He's got some kind of a fantasy in his head, pleases him to think the girl looks like Molly in her young days, okay.

So I'm trying to think now, what was the next thing happened. Yes, the business with the coat. It's a few weeks later, around Thanksgiving, I come into the showroom, Max is sitting there alone by a table, he's making circles with a pencil on an order pad. "What's the matter you're sitting making circles?" I say. "You got time to do that when business is bad. Let's better go down and have a cup of coffee."

"Morris," he says, "I got a problem."

"Well," I say, "you're talking to the right man. From

43

problems I'm an expert." I don't even think it could be something serious, his problem. And me, I'm feeling pretty good, we just got in a big reorder from Carson Pirie, Chicago.

"It's Pat," he says, and all of a sudden it's like everything would fall into place in one of those picture puzzles, the raise, the smiles, the business how she looks like Molly —and the picture is my partner Max, sitting with an order pad, making circles. "I want to get her a coat," he says now. "And I don't know how to go about it."

You know, I read somewhere that in Hollywood, when an important man wants to have monkey business with a girl, he doesn't want anybody should know, he takes always somebody else along wherever they are going, people should think he's the one is having the affair. They call him a Beard, no? It's a crazy idea but this fell into my mind. Max wants I should be for him a Beard. It's like somebody would put an icicle down my back.

"What's the problem," I say, "you can't make up your mind it should be mink or sable?"

"Any kind of a warm coat," he says. "But I don't want she should be embarrassed."

"And what's with you?" I say. "You're not embarrassed?"

It's like he wouldn't even hear me. The sarcasm I'm putting in he certainly doesn't hear. "Max," I say, "what kind of business is this? You're out of your mind a little? What do you want to start up a business with coats, with a model?"

"I can't stand to see the way she comes in in the morning," he says. "Blue from the cold. Did you ever take a look at that coat she's wearing? Gabardine. For winter. This is not a winter coat. It's a spring coat. She must be freezing in it, this weather."

"All right," I say, "so if she needs a coat, why doesn't she go to the stores and buy one? There's not enough coats around?"

"I don't think she can afford it,". he says.

"So let her buy it on time," I say. "Can be arranged."

He gives me now a look, like he just heard what I was saying. "You're getting hard, Morris," he says and he gets up and walks away, I'm standing, looking after him like he just threw a glass of ice water in my face. Twelve years, the first bitter word between us.

Well, it's a few days later, maybe a week, there's a call from Max's daughter Naomi. She is by the doctor and Molly's got to go to the hospital for a few days, for observation. She's got some kind of a condition, anemia or something like it, she is subject to hemorrhages and it's not a new story with her she's got to go to the hospital. Still and all, you're always getting scared from this kind of a thing. The girl is upset, naturally, she's crying and she wants to talk to her father. Well, her father is not in the shop. He's not in his office. I send one of the shipping clerks to see is he maybe having coffee in Solowey's, he's not there. I call the buying offices, Saks, Lord and Taylor, everywhere. Nothing doing.

About four o'clock in the afternoon he comes in with a package and an expression on his face, you would think he's got in the package five of the biggest styles for next season.

"For God's sake, Max," I say, "how many times did I

45

tell you? When you go out leave a number where you can be reached."

"I was in the building," he says. "I met Charlie Aronson downstairs and I went up to see his line. They're making a beautiful line of coats this season." He opens the box and takes out a coat. "Isn't it a beauty?" he says. "Genuine fox collar. A hundred and thirty-nine fifty, wholesale."

Well, you can believe me, I'm burning. I would like to take the coat and the box and knock it on the floor. "And I figured out how I'm going to do it," he says, like he's telling me a great discovery he made, I should give him a medal or something. "It'll be a Christmas present. From the firm. An honest girl can take such a present."

"Since when are we giving Christmas presents?" I ask him. "This is now our holiday, Christmas?"

"No, but it's her holiday," he says, and I see if I'm going to let myself go, just a little bit, we're going to have a real argument, then and there. "Listen," I say, "when you got a minute to stop being Santa Claus, maybe you'll go call your daughter. Molly's got to go to the hospital."

He drops the coat on a chair and his face gets gray like a piece of cardboard. So I'm already sorry, and I take hold of his arms and I say, "Put yourself together, Max. It's not serious. She'll have to have maybe a couple transfusions. And the doctor says he wants her to stay for a few days, for observation." And then I say, this much I can't help myself, "Please, Max. Next time, remember you got a family. Leave a number."

After he's gone, I'm thinking it over for a while and I'm coming to a conclusion. I take the coat into my office and I send for the girl.

"Listen," I say to her, "here is a coat my partner bought for you. He couldn't give it to you personal, he's got a little sickness in the family, he had to go home." I'm looking at her meantime to see does she show maybe a little shame in her face. Nothing. She looks at the coat and then she looks at me and she says, "But I don't understand. I'm sure it's very kind of Mr. Birnbaum—but——"

I'm interrupting her. "What's there to understand? He bought you a coat. I'm sure it's not the first time it happened to you." I can see she's going to make an answer but I'm not waiting. "I'll tell you," I say. "I want you should do me a favor. Take the coat, I'll give you a check for a month's salary, and you'll get yourself another job. Here I think it's a little crowded, with three models. You know what I mean?"

She can't even look me straight in the face. She's holding the coat, with the fur against her face, and now she's putting it down on a chair, like it was made out of, I don't know what, gold lace or something. And she says, "I understand. Will you please thank Mr. Birnbaum and tell him I appreciate it. He'll understand why I can't take the coat. If you'll just give me my check until Saturday that will be satisfactory. I'll leave now."

So that night, I don't have to tell you, I'm not sleeping so good. After all, I am not a butcher at heart. But I'm trying to remember, in life you got to keep your eye on the ball, like the baseball players say. Or maybe it's the golfers. It's true, the girl don't look like the type to be a gold digger. But when you are dealing with a woman, you got to remember there is not a one who's not an actress. I'm including my own wife. My daughter. I'm not against

47

women, believe me. But I'll ask you a question. Did Samson think Delilah was a lady barber? In his eyes she was sweet like an angel, with a heart of gold. I'm not born yesterday. It's only in the movies the vampire looks like Theda Bara. People they break up homes, they always got good reasons.

Well, it's going around and around in my head like this, all night long. But I'm consoling myself. I figure I'll spend a couple bad nights, I'll maybe have a bad time with Max in the morning and then it will be finished. We could go on like before. To keep your best friend in the world from making a fool of himself, it's worth a little aggravation.

In the morning I stop off at the hospital to see Molly. Max is there with Naomi, they're both green in the face, worried, but Molly is lying in bed, her hair is fixed like she would be going to a party, her face is pale but smiling, always with her is a smile, like God made her a present of her life and whatever happens, it's still all right with her. I don't know why, it's nothing to cry, but I feel like crying. Such a woman.

"Look at him," she says, she's holding Max's hand, "he's the one needs the transfusion. Not me. Naomi, why don't you go to school? I'm going to be around for a long time. You don't have to look so green."

Well, afterwards I ask Max how serious it is, what does the doctor say. "Same thing," he says. "It's an old story."

"But can't they do something?" I say. "It's got to go on like this all the time? Must be something they can do."

"They don't know," he says. "It's been like this ever since Naomi was born." He gives his head a shake, big as he is I would like to put my arms around him, cheer him up. "I don't know what Molly ever did, or I did——"

"Don't talk like a child," I say. "You mean everybody who's sick did something? It's a punishment?"

"I don't know, Morris," he says. "It's getting so I'm afraid to touch Molly, I'll send her to the hospital."

Well, this is not a subject you could talk about very much, but I can tell you I'm feeling very disturbed. Again I can't sleep the whole night, next day I'm in the shop, I feel like I'm walking around in a fog, Max comes in about eleven o'clock, he stopped at the hospital, Molly had a good night, the doctor is very pleased.

"So cheer up," I say. "She'll be home in a couple days."

"Yes," he says. "Until next time. What's in the mail this morning?"

"Nothing but orders," I tell him. "I'm afraid to look already. Pretty soon we'll have to send out the salesmen to insult the customers."

So he makes with his face like he would want to smile but it got stuck. Then he goes into the showroom and pretty soon he comes back, his face is even more gray than before.

"Morris," he says, "what happened with Pat? The girls say she went to your office yesterday and afterward she packed up her things and left. What happened?"

I'm not looking at him. I'm busy looking at some samples of silk. "I gave her the coat," I say. "She didn't want to take it."

"Why didn't she want to take it, Morris? Why?"

"I don't know. Maybe she's got bigger ideas," I say. I'm waiting he should give me an answer but he don't.

49

I look up at him and the way he's looking at me, it gives me a funny feeling in the stomach. "What did you say to her, Morris?" he asks me.

"I forget exactly."

"Did you tell her it was a present from the firm?"

"I don't remember. I had other things on my mind, Max. I was thinking about Molly in the hospital and what's going to be with her."

"Morris," he says, "I want to know what you said to Pat, she went away like this. Did you hurt her feelings?"

Now I'm getting real angry. This is his only worry, did I hurt her feelings. "What did I say? I'll tell you what I said. I said she should get herself another job. I said that here it's too crowded for three models and two bosses with families. That's what I said." I'm yelling now a little. Maybe it's the way he keeps looking at me like I would be some kind of a criminal or something. Simon Legree. What did I do after all? It was only to protect him.

"You had no right to talk to the girl that way," he tells me now. "You don't know anything about her. You had no right, Morris."

"I could say plenty about who's got a right to do what," I say to him. "But I don't want we should start any arguments. I did what I had to do. You do what you got to do. If you want she should have the coat, you could deliver it personal."

"You had no right, Morris," he says. "You had no right to do things behind my back."

Well, we are both starting to sound like a broken phonograph. "Don't tell me what I got a right to do, Max," I say. "Better we should stop talking now. I don't want I should say things to you I'll be sorry later." And I pick up the samples and walk away.

I don't see him the rest of the day. The day after, Molly is coming home from the hospital, naturally Sophie is right away over there with the chicken soup. This is with our people a universal thing. You're sick, cascara before, chicken soup afterwards. I go over there later, in the evening, there's tea and cake, I'm trying to act like everything would be the same but it's no use, I can't look at Max, he can't look at me. I try to make a joke, it's like you would try to make birds out of lead. So I sit for ten minutes, I got enough, I get up and I say I'm tired, I'm going home. Molly gives me a look, I know she's wondering what is wrong, I don't want to hurt her feelings but I can't help myself. I can't sit there, with the two of them, and try to act like it would be the same as before. It's spoiled, and that's all there is to it.

When we're walking home Sophie says to me, "What is it, Morris? What's wrong?"

"There's nothing wrong," I say. "I got things on my mind."

"Morris," she says, "don't try to fool me. There's something wrong between you and Max."

"Listen, Sophie, don't nag me." I start to holler a little. "I'm running a business, I got aggravation the whole day long. A man has got a right to get tired. I want to go home and go to bed. Do I have to have an argument with you about it?"

Well, this was after Thanksgiving, I think. Anyway, it's a few days later we're getting the monthly statement from the bank, the accountant comes in with two checks made out to Patricia O'Donel. One is for the salary I gave her, the other is for a hundred dollars, signed by Max. We got an account, you understand, either of us can sign. So the accountant wants to know what is it, this second check, severance pay or what? "Of course severance pay," I tell him. "Why are you asking foolish questions?"

So he goes out, I'm practically shaking, I'm so mad. I'm sitting there a couple minutes to put myself together, then I call him in, Max. "You are really out of your mind," I say. "Applebaum has got to know your business with Miss O'Donel too?"

He looks at me like he wouldn't have any idea what I'm talking about. The scholar. His thoughts are in the clouds. "I'm talking about a check you made out to her," I say. "A firm check. Applebaum wanted to know what he should charge it to. Taxes. Entertainment. What?"

"Maybe he should charge it to conscience?"

Well, I'm burning. "I got no problem with my conscience," I tell him. "My conscience is perfectly clear. All I'm telling you, you want to give out checks like this, use your personal account."

"In the old days," he says, "you didn't use to count so close, Morris. Not between us."

"Better somebody here should count," I say, "before the checks start coming back with extra zeros on the end. And anyway, the whole office has got to know? It should get back to your family yet?"

He gives his head a shake, you would think he's sorry for me altogether. "What got into you, Morris? This is a fine girl. She's in a strange city, she's got no one here. You got to make something dirty out of it if I help her out

52

with a little money, till she gets settled? You never heard a person can do something for a friend?"

"Sure," I say, "it's a beautiful thing, friendship. In Europe there's people haven't got any friends. They just got holes in their bellies. Your people. You got so much emotion to spare, why don't you worry about them?"

In a way, you know, this is not fair what I'm saying now. I know he's giving away plenty for the refugees, just like me. But in this kind of a situation you're not stopping to figure out are you being fair. You are moving like it would be in some kind of a dream, somebody is pushing you.

"What happened to your heart, Morris," he says, "it works only by mail to Europe? You were here that day she came into the showroom with that coat, and that thin face. You know what she had for lunch that day? Crackers and milk. I went down and watched her, at Walgreen's."

"Sure," I say. "And maybe she watched you too, behind a cracker? And maybe when you weren't watching, later, she ate a steak at Cavanagh's, with onions? On your money? And maybe a friend was eating with her too? A friend named McGuire or McCarthy? Not Birnbaum?"

So he looks at me, that same funny look, like I became a stranger to him these past days. "All right, Morris. I'll tell Applebaum to charge my personal account with a hundred dollars. I'm sorry I forgot to tell you. You got me used to thinking we were really partners."

Well, it's giving me a twist inside, what he's saying, if I would try to tell you, you would think I'm exaggerating. But maybe not. You're a writer, you know what goes on with people. I got to give you now a conversation I had

53

with my wife. Fits in. It was a Saturday, I wanted to stay down in the shop, I had a lot of things to do and Saturday afternoon, it's quiet, nobody is banging on my head with the telephone, it's a good time to catch up. So Sophie is coming downtown for some shopping, I meet her for lunch in Longchamps. You know, I got a very handsome wife, did I ever tell you? Maybe you remember in the old days was an actress, Clara Kimball Young? Well, my Sophie wouldn't have to take a back seat for her. But this is beside the question. I don't know why I mentioned it now except maybe that you should understand I got a certain feeling about marriage, pretty old-fashioned.

Well, we're talking over, at lunch, what Sophie wants to get for the kids, clothing, she wants also new curtains for our bedroom, some uniforms for the maid, I don't know what else, all of a sudden she says to me, "I've been thinking, Morris, I'd like to have a Christmas tree for the children this year."

I look at her, I wonder, is this some new wrinkle she got from the PTA, or some psychology lecture, or what?

"It's such a lovely legend," she says, "the whole thing, Kris Kringle, and the reindeer, and the presents and the beautiful songs—and it's such a pretty thing to have in the house—why should we deprive Harold and Jenny——"

"Sophie," I say, "it's not our holiday, Christmas."

"Why not?" she says. "Do we close the door on Passover? Don't we keep it open, for the stranger?"

"It's not the same thing."

"You just want to be stubborn," she says. "You've got some rigid idea in your mind——"

"All right," I say, "we'll have a tree. And we'll hang on it for decoration some model gas chambers."

"Oh, you're terrible," she says. "Just because there are lunatics in the world like Hitler——"

"There's always been lunatics in the world for us. Two thousand years——"

"Oh, don't start with the two thousand years," she says. "All I know is right now all Jenny's friends are going to have a tree, Myra Schwartz and Ellen Caplan and——"

"Don't give me the list," I say. "I know there's plenty Jews would like to forget they're Jews. That's their privilege. Doesn't mean we have to do it too."

"I don't understand you," she says. "It's not as if you made a point of being religious the rest of the year——"

"It's not a question of religious. Do I have to tell you what's going on in the world, Sophie? We could pay the respect at least of not having a Christmas tree in the house." I see she's going to keep on and I say, "I don't want any more discussions about it. No tree."

Well, I'm a little aggravated when I get back in the shop. I don't like to have these arguments, I got to put my foot down, be a tyrant in the house. For me it's a question of principle. But how do I know, after all, I'm right? Maybe it's wrong, to make an issue with the children, keep always alive the difference, the hatred. I realize prejudice could work two ways. Jews ain't immune, believe me. I'm having these thoughts, I'm a little disturbed anyway, I come into the office I see Max is there. He's standing in a corner, looking out of the window.

"What's the matter you're still here?" I say. "It's Satur-

55

day afternoon." He don't answer. I take down an order book, I prepared before a stack, and I go to work. Pretty soon I hear Max say, "Morris, do you remember the day we met, in Solowey's?"

So now I don't answer.

"I was reading one of those little blue books," he says. "Epictetus. You remember?"

"I remember," I say. "I remember it very plain."

" 'No great thing is created suddenly,' " he quotes, " 'any more than a bunch of grapes or a fig. If you tell me that you desire a fig, I answer you that there must be time. Let it first blossom, then bear fruit, then ripen.' "

I look up at him now. "So?" I say.

"What is it, Morris? Why don't we understand each other any more?"

It's giving me again a twist inside, like from a rope. "What is there to understand?" I say. "You want to make a fool of yourself and I can't stand to look on it. That's all."

"Morris, have you ever been alone?" he says. "All alone in the world?"

Maybe it's the window. I told you about that window, you could look down and see your life floating away on the river. Well, I had thoughts too, standing by that window. But instead I should feel sympathetic with him, I'm only getting sore.

"What's the matter you're all of a sudden so alone?" I ask him. "There's only Molly and Naomi and your relatives and the shop——"

"People," he says. "All of us. Locked up in their own bodies. Their own minds. We're alone, Morris. Every

56

important minute of our lives, living, dying, we're alone."

I know who he's thinking about. And I know what else he's thinking. He's thinking how sorry he is for himself, with a wife he ought to be glad just to worship her, like a statue on a pedestal.

"Listen," I say, "I haven't got time for such deep thoughts. I got a business to run and a family to support. Keeps me busy. And any spare time I got, I could think about the people over in Europe, Mr. Hitler fixed it for them so they would never have to be alone again. They could all be together forever, in the gas chambers, the crematoriums, in the cemeteries, or in the barracks, fifty at a time, with one pail for a toilet between them. This is what I'm thinking about, if I got time to stand at a window and brood about who's lonely in the world."

The more I'm talking the more I'm getting worked up. I'm picking up the order books, one after another, and slamming them down on the desk. "Twelve years I know you, you weren't lonely," I say. "Now comes in a girl with a page-boy bob and long legs and an Irish face and all of a sudden you're lonely. Why don't you go home to your wife and daughter if you're lonely?"

He looks at me a minute, then he says, "You had a heart once, Morris. What happened to it? Maybe you lost it? In those salesbooks somewhere?"

"I didn't lose nothing," I say. "Only my patience. I got my same heart, don't worry. Happens I ain't got room in it for everybody. Not for suckers. And not for gold diggers. Not for models who got to be unlonely with married men."

It's a peculiar feeling, you know, you're saying something to a friend, you know you wouldn't ever be able to take it back. You don't want to say it and yet you got to. My heart is knocking in my chest like I would be gambling away a fortune. I'm waiting for him to answer me, I'm wondering what's going to be now, maybe the next thing we'll be punching each other, like bums in a poolroom. Like a nightmare, I'm telling you. But nothing. I wake up, I look around, Max isn't there any more. And inside I got such a weak feeling I got to sit down, like I was maybe running for a hundred blocks.

It's a misery, the next days. I remember in the old country, when I was a kid, the snow. It was coming down in the night like feathers, each one nothing, but in the morning you go to the door, you can't push it open. You know what I mean? The same thing now between me and Max. Every day you got to push a little harder just to say a word. And then one day, you can't say nothing any more. The door is closed and like a mountain is standing against it.

Visiting in the evening, this is a foregone conclusion, finished. In the place we're avoiding each other. We got something to communicate, we're sending a salesman, or the production man, or we let it go altogether. Naturally, at home, Molly can't understand what is going on, she is on the phone every evening, why don't we come over, play some cards, or go for a drive even, or to the movies? I got to make always an excuse. My Sophie can't understand it, she wants to send me to a doctor altogether to find out what's the matter, I don't look good, I'm sleeping so restless, maybe I need a tonic or something. The help in the shop don't understand it, it's a whole different atmosphere. I'll tell you the truth, I would like to stop already. I would like to say to Max, "All right, you want to make yourself cheap, you don't care about your home, your child, your marriage, you don't care about your responsibility as a husband, a Jew, okay. I'm only begging you one thing, be careful Molly shouldn't find out. But between us, at least, let's stop acting like kids, not talking and so on. We got a business to run, after all." But every time I'm trying to say a word to him it's like somebody would put up a hand and grab my throat.

Well, a situation like this you figure the next thing is to call in the lawyers and dissolve the partnership. And looks like this is going to be the only solution. You hear about such things every day on Seventh Avenue. You read about it in the personal column in *Women's Wear*, two lines, you don't think anything about it. A business item. But when it's happening to you, believe me, it's a different story. Such a miserable feeling, I couldn't tell you. You know it can't go on like this, it's no use, still and all you're putting it off every day. Like it would be, I don't know, getting old, dying. And the middle of everything, it's now the Christmas season, the Santa Clauses are standing on the corners with their pails and their bells, jolly, ringing, people running around, busy, happy faces, and your own heart is heavy like lead. Well, you're a writer. It's like a regular play, no?

All right, so now is the last act. One morning, it's a few days before Christmas, I go into the showroom, I see a box is laying there on a table, the cover is off and I take a look, it's a housecoat, quilted, dusty pink, very fine material, satin. So I seen in the morning Max come in with a box, I figure this must be it, and I make up my mind. It's an opportunity. Once and for all, I'm going to give a push that door. I go in to Max's office and I say, like I started the sentence two years ago, "What's that housecoat laying on the table in the showroom?"

"It's for Molly," he says. "A present." He's having the same trouble as me. But he wants also to try. Like we would start to shovel away the snow, each with a teaspoon, we're looking for a house we once lived in it, we know we wouldn't find it any more.

"It's a nice garment," I say. "Maybe I'll get one for Sophie. Where did you get it? Bonwit's?"

"I think Saks," he says.

"What do you mean, you *think* Saks?"

He gives me a look and I'm getting that funny feeling in the stomach again. "Pat bought it," he says. It's like he would hit me on the head. Pat bought it! This man, with his face from the Bible, he lost himself so entirely, he's sending Pat now to buy presents for Molly. For his guilty conscience, I suppose. I could spit in his face, I'm so disgusted. But I'm holding myself in.

"Maybe you got an idea how much Pat paid for it?" I say. "Or she's got her own checking account now?"

Like he's very tired, he says, "Twenty-nine fifty, Morris."

"Thank you very much," I say and I turn around and walk out, I'm so upset I don't know what I'm doing the rest of the morning. Lunchtime the designer comes to me, she wants me to go with her to Fifth Avenue, there's a dress in one of the stores, she thinks somebody copied it from us. Well, this is entirely possible. Since we copied it from somebody, somebody else could copy it from us. The only thing, if they're making it cheaper, I want to see how, so I could at least give my production man the needle. Well, we're passing by a window there at Saks, I forget all about the dress, I see the housecoat, the same one I was talking to Max, only a different color. All of a sudden seems to me very funny the price he told me. You could see it's a very high-class number, expensive satin, quilting, handwork, it's not possible they could sell it for twenty-nine fifty retail. I ask the designer, she agrees with me, couldn't be the price for such a garment. We go into the store and inquire, in the Negligees. Eighty-nine fifty.

Well, it bothers me afterwards, the discrepancy. You would think it's maybe a small thing but it keeps turning around in my mind the whole afternoon. I don't like mysteries. In a book, yes, or on the television. Not in my own head. So I go to the file finally, I take out Patricia O'Donel's card to look for the telephone number. No telephone number. Only an address. Hundred and Thirty-eighth Street. Uptown.

Well, I'm a dress manufacturer, not a private eye. Says in the *Women's Wear*, an article, M. Seidman is getting to be an important man in the garment industry. This is a moot question, I'm sure you could get from my competitors a little argument on this subject but certainly I got more important things to do than drive all the way up to Hundred and Thirty-eighth Street to ask a person how is it she paid twenty-nine fifty for an eighty-nine fifty housecoat. Maybe she knows somebody. Maybe she is a great bargainer. Maybe I'm getting to be a busybody with all the maybe's. So four o'clock, I go out, I get my car and I drive uptown to Hundred and Thirty-eighth Street. Am I crazy? I don't know. Could be. A little. Could be I'm getting for the first time an awful suspicion, maybe I am the villain, what's been going on, not Max. I know I got to find out the explanation or I wouldn't sleep.

I find the house, it's got a gray stoop and narrow windows, it don't look very classy. And the neighborhood is not what you would call high-class residential. On the mailbox I find P. O'Donel, Apartment 10. I go in, there's no elevator, it's on the third floor. I ring the bell and a woman opens the door, thin, maybe thirty years old. Looks like a schoolteacher.

"Is this Miss O'Donel's apartment?" I say.

"She's not home right now," the woman says.

So then I don't know what to say. I say the first thing that comes into my head. "You're her sister?"

"No, just a neighbor," she says. "I come in to mind her boy while she's away."

Now from inside comes up to the door a boy in a sweater, like a little prizefighter, his pants are falling down a little, the whole person is maybe two years old. He starts pulling on the woman and she holds him and says to me, "You want to wait for her? She'll be home any minute now." Well, I'm feeling a little funny. You know how you are getting an idea to do something—so if you go straight and do it it's all right, even if it's foolish, but if you got to stop and wait for traffic signals, you are slowing down and pretty soon the whole thing turns around in your head and you start to sweat a little and you think what kind of a damn fool am I? It's already a little strange, with the neighborhood and the apartment and in my head was an idea, maybe even a hope, I would find something altogether different, I don't know exactly, but a fancy apartment, furs, servants—you know, a love nest. And now, instead, there's this place, I could see it's a room and a kitchenette and you don't have to be an expert from antiques to see the furniture ain't Chippendale and the baby sitter is not an English type governess, she's a poor thing herself in a cotton dress, but the boy—you know, it's a remarkable thing with kids. Older people, you put them in a run-down surroundings, pretty soon they get to look run down themselves. But kids, I'm not talking about if they are being starved or sick, but ordinary circumstances, what do they know about poor, rich, plain, fancy, the hands are grimy, sweaty, the pants are hanging over the chubby knees, the face is dirty a little and they are shining like jewels.

Well, he keeps pulling on the woman's skirt, this little one, in his other hand he's holding a toy. "He wants me to tell him a story," the woman explains me, just like I never had any kids of my own, I had to sit with them for two hours every night, racking my brains for stories for them.

"Lamb," he hollers. She picks him up and I can see he's something to pick up, solid like a little giant. He holds out to me the toy, it's a sheep, made from cotton or something and half of it is pulled out, pretty soon it will be bald altogether. So I take it, I look at it. "Mary, lamb," he hollers. He starts to wriggle around now, the woman can't hold him any more, she's got to put him down. So now he takes hold of my finger and he starts to pull me into the

63

house. I'm looking at the woman and she laughs and says, "Now, Kevin, it's not polite to act that way with the gentleman."

But what does he know about polite? He's got a fixed idea in his head and he figures he's got here another sucker. I'm inside, I see now where he's pulling me. In a corner of the room there is a Christmas tree, a little one, with maybe a dozen balls hanging and on the floor is a cardboard box with straw and little figures around and I see my problem already. It's not Mary had a little lamb, or Mary, Mary, quite contrary, this is another Mary and another story. And I'm figuring for this story he's got the wrong customer. Morris Seidman ain't the man for the job.

He keeps on hollering, "Lamb, lamb," the woman comes up, she says, "Now, Kevin, you've heard the story a dozen times today. You let the gentleman alone." But he don't pay attention. He's holding onto me like with a pliers and I don't know how it is with you but me, a child takes hold of my finger and he looks up at me with his round face, it's so shiny it hurts your eyes—well, I'm finished. I'm standing there, I don't know what to do, he only wants I should tell him the story. So what am I going to tell him? Once upon a time was a Jewish girl, she had a carpenter for a husband, he couldn't make a living, and she had a child, she had to have it in a stable, and for two thousand years we haven't heard the end of it? I'm telling you, my father, the cantor, he should rest in peace, he would have seen me in this situation he would drop dead all over again.

64

Well, my good fortune, just then the door opens and Pat comes in. She don't even see anything in the room, only the boy. "Kevin," she says to him, and the boy is scootling over, right away he wants to see what's in the package she's carrying, is it something for him.

"Oh, you little cash register, you," she says. "Don't worry, it's for you." And she picks him up and gives him a hug and says, "Martha, how was it this afternoon?" And then she sees me and her face gets a little pale. She puts down the boy. "Mr. Seidman," she says. "Is something wrong?"

Fine thing. I worked myself up to this, somebody sees me in their house, the only thing they can think is that something is wrong. "You'll pardon me for dropping in so informal," I say, "I couldn't find in our file the phone number."

"I don't have a phone," she says. "I've been trying to get one——"

"I understand," I say, I see she is embarrassed I shouldn't think she can't afford it. "They're scarce now. You got to have a priority for everything these days. I know people, they've been trying for months——"

"What is it, Mr. Seidman," she says. "Is anything wrong with Max—Mr. Birnbaum?"

"Nothing," I say. "It's nothing important. I just got a question, something I couldn't figure out, maybe you could explain me."

She looks at me a minute, then she turns to the woman, she says, "Thank you, Martha. Do you mind if I give you the money tomorrow?"

65

And the woman says, "That's all right, Mrs. O'Donel. Kevin was a very good boy today," and she gives him a squeeze and goes out.

"What is it you want to know, Mr. Seidman?" Pat says, she goes meanwhile to the table to put down the package and she takes off her hat and coat. I can see her back is stiff, she's not intending to make it easy for me, my visit. Well, you couldn't blame her. The same time, I'm still trying to figure out. What is the angle here? Couldn't be just what I see, a young working woman trying to get along, with a small child, a poor apartment, a neighbor who helps out. Please. Got to be an angle. Couldn't be I've been crazy all these weeks, months, building up a fantasy . . .

"It'll maybe sound to you foolish," I say, "but I understand you bought a bathrobe for Mrs. Birnbaum——"

She hears this she turns around, quick. "Isn't it all right? Max gave me the size——"

"It's fine, the size," I say. "It's fine, the whole robe. First-class workmanship. I thought I would get one for my wife too. Not a Christmas present, you understand. We don't give presents, Christmas. It's not our holiday."

I'm waiting to see, will she say something. But she doesn't. She just looks at me very straight.

"Some Jews are forgetting this," I say. "They think maybe it's like being a member of a club, to be a Jew. You could drop out by changing your name or putting up a tree in the living room. The Jews in Germany, they made always a big fuss about Christmas. You could see how it helped them. Peace on earth. Good will to men."

So the child hollers now, "Lamb, lamb." She puts out a

66

hand to the toy. "Yes, darling," she says. "He must be tired now. Why don't you put him to sleep with the others?" So he stamps away, the little man, to the corner, and Pat looks at me. "Christmas is something very precious and beautiful to us, Mr. Seidman," she says. "I'm sorry if others can't share it. But just what is it you want of me?"

So now that I got to tell her, in so many words, I feel like an idiot. How could a sane person, a businessman, supposed to have some judgment, get himself into such a ridiculous situation? "Well, anyway," I say, "Christmas or not, I would like to buy a nice robe for my wife. Just like this, a present. You got it at Saks?"

"Yes." That's all. Yes. We're looking at each other, like two cats over a fence.

"So I went to Saks," I say. "I priced it. Eighty-nine fifty they want. Max told me you paid only twenty-nine fifty."

I see she's getting now a little red in the face. "Did you tell Max?" she says.

"No. I wanted to ask you first. If you don't mind."

She turns around now and picks up from the table a package of cigarettes, she takes out one and starts to knock it against the table.

"So how about it?" I say. I'm still hoping there's some answer. Not just that I'm an idiot. And a mean-hearted idiot into the bargain. "You got it maybe someplace wholesale and put it in a Saks box? Or maybe somebody gave it to you for a present? And you didn't want to keep it?"

She gives me now a look, like I would be on exhibit. "You have a rather low regard for people, don't you, Mr.

Seidman? Are you in the habit of selling the gifts people make you?"

"I'm not accusing you anything," I say. Not much! "I just want to find out."

She keeps knocking the cigarette on the table. "Frankly," she says, "I don't think it's any of your business. But since you troubled to come all the way up here, Max gave me a check for a hundred dollars. It was to buy something for myself and Kevin for Christmas. I didn't feel right about it. I never do. But he gets so hurt when I say anything about it, I just can't refuse."

I'm thinking, it sounds good but after all a person could say the same thing with a sable coat. "That's very nice," I say, "but I still don't understand, where does the housecoat come in."

"I told Max I'd feel better about accepting the money if he'd agree to my dividing it in three, and getting something for Mrs. Birnbaum too. That's all."

That's all, she says. My head is turning around inside like a merry-go-round. "I still don't understand," I say. "In three is thirty-three dollars. All right, so it's twenty-nine fifty, like you say. But in the store the robe is eighty-nine fifty. Maybe I'm dumb. Please, you'll enlighten me."

"It's really not very complicated," she says. "I couldn't find anything really nice for less. And I wanted something very nice for Mrs. Birnbaum."

It's like bells are ringing in my head now. "You mean, you spent the whole thing? The whole hundred dollars for Molly?"

"Well, not the whole thing. Just eighty-nine fifty."

"And what's with the tax?" I say.

She gives a smile with one side of her face. "There was still enough left over to buy that crèche for Kevin. I think Max—Mr. Birnbaum—would like him to have it." She's looking me straight in the eyes. "He seems to feel differently about Christmas than you do."

Yes. About Christmas. About a lot of things.

"Now I've told you," she says, "I'd be obliged if you didn't tell Max."

Well, there's only one thing would help me now, if I could find a place to fall through the floor. But it's very solid, the floor. And it's always happening like this, good things always come in bunches, I'm getting somehow all mixed up with my hat and my coat and my cigarettes, my hat is falling down, I'm starting to pick it up, then some papers fall out of my coat pocket and she helps me pick them up, I'm sweating and my hands are like from ice. So finally, finally, I'm starting to walk to the door, it's like I was there a year already. "You'll pardon me," I say, "for butting in like this——"

"That's all right," she says. "I'm sorry you had to trouble. I've been trying to get a phone put in. They told me at the plant that I was entitled to one as a defense worker——"

"You're not modeling any more?"

"No. I may go back to it sometime. Right now I feel better doing something with my hands. I feel as if I'm contributing something."

The boy comes up again and sticks the sheep in her hand. "Lamb, lamb," he says.

I look down at him, that little shiny face that don't know nothing except he wants a story, he don't know the trouble

69

stories can make in the world, he don't know from jealousy, from caring for a person so much that you get a sickness in the head from it. "That's a fine boy you got," I say.

"Kevin's a big boy," she says. She pulls him back and holds him against her, in front.

"That's his father?" I ask her, pointing to a picture, I noticed it before, by the tree.

"Yes, that's Kevin's father. He was killed last year. In Italy." I'm looking at her hands on the boy's shoulders and I'm thinking, like I was out of my head or something, what the teacher says about my Jenny, she's got natural piano hands. It looks, actually, like the kind of hands you would see on a piano. But there's like ink around the nails, from the machines I suppose. "It hasn't been easy for Kevin," she says.

So now I would like to go already because I'm feeling funny in the chest, like I would need some air, but it don't seem right I shouldn't say something. "And what's with you?" I say. "For you it's been easy?"

Again she gives this funny smile, with one side of the face. "Well, not exactly. New York's not an easy place to make friends. I don't mean the kind you have to hold off with a club. That's one of the reasons I gave up modeling too. Maybe it's my fault. One thing that makes it difficult —Matt and I knew each other so long. Since we were children. I never even went out with another man." She looks at the boy and we're both looking at him, not looking at each other. "It's meant a great deal to Kevin and me, having someone like Max and Molly take an interest in us."

"Molly," I say. "You know her?"

70

"She's been up here with Max, to visit. She's a lovely person. She's been so sweet to Kevin."

The kid pulls away from her now and comes and stands against my leg. I put my hand on his head, it feels like a good-quality straw, and he looks up at me and says, "Lamb, lamb," they could make you crazy, those kids, with their fixed ideas—like their papas, they also get a fixed idea in their heads, they could ruin a friendship from a lifetime.

"I've never known anyone quite like them," she says. "Anyone so really good." And then she says, like she's talking to the boy, not to me, "Max thinks the world of you, Mr. Seidman. I'm afraid you've made him very unhappy."

"Yes," I say. I'm looking down at the boy with his little sheep in his hand and I look over at the box with the straw and the cradle and the Wise Men, and I'm thinking, what is it with people, year in and year out, century after century? The door is open and they are standing always outside, in the dust, in the dark.

"Pat," I say, "you want to make me a big Christmas present? Tell me you'll excuse me, how terrible I misjudged you."

"Are you sure you did?" she says. She looks me straight in the face and I see that Max was right, it's something around the eyes, the same kind of sweet expression, like Molly. "I'm in love with Max, Mr. Seidman," she says. "It's with me every minute of the day. And every minute of the night."

It's a funny thing, it's like I would know this already. Only all of a sudden I got a telegram: *Repent. I gave you the power to love. And all you did was judge.* "I wish it could bring you happiness, Pat," I say.

"It has," she says. "In a strange way. You know, the only really terrible thing is to feel nothing. Not even longing."

So I can't say anything for a minute, it's like my throat would be full of chalk. Then I say, "Listen, Pat, maybe you would do me a favor. I'm going to get this Christmas a tree for my kids. Would you come for a visit to our house, Sunday, maybe show Mrs. Seidman how to make with the decorations? And bring the boy? It's a few years since we had a small child in the house. Will be a big treat for us."

She looks at me a minute, then she says, "We'll be glad to come."

"You know Max lives only a couple blocks from me," I say.

"I know," she says. "I hope Molly will like the robe. I wasn't sure of the color."

I put out my hand and take hers, I wish I would have the nerve to put it against my heart. "She'll like it, Pat," I say. "It's a beautiful thing. I wish she could know how beautiful."

Well, you asked me what are my thoughts about Christmas. You didn't expect to get a whole *megillah* like this, hah? But I guess you can understand, I got a full heart on account of the news about my son. I wish I could say to everybody, this Christmas, put away the hatred, put away the misunderstanding, it should mean something in the world, finally, finally, peace on earth, good will to men.

three

Come in, come in, I'm glad to see you, sit down please, make yourself comfortable, can I get you something, a drink, a cup of coffee, I'll send down, have a cigar at least. So how's the writing business these days? Yes, I've been thinking what you said. In fact, I couldn't sleep the whole night after you called. Naturally I'm flattered a big national magazine should want to publish an article about me. But it makes me nervous too. I mean, what's to write about? If I invented something, or I discovered a new star in the sky, or if even I was a politician with big plans how to make more of mishmash in the world than there is already—but a dress manufacturer? I could write you the whole story in three words; styles, bicarbonate of soda and aggravation.

And this title you told me on the telephone, "Dior to the

73

Masses." I'm blushing every time I think about it. No, I'm not modest but I don't like people should think I'm blowing myself up with big ideas about who I am and what I accomplished. Dior at least is a genius. Not a genius like Beethoven or Rembrandt, but in his own line it's also something. But me, I had only a little luck. Happened, a few years ago, I got fixed in my head an idea that a working girl with twenty dollars in her pocketbook that she saved up for a new dress wants just as much to be smart, to make a big impression on her friends, or her sweetheart, or her husband, as a society lady who drives up to Bonwit's in a Rolls-Royce. So this is not "Dior to the Masses." It's simply a businessman's idea. All right, I made out pretty good with it. But there's people made a fortune from other things. Lipsticks, can openers, Scotch tape. This is a reason to write a history about them?

Yes, you want to say I took a gamble, this is true. Is this something that's a credit to a person? I don't know. I had a good business, I was getting along fine, making a nice living, I got all of a sudden this ambition to have a Style Show with dresses that retail for twenty-nine fifty, and to make this a big fashion event, with beautiful models and champagne, just like they are doing with individual-designed dresses for five hundred. Lots of people, even in the family, thought I was crazy. They tried to talk me out of it. You should have heard my sister Bessie those days. I was insane, I would land in the poorhouse, with the children together. You should hear her now. She's only worried I will land in Menninger's Clinic, the money is going to my head.

Well, wasn't so bad, what people said, but the bankers,

this was something else again. It was a struggle, to gain the confidence. Wasn't so easy with the credit. I remember plenty nights I would stay late in the shop, working, figuring, I would be so tired I would sleep there on a couch in my office instead of going home. And I ate up enough aspirin and Alka-Seltzer those days, they could declare on me a dividend alone.

So it came out all right. I made a success. People are coming now from all over to my Style Shows, even from Australia. I get fine write-ups in the papers. I am invited to be president of the Garment Manufacturers Association. Nowadays I walk into the bank, nobody looks like they wished they would be somewhere else. I got valuable opinions about conditions, politics, labor relations. Now that I don't need it, I could have all the credit I want, at special rates. I don't blame them, you understand. This is the way business is. But I'll tell you something, I'm wondering sometimes what is it all about. There is a certain satisfaction, I suppose, to make a success, to have an idea, fight it out, prove you were right with it. But doesn't last, the satisfaction. In a funny way, it's only the struggle lasts. The memory. I'm still reaching for the aspirin in my desk. I'm still getting up sometimes in the middle of the night, sweating, I'm afraid, I don't know of what. And in the shop, so it's on a bigger scale now but it's still the same business, the same problems, the same aggravations. If I want to go away for a while, I still got to worry what's going to be while I'm gone. Or maybe I don't have to worry. But I worry. You know what I mean?

My son? Well, this is a question. I couldn't answer you in one word. I had for him other ambitions than to be a dress manufacturer. You know, a lawyer, a doctor, something in the professions. But three years in the army, away from home, it changes a boy. You couldn't expect he should come back the same as when he went away. So there's problems. I'll tell you the truth, we had with him a few months after he got back from Korea, I thought I would lose my mind. It's anyway a touchy situation with the children nowadays. Like there would be a revolution, not only in politics, economics, science, but the whole family relationship. But parents are still parents. They're sitting with their worries. How many years it's been going on now, one thing after another—Hitler, the war, communism, Korea, the atomic bomb—and then what you're reading every day in the papers, what's going on with the young generation, hot rods, cold propositions, gambling, dope, stealing, killing—honestly, sometimes your mind, it's too much to take in, you would think the world is turning into a Dante's Inferno altogether.

I suppose in my young days it was the same thing, different names only. Hijacking, low-lifing, bootlegging— there's always some kind of problems like this. But who had time to notice? I came over to this country, I was thirteen years old, right away I had to make a living. Not next week. Next day, if we wanted to eat. So I had a job in a grocery in the morning, in the afternoon delivering for a florist and three times a week, in the evening, pin boy in a bowling alley. The rest of the time I had for myself, except when I would go to night school. You know what was my biggest problem those days? How to save up six cents for a malted once a week, Saturday night. And maybe how to sit on the bench in night school so the teacher shouldn't know I'm catching up a little sleep while she's reading to us.

We had in the neighborhood, I remember, bums too. I'll tell you the truth, I would maybe have liked to be one myself. But the first thing, my mother wouldn't let me. She was a plain woman, she had for the children plain ambitions. A lawyer, doctor, violinist, yes. A bum, no. In the second place, it's a very tough career, you know, to be a successful bum, and I didn't have the gift for it. Maybe just to be a regular bum, yes, but to work myself up to be a politician, a Tammany boss, maybe even the mayor, for this you got to have the right stuff. Nowadays it's different. It's no future for a bum. A kid steals an automobile, right away they rush him to a psychiatrist. They don't figure this is maybe a boy who's got a real talent for being a crook, he's practicing on automobiles, gradually he could work himself up, someday maybe to steal a bus or a street-car or maybe even a whole traction company. Then with the money, he could start up a big foundation, with a staff of psychologists who are making research about what to do with the problem of juvenile delinquents.

Well, I'm making a joke, you understand, but not entirely. I'll tell you the truth, maybe I'm a reactionary, you should excuse the expression, but sometimes I'm getting fed up with the psychology business. I'll give you a for instance. My daughter Jenny had a birthday a few months ago, she was fifteen and we made for her a party, fifteen couples, like for her age, it's a nice idea, no? Everything was fixed up beautiful in the house, the buffet, with the cake, candles, sandwiches, and the children enjoying, laughing, having fun, no carrying on, no drinking, only

77

soft drinks, and my Jenny, she looks like a little princess in the white taffeta I made for her and I don't mind telling you I'm feeling like a king in my heart; I turn to my wife and say, "Well, Sophie, looks like a plain old-fashioned party, no gin, no cocaine, no problems, complexes, repressions, just nice kids enjoying." I've just got it out of my mouth, Jenny comes up, she says to me, "Pop, why don't you take Mom out to a movie? We've got to turn out the lights now and neck."

How do you like it? Fifteen years old. She's got to turn out the lights and neck. It's a law. It was passed by Sigmund Freud. Maybe to you he is a god. For my part, he should better have gone into the chicken business, like my father-in-law. My opinion, there's sex for chickens and sex for people and, libido shmido, it's not the same thing. Not two years old, they're already stuffing in the kids' heads about flowers and seeds and Mama and Papa, God forbid you should grow up and think a flower is a flower and Mama is Mama.

I was twenty, I was engaged, I didn't know a thing. Ignorant, like from a convent. Who knew about sex? Until I graduated from night school I thought it was a department store on Fifth Avenue. My wife? No, she was a New Jersey girl, from Perth Amboy, our cousin's a friend. Their family was in the chicken business. Nowadays, since the war, I understand it's a pretty good business but they could never make a living from it. My father-in-law was anyway a very impractical man. Ask him something from the Talmud, he could give you six different answers. But if a chicken was sick, he would be helpless. Take it in the house and give it some calomel. But for Sophie and me, when we first got married, it was a picnic. We had chicken for dinner three nights a week and always fresh eggs for breakfast. I would have settled for less. She was a very beautiful girl, my Sophie.

No, the dress business came later. I was working then in a stationery concern, a responsible position, fourteen dollars a week. For a couple years my mother, she should rest in peace, was after me I should be looking around for a girl. "It's time," she said, "you should be thinking about a family, a place of your own, leaving the nest." You should have seen that nest, there were feathers, plenty, from the poultry store next door. What I was thinking all the time was how could I get *her* out of this nest. "Morris," she would say to me, "stationery and twine is a good business, don't be stuck up, don't walk around with your nose in the air." My nose in the air, if the boss would ever see me lift it up from the packages he would chop it off entirely. "Give a look the boss's daughter sometimes," she would say. "What can it hurt?"

What can it hurt? It can hurt plenty, believe me. I got a friend, Joe Wachtel, he was a cutter in those days in a skirt factory, he gave a look the boss's daughter, twenty long years he's been suffering. Not only she looks like a lemon but such a disposition—and the irony, the way it's happening in life—the father lost his business and for quite a few years now Joe's got to support *him* into the bargain.

Me, I wasn't smart, I didn't know anything, I only followed my heart, like they say. And I am a happy man, twenty-seven years. What happened? You want to write a scenario? Nothing. We met, I wrote her a couple letters,

79

with some nice quotations, Tennyson, Edgar Allan Poe, I sent her for her birthday a book, Victor Hugo's *Les Miserables*, we went finally to a concert, Mischa Elman, and we were courting, like they said in those days.

When I see what's going on nowadays, kids they just met, they don't even remember the names, they're smooching, petting, necking—I was lucky I could sometimes hold Sophie's hand, with a glove on it yet. And believe me, with her family there was no monkey business. We went sometimes to the movies, home eleven o'clock. Once in a while, the opera or a show, home twelve-thirty. Sharp. But sharp. You come home later, a half-hour, Sophie's father is waiting, he gives her such a crack in the face you could hear it in Newark. And mind you, we're practically engaged. So, according the psychologists, this is terrible. From this you could get all kinds of complexes, hostilities, traumas, God knows what. So we're married twenty-seven years, we got yet to have our first real quarrel, we got two beautiful children, nobody had to explain us how, hormones, inhibitions, all the nonsense, whatever I was supposed to know I found out and what I didn't know I wasn't missing.

All right, I'm not saying for everybody it's got to be the same way. Happens, a person like me, monogamy fits me like a glove. Some other people, after a few years, they are making jokes, they're spelling it "monotony" and flopping around in their marriage like flounders in a basket. So live and let live, that's my motto. Only a person should have a little dignity about himself, a little self-respect. But when I have sometimes an argument with my star salesman, Larry Kogen, about this—like when I got to

throw cold water on a customer who wants to be a play-
boy, make dates with the models—he says to me, "Morris,
you're a regular pamphlet from the YMCA. Tell me,
you've been married almost thirty years. Vanilla, vanilla,
vanilla. Don't you ever get tired? Wouldn't you like to try
maybe a little strawberry sometime? Chocolate?"

"Larry," I say, "you got a big territory. The President,
Congress, Jews, colored people—okay. Make jokes. But
me and my love life, leave us out of it. I got in the world
one place where I would like to keep the respect. My
home and my family. Please."

So he gives me a look like I would be something in a
cage and he says, "Morris, either you are the biggest faker
that ever lived, or you belong in a book."

"I'm in a book," I say. "Dun and Bradstreet. I would
like to be a hero there, with a triple-A rating."

He gives his head a shake. "Galahad Seidman in the
Rag Business," he says. "But never mind. Stay as sweet as
you are, baby." And he gives me a clap on the shoulder.
"You know, wouldn't look bad on our letterheads. Galahad Seidman, Inc. Frocks for the Expectant Virgin." And
he starts in to laugh like a hyena, he goes into the showroom, he's got to tell the models the big joke.

Well, he's not a bad boy, Larry. Goodhearted, he would
give you the shirt off my back. But what do you think?
You know me already a little. You're a writer. You got the
idea also I'm maybe a Knight from the Cutting Table?
Don't fool yourself. You think I don't know I got in the
place half a dozen gorgeous girls, running around all day
long in their little panties and bras? You think maybe I
don't get ideas sometimes, even an old kay like me? You

got another think coming. But in this world I know you got to pay a price for everything. I'm not talking about big tragedy, *Camille, East Lynne*. I'm talking about a piece of satin, a fine piece of taffeta, you drop it in some dirt, finished. You can clean it, clean it, clean it, it's not the same. Never. That's all. Simple. Somebody else wants it, fine. God bless them. I know there's millions of people are living like this. They should only live and be well. I don't want it.

But am I going to say this to Larry? To the buyers who are coming into my place with their tongues hanging out? They would think I'm accusing them, I feel superior, something, they would say Seidman is all of a sudden a Holy Joe, maybe he caught something, or maybe he's a radical altogether and anyway his styles ain't so good this season.

So like I was saying, Psychology. This is the big issue today. And my wife Sophie has become the professor in the family. You want to know maybe from the Oedipus complex? This is where a boy chops his father in pieces and elopes with the mother. You want to know from fixation complexes, eating complexes, not-eating complexes? You only got to ask Sophie. She's got all the books, she goes to all the lectures. And her friends, they are all going to the Analyst. *This* is a profession. In my days, before a person would call in the doctor for two dollars he had to be practically dying. Now for the analyst, twenty-five dollars, and you are getting a bargain. And for what? You are nervous. You are walking around in the world like it was filled with tigers. Who isn't? When was it different?—You can't sleep. So you go to the Analyst, what does he do for you? He sits in a chair, you lay on a couch, you talk to him, he listens politely, an hour, fifty minutes, then he gets up, I'll see you Thursday, he says, and twenty-five dollars goes on the bill. You know what my mother, she should rest in peace, would do if she heard such a thing? She would call a policeman. Honest to God. Highway robbery!

Well, I don't want to say nothing against it, maybe there's people need it, or think they need it. But take when my boy Harold came back from the army. One time he decided to go away from the house to stay in a hotel. This is, I suppose, a psychological situation. I mean, it's not like he had to run away from a house where there is garbage on the floor, or his father is a dope fiend, or there's seven kids sleeping together in one room. We got in the house ten rooms, and a rumpus room besides, he could have there a suite if he wanted, with a separate entrance, he doesn't even have to talk to anybody if he doesn't want. No, he decided he wants to live by himself in a cheap hotel. All right, he wants to live his own life. Fine. Ask me, why is it, in a room ten by twelve, with wallpaper like for inside a casket, this is his own life? And in his own house, a big room, with a yard outside, and a tennis court, this is somebody else's life? And if he's having in the morning a good breakfast with his family, instead of swallowing down a cup of coffee with a doughnut in a drugstore, this is losing for a young man his whole independence? But all right, this is how he wanted it, no argument.

But his mother, God bless her, she says to me, "You

know what is this whole business with Harold? It's because his emotions are bottled up and they come out in the wrong place."

"What are you talking about, bottled up?" I say. "What is he, seltzer? A balloon? This is a boy, flesh and blood——"

"I know what I'm talking about," she says. "I told you before, when he was in school yet. He never took enough interest in girls. You should have talked to him more, it's a father's place, with a son."

Sure. I should have talked to him more. Maybe I should have run to Korea, altogether, to Japan in a ricksha, tell the general I got to see my son right away, he should send a telegram to the Communists, stop the war, the whole thing, Harold's mother wants I should tell him about sex.

I'm telling you. It's a lucky thing *she* didn't find on Harold's dresser the picture of the baby. I would have had with her some excitement. You know how it is with a mother. Like with the psychology, all kinds of theories. Freedom of the sexes, trial marriage, intermarriage, no marriage—but let it be their own child that's involved and there's right away hysterics. I'll tell you the truth, I wasn't so calm myself. This is quite an experience, you know, to pick up a letter and read, and all of a sudden it hits you you are a grandfather and you never even received a notice your son was engaged.

It was my own fault, of course, what happened afterwards. I should have come right out, talked to the boy. But it was such a peculiar situation, it wasn't only Harold who was mixed up. I was plenty confused myself. You know, the father-son business, it's anyway a very complicated thing.

You want to hear? It's a long story, I'm warning you. Me, I don't mind at all; as a matter of fact, I would like to go over it again, just the way it happened. For my own sake. I'm wondering sometimes, even now, how a person like me, a practical businessman, could get himself in such a predicament with a son.

So. I got to give you a scene in the house when the letter came from Harold that he was coming home, definite, from Korea. You can imagine, it's quite an excitement. Even Samson—must be some kind of communication, you know, vibrations, I don't know what—but he's running around the house, barking at everybody, I swear I could hear him saying, in dog language, "My boss is coming home." Me, you understand, I'm not so calm myself but I'm trying to hold myself in, one person in the family at least should keep a perspective. I say to my wife, "Listen Sophie, you are the one who's always making with the psychology, I want to say just one thing. We've got a boy who's been away from the house nearly three years. It's going to be a big temptation for us to make a fuss over him, like he was a baby. But we got to remember, he's a young man now. Twenty-one years old, nearly twenty-two. We got to control ourself, or it's going to be problems in the house. I'm warning you."

So what is her answer? "*You* control yourself," she says. "I'm going to clean him up a little, three years in the army, I can imagine, and I'm going to make him a devil's food cake and I'm going to watch him eat the whole thing, with two quarts of milk. And you know what else? I'm going to tuck him in at night."

"For this you needed to become a professor of psychology?" I ask her. "Listen to me, Sophie. This year is going to be an election——"

"I know," she says. "You want Harold should run for mayor? I'm willing."

"Don't be so smart," I tell her. "I want you should use some judgment. Your baby is going to vote in the next election. He's a young man, with a whole future to decide. A citizen. You realize what that is?"

"Yes," she says, "it's someone I'm going to clean up a little, make him a devil's food cake and tuck him in at night."

Her eyes are like stars in her face, shining. A very handsome woman, my Sophie. And sassy too, believe me. "What's the matter," she says, "you're jealous?"

"Not yet," I say, "but you'll show me the chapter in Mr. Freud, I'll read it, maybe I'll work myself up to it."

So now we both got to laugh finally and I put my arm around her and we are dreaming a little, you know, the things a parent is remembering, a sled, a graduation, the first time he put on a tuxedo to go to a formal dance . . . Well, it's a funny feeling, I'm telling you, when he comes down from the plane, all of a sudden so tall in his uniform, he looks maybe seven feet, it's already too much, you know, with a father who is altogether five six and a quarter with stockings. But it's all along like this, the history with a son. Like when he went away to summer camp the first time, a chubby boy, and he comes back, stretched out, skinny like a string bean, and the hair all chopped off short, Sophie wanted to sue the camp, they sent back the wrong merchandise.

And here, fifteen years later, at the airport, it's the same thing. What happened all of a sudden? Who changed the bobbin in the machine? I turned my head away a second and the boy is gone and now I got to shake hands with Lieutenant Seidman, a fine-looking young man but are we acquainted? Did we have, once upon a time, maybe breakfast together in the same house? I fixed for him once a bottle, with a formula, not bourbon on the rocks?

Well, maybe I'm not explaining myself very good. I'm not a writer, and with the emotions, it's easier to feel them than to explain them. But it's like every time you turn around you're losing a little your footing. You're standing in the same place and, like on the beach, the sand under your feet, the same way the life is slipping away while you're standing.

Don't misunderstand me. This is not a tragedy I'm talking about, a boy comes home from the army, a soldier, straight, tall, handsome like a regular movie actor. But I'm thinking very serious now. It's a long time I didn't have a real talk with Harold. This was for me the biggest pleasure, when he was a boy. You know, school, the homework, or he's got trouble with a friend, or a teacher, one time there was a big thing with a dog, I think I told you this story. Now, the last years, there's only letters. What can you say in a letter? A joke, an incident, a piece of philosophy maybe. But talk—the real stuff? It's no substitute. It's a whole new situation now. All of a sudden I got on my hands a young man and I don't know any more what's

87

going on in his head and his heart, what are his plans, his ideas, his interests, like they say. All I know is I'm not worried. I know my Harold is a good boy, a clean boy, a serious boy. A parent can have from such a son nothing but pleasure, if only there shouldn't be any more wars, they should only let him alone.

Well, in the house, you can imagine. Samson we got to give a phenobarbital altogether. This dog, it's either he's scratching himself to death from worry, or else he is shaking himself to death with happiness. So much emotion, these little creatures. My daughter, Jenny, of course is right away pestering him, what did he bring home, souvenirs, has he got any pictures, what about the nurses over in Korea, and what about the Korean girls, are they pretty and so on, a blue streak. And Harold is very patient, yes, he says, the Korean girls are pretty, some of them are beautiful and he looks for a minute with faraway eyes, you would maybe think he's thinking about somebody particular. So Jenny says, "Did you meet any of them, did you date?" And Sophie says, "Jenny, let him alone already with the Korean girls." And to Harold she says, "How about tasting a piece of cake. Gladys made it special for you."

"Later, Mom," he says, "but I will have some more coffee."

"You had three cups already," she says, "and nothing to eat."

"Sophie, stop bothering him," I say, "he's twenty-two years old——"

"Twenty-one," she says. "Don't add on years."

"So he'll be twenty-two in a few months. You're still going to tell him how much coffee he should drink?"

So Harold puts an arm around his mother, he says, "Never mind, Pop. Feels wonderful for a change, to be fussed over." And he gives his mother a hug.

Jenny says, "Now you're home maybe I'll get a little less of it."

"Poor you," I say, "you got such trouble with your parents. Let me tell you," I say to Harold, "how grown up your sister is. We had a birthday party a few months ago——"

"Oh, Pop, don't start that," she says.

"So in the middle of the party," I say, "your sister's got to send me and your mother to the movies because she's got to neck."

"No fooling," Harold says. "Little Jenny. I remember when you gave Leon Sapperstein a black eye just for——"

"Now don't you start," she says and she starts punching on his chest and he grabs her hands and pulls her to him and gives her a big hug and he says, "If you're old enough to neck, I'm entitled to some consideration," and just now the bell rings, the first one of the family is arriving, naturally we're going to have a big gathering, a celebration. So who is it? My sister Bessie and her husband, Myron. We hear her from the hall already, she says to Gladys, she's practically screaming, "So where's the General?" And she comes in, she's got on a special hat for the occasion. This woman, with her hats, you could have a conniption.

"Look, look," she hollers across the room to Harold. "A regular movie actor he became."

"Oh no," Jenny whispers to her mother. "That hat. What are those, radishes?"

"Sh," says Sophie.

"So tell me already, Harold," Myron says. "Is it true about the Korean girls?"

This is a very subtle fellow, you understand, this brother-in-law of mine. A real member of the intelligentsia.

"What kind of questions are you asking," Bessie says. "You're in a house two minutes. What is this, a pool-room?"

"Don't get excited," he says. "I forgot, you are the interlocutor in the family. You ask the questions. Excuse me for living."

She gives him a look, you could fry an egg on it, then she says to Harold, "Let me look at you already." So Harold goes over to his aunt, he gives her a kiss, she looks him up and down and she says, "You're home, what's the matter you're still wearing your uniform?"

"Give him a chance," I say. "He just got here."

"He's grown," Sophie says. "I'll bet he can't even get into his old suits."

"So get him some new suits," Bessie says to me. "What better have you got to do with your money?"

"I can think of a lot of things, Aunt Bessie," Harold says to her, but with a smile, very polite, then he says, "How's Uncle Nathan? How are things in the old neighborhood?"

"What old neighborhood," she says. "There's no more old neighborhood. There's only immigrants and more immigrants."

90

I see Harold and Jenny give each other a look and I say, quick. "So take off your hat and stay a while," but mean-time Harold is already saying, "What do you mean, immigrants, Aunt Bessie?"

"You didn't see?" she says. "They turned the whole West Side into a slum. They ought to send them all back where they came from."

"Where did I hear that tune before?" Jenny says.

Sophie says, "Jenny." And Harold says, "You mean us immigrants too?"

"What are you talking about?" Bessie says. "Us immigrants. We came over, we tried to better ourselves, give the children an education, improve things——"

"Well, give them a chance," Harold says. "Don't you think that's what they want too?"

"What is going on here?" I say. "This is a time for a big sociological discussion?"

But Bessie don't listen to me. She's got a chance for an argument, she's always Johnny on the spot. "What do they know," she says. "Porto Ricans. Kids, twelve, fourteen, running around all night, with knives, dope——"

"Listen," I say, "stop already. I got Porto Ricans working for me in the shop. Simple, nice people, good workers——"

"Sure," she says, "for you it's fine. Jim dandy. You pay them cheap wages and you don't have to live with them. Eight, nine, ten people in an apartment——"

So Harold raises now his voice. "Aunt Bessie, you think they *like* to live that way?"

I see Bessie ruffles herself now like a chicken. Sophie sees too it's going to be trouble pretty soon so she takes her arm and tries to pull her to the dining room. "How do you like it," Bessie says. "Home ten minutes, already he's hollering on his aunt."

"Come on, Bessie," Sophie says, "have some coffee and a piece of cake. Gladys made it, it's delicious." And she takes her away to the dining room.

"Immigrants," Jenny says, disgusted. "How dumb can you get?"

"Jenny," I say, "stop it. She's still your aunt."

"I'm not bragging about it," Jenny says.

"Okay, cut it out, Jen," Harold says. "I'm sorry I let go, Pop. Guess I'll have to start learning manners all over again."

"From her?" Jenny says.

Well, I got to agree, even if she's fresh. This kind of an education Harold doesn't need. So I take his arm and say, "By the way, speaking of education. You thought maybe a little about college while you were away?"

"Not much, Pop," he says. "College seemed awfully far away, over there."

"Well, now you're back you got to start thinking about it," I say. "I wrote away to a few schools meanwhile, I got some forms for you to fill out, applications, you'll look them over——"

"Not yet a while, Pop," he says. "I'd like to look around a bit, get oriented."

"Oriented?" I say. "You didn't have enough of the Orient?"

Well, I'm trying to give you an idea how it's getting fixed in my mind, not all of a sudden but little by little, that something is different with Harold. True, I'm prepared, like I spoke with Sophie, there should be some difference. I expect it. This is no longer a boy, he's been a soldier, he had some pretty tough times over there too, I don't expect it should be any more like when he had a graduation or a birthday party. So what is it? I'm looking at him, how he acts with the family, nice and polite like always, and I'm wondering, why am I feeling disturbed? Why am I feeling with him a little strange, myself? One thing I notice. Hurts me, kind of. He had all the time such a quick sunny smile. Like the world's got nothing for him but surprise packages waiting. Now it comes out slow, like he's got something else on his mind, he's remembering something for which a smile isn't the answer and the only reason he's smiling is the company, his family, relations, and he's trying to be sociable. You know what I mean?

Well, what could it be? I don't want to start in asking questions. Maybe he would be embarrassed, it's something he doesn't want to talk about. The same time, I want he should know he's got somebody he can discuss with, if he feels like, who can help him if he's got some kind of trouble, problems. But for this you can't send out invitations. You've got to wait, the right time.

The first thing, I figure I got to take him to the stores, get him outfitted with some clothes. Right away he says, "I don't want to spend a lot of money on clothes, Pop. I can wear my old suits." And he tries them on, it's to laugh. He's grown maybe three inches, the pants are sticking up over his shoes and the shoulders are narrow like for a chicken. So I say, "Come down to the place tomorrow, we'll have lunch and we'll go afterwards and buy some things for you."

93

Next morning, he comes in, I'm having a conference—you should excuse the expression—with a certain Mr. Wilenski, a delegate from the union, a very fine gentleman, you could get from him in five minutes an ulcer. It's got to do with the price on certain new numbers we're putting in the line, I mean the price for labor, operating (this is sewing, on the machines), cutting, finishing, pressing—this is in our business a very crucial thing, you know. If you can't figure a reasonable price for labor, you can't make the dress. I mean, you can make it but you can't sell it, because you will lose money. So you got to figure out what is a fair price for the different workers and there should be left a little profit too.

So you're having on every dress, besides the headaches you got in the first place, to get the style, to get the material, to get the customers, to get the deliveries—you also got to have a Geneva Conference with the delegate from the union to decide what is a fair price. And for him a fair price is the retail price of the garment, divided among the workers, plus a bonus, two weeks' vacation for everybody including the officers of the union and his own grandchildren, and besides this, I should turn over my stocks and insurance policies. Well, you understand, capitalists got no conception of what's fair, they only want to grind up the workers into meat balls, so there is always a little difference of opinion. And from this difference of opinion there is being sold on Seventh Avenue I couldn't tell you how many tons of aspirin and bicarbonate of soda.

So I'm standing with this Wilenski, and Miss Youssem, my designer, we just made a connection, a very talented

woman, very original ideas, and my production man, Sam
Rosenzweig, he's been with me a good many years, and a
model, Marie Anderson, a lovely girl, she's got on the
dress in question but nobody is looking at it any more, we
are too busy arguing. Harold comes in, I introduce him
to everybody, he knows Rosenzweig from the old days,
and when I come to Wilenski I say, "You maybe heard
about Mr. Wilenski in the army. He is from the Blood
Bank Department, from the union."

"Mr. Seidman," he says, "no insults. You'll start with
the insults, I'm walking out."

"So walk," I say. "Who are you threatening?"

"I'm not threatening," he says. "I'm just saying. No
insults."

"You are not going to stop me from talking, Mr.
Wilenski," I tell him. "Make up your mind. You want to
walk, walk. It'll be good for you, a little walking. You're
getting anyway too fat."

Well, I see Harold is looking at Marie, she's something
to see, a beautiful girl and a fine girl too, nobody could
say against her a word, and they're smiling, the two young
people, but I see Harold is a little embarrassed and I realize, in the garment business, shouting is a natural tone of
voice and an insult is like for somebody else saying "Ge-
zuntheit," but if you're not in the business and you're
not used to it, you could think maybe somebody is going
to get killed. So I say to Marie, "Take my son and show
him around the place, introduce him to the other models,
it'll be more interesting for him than to stand and watch
Mr. Wilenski extract from me a quart of blood."

95

So Wilenski says, "I told you, Mr. Seidman, stop with the insults. I mean it."

"And I told you," I say, "if I got to take orders from you, I'll sell out the business altogether and go raise oranges in California."

"Please," Miss Youssem says, "can we talk about number 712. I can't understand, Mr. Wilenski, how you can come up with a price of four dollars for the operators, for four seams and——"

"There's five seams," Rosenzweig says.

"Are you telling me how many seams there are," she says. "I only designed the dress."

"And I'm only the production man," Rosenzweig says, "and number 712 has got five seams."

"And I'm only the boss," I say, "and you are both wrong. You're talking about two different styles. 712 is the lightweight wool, with the dropped waist in back."

"In my book, it's marked 713," Miss Youssem says.

"So I changed the number," I say.

"Well, I wish somebody would tell me these things," she says. "There are enough other ways of losing one's mind around here."

Well, this is just to give you an idea, what goes on. We're arguing for about an hour, finally we get the price settled and Wilenski says to me, "You want to come down, have a bite with me at Solowey's?" and I say, "You are taking no chances with this invitation, Wilenski, you know whenever I got to talk to you I can't eat afterwards for two days," but the real reason is I'm expecting for lunch a Mr. Pankhurst, a very fine gentleman from Baton Rouge, he owns there a big department store, he's been

96

buying from me for many years. I got a few customers like this from the old days, they like I should wait on them personally. It's a funny thing, I was thinking just the other day, this Mr. Pankhurst, we've got absolutely nothing in common. His family owned plantations from way back, they are from the high aristocracy in the South. And in the early years, when I was still on the road, whenever I would be in Baton Rouge, he would always invite me to his house, for dinner or for an evening, sometimes with his wife only, sometimes with other people, and you know I'm not using the language so perfect and these people are all high educated and still and all we're talking about books, music, history, and always I got from them respect.

You know, you always hear how in the South there's a lot of prejudice. But you go sometimes to Mr. Pankhurst and try to say to him, this Seidman is a shyster, a sheeny. You'll see how long you are standing there. Well, I got like this quite a few acquaintances in the country, and this is for me America, and nobody is going to tell me different. All right, why do I tell you this, I'm not making a speech, I don't want to get elected nothing, I only want to explain what is happening. I introduce Harold to him, he heard me talk many times about the boy, he's glad to meet him, he asks questions, after a while we go for lunch, a fine restaurant, Longchamps on Thirty-fourth Street, I take Marie along too, for the scenery, and I order up a good lunch on the expense account, you understand, I got no objections the government should help me entertain the customers, it's got a hand in my pocket plenty, so everything is fine, friendly, Mr. Pankhurst had also a son in Korea but in the air force, a major, and he's got stories to tell and Harold's got also stories, like the time he got lost from his company near the Yalu and he ended up in the hospital in Pusan weeks later, he don't even remember how. Terrible thing. But he makes from it like a travelogue, like he was seeing the country and it was a big lark for him, you could never tell which Korean was friendly, which not, and any minute you could get shot, chopped in pieces, and I'm getting hot and cold just to listen but the same time I got to confess I'm proud of him the way he is talking.

And then, don't ask me how, it's like you're driving along nicely in your car, enjoying the scenery and all of a sudden the horn starts blowing, by itself, like the machinery went crazy—the same way I hear in the middle of the crab meat, Harold is talking about minorities and Negroes and segregation and I'm getting pale, I try to change the subject, but the boy is talking very fast, I never heard him like this, he was always a boy talked kind of slow, sometimes you would think he's dreaming altogether. And what is he saying, so excited? Racial differences are a fraud kept alive by the big-money people in the South! The army proved it. In the army, where the white boys saw that the colored soldiers were just as intelligent, just as brave, just as loyal as anybody else, the prejudices were forgotten, they got along fine, no nonsense. And if it wasn't a question of money and greed, the whole thing could be washed away in no time. Can you imagine such a thing? I tell you I can't even look in Mr. Pankhurst's face, I'm dying. Some lunch I fixed up for this gentleman from the South.

So finally, finally, it's like a year later, we get back to

the place and Marie runs quick to the showroom, they're waiting for her to show some dresses, and Mr. Pankhurst says to Harold, "Well, son, I don't think you'd be a very popular lecturer down our way but I'm always glad to listen to an honest, fearless opinion." And he turns to me, he says, "He's a good boy, Morris. Don't you dress him down now." You see, really a gentleman. But I still got a bone to pick with Harold.

"Tell the truth," I say to him, after Mr. Pankhurst goes away, "you got a million subjects to talk about, why with a man from Louisiana do you have to pick out segregation?"

So he says to me, "Why not? It's important, isn't it?"

"Sure it's important," I say, "but I got also problems that are important. I've been doing business with this man fifteen years, he's a very good account, I don't know from his personal affairs, he don't know from mine, what do I need to mix in in his business? Segregation is a problem for the people in the South, they're stuck with it for a hundred years. Do I know what headaches they got with it? It's not my business. We got respect for each other, we trust each other, but I don't ask him about segregation and he don't ask me if I am kosher."

"Pop," he says, "you know why there's war in the world? Because we don't make other people's problems our business. We don't care."

"Yeah?" I say. "Seems to me it's just the opposite. If we minded our own business, and didn't mix in, maybe we wouldn't have been in no war in Korea at all. Anyhow," I say, "what kind of nonsense, we should argue about this.

99

Let's go out better, we'll buy you some suits at Rogers Peet."

So we go out in the street and start to walk toward Forty-first Street, there's a Rogers Peet, I traded there for many years. I see Harold is looking around and I say, "Looks pretty good to you now, hah? New York?"

"Yeah, pretty good," he says. "What was this stuff Aunt Bessie was giving me about the Porto Ricans ruining the neighborhood?"

"Well, ruining I don't know," I say. "It was pretty ruined already. But it's a big problem, no question."

I see right away he don't like my remark. He takes away his hand from my shoulder. "How do you mean?" he says. "Why are Porto Ricans more of a problem than anybody else?"

"Harold," I say, "let's not start up an argument. I assure you I got nothing against Porto Ricans, personally."

"Only they're gooks," he says.

"What kind of a word is that?" I ask him. "Gooks?"

"That's what a lot of fellows called the South Koreans," he tells me. "The ones we went over to defend. From the other gooks."

"Harold, I didn't call anybody names," I say. "But facts are facts. Since they've been coming in, it's made a big difference in the city. You could read in all the papers, editorials, complaints, incidents."

"For instance," he says.

"Well, for instance the Rappaports. They're living on West Eighty-seventh Street. They got a boy, fourteen. Twice he got beaten up. Even themselves, they're afraid to walk home from the theater at night."

"So they can take a taxi," Harold says. "They can afford it."

"Harold," I say, "this is a sensible argument you're giving me?"

"No, I'm sorry," he says, "I didn't mean to get ratty. But I hate it when people get things twisted up. Capone was a gangster so all Italians are gangsters. The Jewish shopkeeper on the corner is a sharpshooter, so all Jews are sharpshooters. A Porto Rican boy attacks a girl in the park, so all Porto Ricans are murderers and they're ruining the city. Deport them."

"Harold," I tell him, "I don't want to deport anybody. All I'm saying, you take people from their own country where they're living in a certain way, with certain ideas, you bring them over here in the tens of thousands, an entirely new environment, you got to have from this problems. That's all I'm saying."

"So the Irish made problems when they came over, and the Italians and the Germans and the Jews——"

"That's right," I say, "but you got to remember, Harold. The people that were here at that time, they didn't like to see them come in, neither. They hated us, with our pushcarts, synagogues, rosaries, stilettos—and you know something? You couldn't blame them, in a way. But the economy, at least, needed us. It was a whole different story."

"So what are you going to do?" he says. "Shut the door now? You can't. Happens these people are citizens. They're entitled to go where they want."

"I'm not stopping them," I say. "Let's go in here already and look at a suit."

101

"And in the second place," he says, "people aren't just statistics. They suffer when they're hungry. They die when they haven't a little hope, a piece of dream to cover themselves with. They're *people*. You're supposed to care what happens to people."

"All right, I care, Harold. But we're going now to look for a suit for you."

"This country got big and great on its immigrants. If they bring problems, we've got to take hold and solve them, that's all."

"Harold," I say, "you just got back from solving the Korean problem. Give yourself a couple days rest at least before tackling the Porto Rican question."

So he stops now and he gives me a grin, a little lopsided, and he says, "I'm sorry, Pop. I didn't mean to sound like a wise guy with all the answers. But I get steamed up about this sort of thing. I guess I've developed an allergy or something. I spent three years of my life, listening to that stupid gook talk——"

"Please, Harold," I say, "you didn't hear from me no gook talk. What am I, crazy? You think I don't know on the same list with 'gook' is 'kike'?"

So he gives my arm a squeeze, we go in the store finally and I get my usual salesman to wait on us. He makes a big fuss over Harold, partly it's business I guess but partly personal too, he knows Harold from when I was buying him suits with short pants. And Harold is again polite, with that smile on his face like he's not really there, he's a thousand miles away. Mr. Peters shows him jackets, very nice, one after another, finally he tries one on, gray cashmere, he looks wonderful in it, I shouldn't say it I'm his father but he looks sometimes terrible handsome, this boy. Where did he get the blue eyes in his dark face, I couldn't tell you. He goes to the mirror, to see how the jacket fits, he stands there a minute.

"This is one of our custom models," Mr. Peters says. "It's been reduced to a hundred and ten dollars."

I see Harold gets a funny look on his face, he turns away from the mirror and takes off the jacket.

"You don't like it?" I say. "I think it looks very good on you."

"It's fine," he says, "but do you mind, Pop. I just don't feel like looking at clothes today. I'm sorry, Mr. Peters," he says to the salesman, "I'll be back some other time." And he don't even wait for me, he walks to the door like he's anxious to get out in the street and get some air.

I'm walking along with him back to the place, I don't know what to say to him, he's acting so peculiar. Finally he turns to me, he says, "I guess you must think I'm a little cracked, Pop. I liked that cashmere number a lot."

"So?" I say.

"So," he says. "I was standing there, looking at myself and all of a sudden I felt, I don't know, as if I hadn't the right, as if it shouldn't belong to me."

"Harold, I don't understand you. You mean maybe because it's *my* money?"

"No, that's not it. I wish I knew just how to explain. You know I've always liked clothes, Pop. You know the kind of things you think about when you're sitting in a dugout, or bouncing along in a jeep? Corned beef sandwiches, or rummaging around that second-hand record shop on Broadway, looking for old Ella Fitzgerald records

—well, one of those sweet dreams was getting into expensive clothes again, all silk inside and cashmere out—and here I am, decked out in a hundred and ten dollars' worth of cashmere, marked down, and all I can think of are people on a road, women, kids, fighting over scraps that fell off our garbage trucks. You don't know what it's like over there, Pop."

"I could imagine. But Harold, if you don't buy the clothes, will this change?"

"I know, Pop. But all the same, the price of that one jacket would feed I don't know how many of them, for a year. I just don't feel like buying suits now for a hundred dollars. I'd rather buy one for thirty dollars and feed a few hungry people over there with the rest."

So now I'm getting a little annoyed and I say, "Harold, you've been home twenty-four hours, already you gave a couple lectures, sociology, segregation to a man more than twice your age—now you're going to give me a lecture how to spend my money? If I want to send money to Korea, I'll send it. I'm giving away plenty for charity every year. One thing's got nothing to do with the other. If I want to buy suits for you it's my business, no?"

So he says, "I'm afraid not, Pop. I'm afraid it's my business. I'm not a kid any more."

"All right," I say, "you want to be independent? I'll give you the money, get for thirty dollars a suit, second-hand for ten dollars, dungarees, whatever you want. Go by yourself. Private. I don't have to go with you."

"Pop, it's not that," he says. "Please try to understand. It's just that I've got to start looking out for myself. It's time, don't you think?"

"All right," I say. "You got some ideas *how?* I'm your father. I would like to hear."

"I'd like to tell you, believe me," he says. "But right at this point my ideas don't amount to much."

"But anyway, you got to be dressed, no? You're going to sit waiting for opportunity in your underwear? Or maybe go looking with those pants, they're up over your shoes?"

"I'm sorry, Pop," he says. "I didn't mean to make you sore."

"I'm not sore," I say. "Why should I be sore? You're a young man, you're entitled to your own ideas. I'm not going to interfere, this I promise you. But you got to make up your mind. Yes or no. With speeches you wouldn't get anywhere."

"I wasn't making speeches," he says. "I was just—oh, let's skip it."

"And college," I say, "now that we're talking. You want to skip that too?"

"I don't know," he says. "I've been thinking about it a lot. I can't seem to make up my mind." He's twisting up his face now like when he was a little boy, thinking. "I always figured when I came back I'd go back to school, all nice and relaxed, on a good allowance, no worries, go on to become a lawyer or a doctor, come out to a ready-made practice waiting, with you, the family, friends. All nice and cushy. But I don't know any more, Pop. I'd like my life to count for something more than that."

"I don't understand you, Harold," I say. "A doctor doesn't count for something?"

"I suppose so," he says. "I just don't feel any more it's what I want. I don't want to just settle into a mold, writing

105

prescriptions for Aunt Bessie's sinus, for kids with measles and people with bellyaches. I'd like to do something about the real sickness of the world—war, poverty, injustice . . ."

Well, it's very fine what he's saying, high ideals, but to me, I wouldn't lie to you, it sounds like a lot of nonsense. You could be a doctor and make a success, and you want to be an idealist also, you got time week ends, you could give spare time to a clinic, so many things. I don't want to tell Harold he is talking like a fool, I don't want to show him how disappointed I'm feeling, still I can't help saying, "You mean you want to be a doctor to the whole world? You wouldn't be satisfied with just separate countries?"

So he puts on his face this new type smile, it's like a piece of haberdashery he picked up somewhere to cover his face, like you are putting on a shirt to cover your chest. It would be good for a headwaiter, a public relations man in an undertaking parlor, but for a son with a father, no. It's making me, even, a little angry. Well, not angry exactly. Maybe it's more worried. Or even a little hurt. I don't know exactly.

"I think I'll shove off, Pop," he says. "You must have lots of things to do. We can talk about this some more at home."

He goes to the door and meanwhile Marie opens and comes in. She's got on a sample from the new line, a little tailored suit, and she looks like a doll.

"Oh, I'm sorry," she says, "I didn't mean to interrupt."

"It's all right," Harold says. "I was just leaving."

"I could come back," Marie says to me but she's looking

at Harold. "Miss Youssem just wanted you to see how this looks on."

"Very pretty," Harold says. "You ought to sell a million." He gives her a smile and she gives him one back, and he goes out.

"My, he's good-looking, Mr. Seidman," she says. "Is he coming into the business?"

"I wish I would know what he's going to do, Marie," I say. "You talked to him a little? What is your impression?"

"How do you mean, Mr. Seidman? He seems very intelligent."

"To me he seems very confused. You heard, at lunch. With Mr. Pankhurst."

"Well, I happen to agree with him——"

"This is not the question. Maybe I agree with him too. But a customer. From the South. Time and place department. No?"

"It must be a little strange for them, Mr. Seidman," she says. "Coming back. I mean—capturing a hill. Staying alive. Staying warm. And then back to a world where relationships are a kind of minuet. Or masked ball. It's not surprising if they've lost the rhythm. Or don't think it's very important."

I look at her, I wonder from where does this lovely girl get such wisdom. Maybe twenty years old.

"But he doesn't seem the sort of boy you'd have to worry about," she says.

"Worry?" I say. "Listen, I know that boy like a book. He'll settle down, he'll be fine. Perfect."

"I'm sure of it," she says.

"So give me a little water," I say, and I take an aspirin from the drawer. She pours for me some water in a glass and hands it to me. "The girls all think he's terribly nice," she says, and I say, "His mother will be very glad to hear it," and I don't know why, we both start to laugh.

"All right, let me see," I say. "Let's get back to business." She walks for me up and down. "Looks pretty good," I say.

"I think it's stunning," she says.

"On you, certainly," I say. "If I could only send you with the suit I would know we got a winner."

So she blushes a little. Actually blushes, imagine in this day and age, a modern girl, and I say, "All right, I'll tell Mrs. Seidman what the girls think about Harold and you'll tell Miss Youssem I think she's a genius and Larry will go out and sell a million and we got here a whole mutual admiration society."

So from feeling rotten, I feel now pretty good. After all, I figure, what's to worry? A boy with a good mind, a pretty good education, even if he don't go on with college it's already more than most boys got. Looks, a wonderful personality he's certainly got. And is it so bad he's got also a good heart, sympathy for people, Negroes, Porto Ricans, Koreans? All right, he's a little confused now about the future, what he wants to do. He wants to be independent. Well, this is what we are all striving for with the children, no? To stand on their own feet?

So I make with myself a resolution. From now on I'm going to let him alone, with the college business, clothes, whatever it is. Let him adjust himself, get back into a normal routine, like Marie said. If he wants from me money, or an advice, that's another story. He could always come to me, I'll always be there to help him. But no interference. Let him find his own way, whatever he wants.

A fine resolution, no? Still and all, I'm expecting there will be a *little* communication between us. A boy is away from his family three years, he went through so much, it's not unreasonable his father should want to hear from him a little something about his experiences, what went on over there. But nothing. I get home in the evening, he's out for a walk, or he's sitting in his room with the door closed, listening to records, or the typewriter is going a mile a minute—this boy, you know, whatever he does, even typing, it's like for a prize. What is he writing? He don't say and I don't ask. I made up my mind, I'm sticking to it. Hands off.

Well, I'm sitting one evening, after dinner, with the paper, it's a Thursday, our Gladys is off and Harold says to his sister, very nice, co-operative, "Come on, Jen, K.P. Let's clean up the dishes," and Jenny says, "Why don't you enlist again?" and Sophie says, "Don't be fresh, Jenny," and to Harold she says, "Never mind the dishes, dear. Why don't you sit down here with me and we'll have a little talk. Just you and I. We haven't really, you know, since you got back. I've got so many questions to ask you."

"Could we make it some other time, Mom?" he says. "My head's full of a lot of stuff I want to get down."

So she says (not like me; with her, the psychology

business, you always got to come right out with everything, otherwise you could get a repression) "What are you so busy writing all the time?"

"Oh, some stuff," he says and he gives her this smile he got in the PX, I feel like telling him he should better frown already. From this kind of a smile parents could only get lonesome.

Later, when Sophie and I are in bed, I'm reading a book, she's looking at the paper, neither of us knows a word we're reading, you can believe me, finally she puts away the paper and she says, "He's certainly changed."

"So why are you sighing so hard you could blow away the quilt?" I say to her. "Naturally he's changed. What do you expect? Three years in the army. Takes a while for a boy to adjust himself."

"I don't know," she says. "I wish he had a girl. That's what I wish."

"How long is he home?" I say. "Already you got to start the matrimonial agency? Give him a chance to breathe at least."

"I'd just like to see him enjoying himself a little," she says. "Not so serious."

"Stop worrying," I tell her. "You should have seen him in the place the other day. With the models. They think he is terribly nice. And he was enjoying himself plenty."

So she sits up in the bed like a jack-in-the-box. "Morris," she says, "this I don't like. This is not the solution. You leave him alone with your models, you hear?"

"Don't get so excited," I say to her. "One minute you're wishing he had a girl, the next minute I tell you I introduced him to some girls, you turn on me like a tiger. Where is the logic?"

"I was talking about a girl he can take out, nicely, dancing, for a walk, a soda, something. Not a model."

"Sophie," I say, "you're a beautiful woman. And not only beautiful. Intelligent too. And educated. But I got to tell you—what you are not learning in your psychology courses would fill some book."

"All right, Mr. Universe," she says. "You have the big opinions. All I want is a good life for my family."

"I know, Sophie," I say, and I put my arm around her. "But this you can't order from a catalogue." And she sighs again and I say, "You know something? All of a sudden I got something else on my mind than the children."

"You're hungry," she says. "You want a sandwich."

"Nope," I say. "You're not getting off so easy."

"Morris," she says, laughing, "stop, it's late."

"For you it's late," I say. "For me it's early. I'm altogether twenty years old and I think you are the sexiest woman I ever saw in my life."

"Morris," she says, she's still laughing, "at least put out the light."

"What are you afraid of," I say, "you'll see that I love you?"

"It's not nice," she says, "parents of grown children."

"Nice," I say, "is no word for it."

Well, what I mean, I don't want to get too personal but I want you should get the picture. Not like there would be a big crisis, explosions, arguments. Nothing. Just a regular family life, everything going on like before. Only every day goes by, there's something with

Harold to make Sophie and me upset. And we couldn't put our finger, exactly, why. For everything there's an explanation. He likes to walk by himself till two, three o'clock in the morning? Well, he's got things to figure out. Maybe in the middle of all the shooting, running, killing, he thought of this. To walk by himself in the old neighborhood, everything quiet, friendly, nobody's going to start screaming all of a sudden like lunatics and throwing bombs. Maybe he needs it, something like this. Could be very soothing for the nerves.

So that's one thing. He doesn't care to look up his old friends again? Well, after three years, you lose the contact. Maybe he feels he hasn't got too much to say to them now. They got different ideas, plans, I don't know what. He sits in his room sometimes a whole day long, the records are going, well, this also could be something he dreamed about it when he was away. He always loved music. Or the typewriter is going like crazy? So he's writing letters. Or whatever he's writing. In the morning he rushes right away to the mail, to grab a letter, sometimes a package, it's a little like there would be some secret, he's got to keep it from the family? But this too, it's nothing to make a production. Maybe he had there a little something with a girl, a nurse, he's carrying on a correspondence.

You see what I mean? In my mind I'm asking the question and there's always an answer. I got to tell you now a telephone conversation, fits into the picture. But first I want to give you a scene, in the morning, breakfast. We're at the table, the family, the doorbell rings, it's the mailman, Gladys goes to the door, brings in the mail, Harold right away grabs, looks for himself, takes out a letter. He opens it, looks at it quick, it's hardly time to read anything, then he puts it away in his pocket and starts to eat his egg like it was made of rubber chopped in with a little sawdust. And all of a sudden I got enough, being a diplomat. This is not a star boarder in my house and I'm not Lord Chesterfield.

I say to him, "Harold, what's in the letter?"

"The letter?" he says. "Oh, nothing."

"So if it's nothing why are you looking like you lost your best friend?"

"I'll bet it's from a babe," Jenny says.

"Listen to me, young lady," I say to her. "I know you had a birthday party not long ago, you had to send your parents away they shouldn't find out how grown up you are. But here and now I'm giving you a notice you are not too old to have your mouth washed out with soap."

"What does he want from me, Mom?" Jenny says. "Babe is a dirty word all of a sudden?"

"I want everybody in this house to change the subject," Sophie says. "Immediately. A letter is a private thing."

"It's not that private, Mom," Harold says. "I just don't see any point in talking about it, right now."

"So when could you see the point?" I ask him. "You're home already quite a few weeks. Maybe you could give us a date when you're going to start acting human again?"

So he jumps up and starts to go away from the table.

"You're not finished," I say. "Sit down and eat your breakfast."

"I don't want any more," he says. "Do you mind?"

"Yes, I mind," I say. "And if it will make it easier for

you to remember where you are and who you are, you can call me colonel. Or general. Sit down."

So now comes in our housekeeper, Gladys, she knows always the right time to put in her two cents' worth. "You want some more coffee, Colonel?" she says to me.

"Listen, my dear woman," I answer her, "when you came to us eleven years ago, you weighed maybe ninety-eight pounds. Now you weigh a hundred and ninety-eight and this I'll tell you, the next hundred pounds ain't going to be so easy for you, if you don't show a little respect for who's running this house."

"Yes, sir, General," she says. "I got nothing but respect for Mrs. Seidman," and Jenny is spitting out half her coffee in her napkin and I'll tell you the truth, I got to hold myself in also, I shouldn't laugh. This is a character, this Gladys, I could tell you stories about her too the whole day. One time the children were sick, both together, they had scarlet fever and in the middle of everything, doctors, medicines, charts, Gladys brings in two little bags made from muslin, inside is seeds, herbs, I don't know what, and she ties them around the children's necks. Sophie is plenty worried, it's no joke, scarlet fever, and she says, "Gladys, what are you doing?" and Gladys says it's something, a charm, her grandmother told her it's good against the red sickness. So Sophie says, "Shame on you, Gladys, you're an intelligent woman, you don't believe in this nonsense," and Gladys says, "No, I don't believe in it but maybe there's spirits hanging around here, they do."

I'm telling you, a real character. Sometimes I'm thinking the colored people and the Jews got a lot in common,

I don't mean only broken heads. But the songs, and the humor, and the way they are thinking. King Solomon must have done plenty traveling, besides the homework. Anyway, what was I saying? Oh yes. Harold is standing by the table, and Gladys says to him, "Those eggs must be cold, honey. Let me fix you a fresh plate. You got to keep up your strength, boy. You getting puny from all that writing."

So now Harold too can't keep himself from smiling and he sits down again and I say to him, "What's the matter, Harold? You got to be such a big man, a soldier, you can't take us into your confidence any more? It's not a family any more? You got to shut everybody out?"

So now he looks a little funny and he swallows down some coffee, like it would hurt his throat, and then he says, "It's not a matter of shutting anybody out. If there was something good to tell you, I would. But I can't keep you posted on every move I make. There's some things I've got to figure out for myself. Work it out myself."

"Hurray," Jenny says. "Can I have three dollars, Pop? I have to have a haircut and wash today. I'm just a hopeless dependent."

Well, it's very much on my mind, this little scene. I go down to the place, I'm there an hour, comes in this call from my sister Bessie, in Flushing. What's on her mind this time? Her sinuses? How much money I'm making? No. She's worried about Harold. "What's going to be with him?" she says. "Sitting around the whole day, making himself crazy?"

"Who told you he's sitting around the whole day?" I say.

"I know, I know," she says. "You think you're fooling me? The very first day, I saw what was going on. I said to Sophie afterwards, 'Sophie, this is not the same boy, he's changed,' I said——"

"Bessie, please. You want to say something, say it. I'm busy here."

"Never mind," she says. "You got nothing more important than this boy. Why don't you take him into the place if you're so busy? Give him a chance to learn the business?"

"He's got to want it first."

"You could use a little persuasion. Listen, Morris, I'm warning you. It's a very serious problem now with the boys coming back from the army. My next-door neighbor, Mrs. Finkel, she's got a nephew who came back from Korea six months ago, he was hanging around also like this, so the other day his mother found in his closet maybe twenty pocketbooks he's stolen."

Can you imagine this woman? She's making such an analogy with Harold?

"And you know what else?" she says. "Thermometers. Dozens."

"So what do you want from me, Bessie," I say. "Let him use them in the best of health."

"Always with the jokes," she says. "Some day you will laugh out of the other side of your face. You know what happened with this boy? His father was also busy, busy, let the boy alone, he's entitled to a rest, so when he found out about the pocketbooks, naturally he was afraid the police will be knocking on the door any minute, he tried to talk to the boy, reasonable, he should bring the stuff back and the boy starts to holler, like an Indian, the father shouldn't pry into his private life, if he wants an advice he'll ask for it and he runs out of the house, this was a week ago, they haven't heard from him yet, not a single word, the parents are going frantic."

"All right, Bessie," I say. "It's a very sad story. But it's got nothing to do with Harold. Harold is not stealing pocketbooks. He don't collect thermometers. And I'm not prying in his affairs. And you'll do me a favor, save your stories for somebody else. Good-by."

Well, it's a ridiculous thing. All the same, I can't help thinking. You pick up the paper, every day there's stories about kids from fine families, high educated, the terrible scrapes they're getting into. Comes into my mind, the way Harold is always grabbing the mail, the look on his face when he opened the letter this morning at breakfast. So I give myself a lecture. What could it be? He's figuring out to rob a bank? He's making a conspiracy to blow up the Brooklyn Bridge? He's peddling dope? He's getting mixed up with gangsters? What could it be? The whole thing is nonsense. But the same time, I got this funny feeling in my stomach, like I ate some bad sardines or something.

I get home in the evening, Harold is not there. He ate dinner early and went out. "You're late tonight," Sophie says. "Is anything wrong?"

"What should be wrong? We're getting out a new line. You know there's always problems. So where did Harold go?"

"Do I know?" she says. "Walking again, I suppose. Or whatever he's doing."

"What do you mean, whatever he's doing. He's maybe out stealing pocketbooks?"

She looks at me like I would be crazy and I realize how it's still on my mind, this ridiculous thing Bessie told me. But I'm not going to tell Sophie now, she should start worrying more. "I was just making a joke," I say.

"I wish you hadn't yelled at him this morning," she says. "It upset him."

"I'll tell you the truth," I say, "it upset me too."

"Morris," she says, "I'm worried about him. He doesn't seem like the same boy since he came back. He's so closed in. Introverted."

"Ah ha," I say. "Another two-dollar word. Introverted."

"Well, you don't know," she says. "You're in the shop all day. But I see him, how he acts. All day in his room, listening to records, or the typewriter is going——"

"So what?" I say. "Before he went away he listened to records too, in his room. And he wrote on the typewriter."

"But not so, I don't know, secretive. Always with the door closed, as if he's got something to hide. Or he doesn't want to talk to us. I don't know. I just don't know."

"So what are you doing there?" I say. I see she's fussing with some socks in a basket.

"Fixing some of his socks," she says. "Some things are still the same. He still wears holes in the same places." And she gives me a smile, it's like she would paste it on for Hallowe'en. I'm telling you, such a houseful of smiles, a person could get very nervous about his family, what's going on.

She gets up now to put away the socks in his room, and I

follow her in there. Well, I don't have to describe you. The accumulation, pennants, an exercise machine I got him one time, his record player, records lying around, books, the typewriter on a table, papers lying all around —well, a boy's room. A whole lifetime of memories packed away.

She goes to the dresser to put away the socks, I follow her there, I pick up some papers from a chair. "Remember, Sophie, in English, the themes? Always A's?"

She doesn't answer me. Only a sigh.

"Can you blame him," I say. "He likes it, to be in his room again, like in the old days?"

She closes the drawer with the socks and she sees now a pair of shoes on the floor, she picks them up and takes them to the closet. Meanwhile I noticed on the dresser a letter, with a snapshot sticking out, I'm curious and, automatic, I pick it up to look at the picture. It's a little Korean baby, a boy, chubby, with big dark eyes in a round face. I see the name is printed on the picture: Kim Sung. So I don't know why, maybe it's because it looks a little like Harold when he was a baby, the picture, but all of a sudden an idea comes into my mind. I pull out the letter, I know it's not right but I can't help myself, and I start to read. The writing is slanty, looks foreign, but very fine, like a student, some high-type person, and I read a few words: "*The clothes and toys arrived and were most welcome. You should see your little boy playing with the mechanical duck, it would gladden your heart.*"

I'm standing, my head is turning around inside like a pinwheel, I hear Sophie say, "What are you looking at there?"

"Nothing," I say. I quick put the letter down, I turn

around, lucky she's not looking at me, she's picking up a sweater from the bed, folding it.

"His room is such a mess lately," she says. So I say, "Listen, Sophie, stop with the straightening already, we got Gladys for this. You got better something for me to eat? I'm hungry."

"You didn't have dinner?" she says.

"No, I forgot," I say.

"What am I going to do with the two of you," she says. "There's some pot roast, from dinner. You want some?"

"Fine. Make me a sandwich. I'll be right down."

So she puts down the sweater, she goes out and I wait a minute, then I pick up the letter again, my heart is knocking in my chest, I feel like a spy altogether. I start to read, I can't focus my eyes so good, the letters are swimming in front of me. ". . . *the mechanical duck,*" I read again, *"it would gladden your heart. He can wind it all by himself. We know how happy you must be to be back with your American family. But your Korean family misses you. Please don't forget us."*

Well, so now I understand everything, the confusion, the way he is grabbing his letters, the walking by himself, everything. His Korean family. And my Korean family too, God help me. I got a grandson, it's not enough his name should be Seidman, it's got to be Kim Sung Seidman.

I hear a bell is ringing, seems to me it's in my own head, for my own funeral, then I realize it's the phone. I hear Sophie call, "Morris, it's for you. Mr. Rosenzweig."

I put back the letter, like in a dream, I cover it over with an ash tray, Sophie shouldn't see it in case she comes back in the room. Then I take off the ash tray because I'm afraid Harold will notice. Then I can't make up my mind altogether, I'm standing there like paralyzed and I hear Sophie is calling again. "Morris, you going to answer or not?"

I go out to the hall, I pick up there the phone. "Hello, Rosenzweig." My voice is like a dying chicken. So he tells me he's still in the shop, he's got some kind of a problem with a pattern, the yardage doesn't come out right, I don't know what but he's aggravated. What should he do? So I say, "Sam, I can't talk to you now, take it up with me in the shop tomorrow, please."

"What's with tonight?" he says. "Aren't you coming to the Turkish bath?"

Well, we got a thing, for a number of years. Rosenzweig and my head presser, Simon Karp, Thursday nights we go always to the Turkish bath, take a little steam, maybe play a little pinochle afterward. I had my mind so occupied with Harold the whole day, I forgot entirely. Like I forgot to eat.

"Not tonight, Sam," I say. "I'm not feeling so hot, I think I'll skip it."

"What's the matter?" he says. "You got a cold?"

"I don't know, Sam. The nerves."

"It'll be good for you, a little steam," he says. "Especially for the nerves."

"All right," I say. I realize I got to talk to somebody or I will explode. "I'll meet you at Libby's, in half an hour."

I get my coat out of the closet, Sophie comes in from the kitchen, she says, "Where are you going? I fixed you a sandwich."

"I'm not hungry," I say.

"But a minute ago you said——"

"Sophie, please, I got a lot on my mind. I'm going down to talk to Rosenzweig. Maybe I'll take a little steam. I'll be home later."

I go out, I get in the car and start to drive. I feel as if I aged a hundred years in the last five minutes. How many times I thought how it would be—the feeling you're a grandfather. And before this, when Harold would come to me and say, "Pop, I'm in love, I want to get married." To a fine Jewish girl, beautiful, or even not beautiful, from a substantial family, or if not substantial, at least people with the same background, the same religion, we should have at least a mutual meeting ground. Not to come into a house where they got maybe a Buddha in the vestibule, and incense burning, and you got to take off your shoes and sit on the floor or whatever they are doing over there, and an interpreter should have to say for you how-do-you-do to your in-laws.

Well, I could make from this a production but I'm not a Dostoevski. I just want to give you a general idea, what's going on in my mind. You could picture this scene, I'm in the steam room with Karp and Rosenzweig, I told them the story and they are sitting with the towels on their heads, and they're also like stunned. Rosenzweig forgot even to hit himself with the besom while he was listening, so you can imagine. "Could it be a mistake altogether?" he says finally.

"What mistake?" I say. "How? Your Korean family, she says. There's a picture of the boy. Even looks like Harold. A little boy, an infant, with a sad little face——" All of a sudden I can't talk any more.

"Morris, please," Rosenzweig says. "Must be a solution. Don't be so upset."

"No, I shouldn't be upset. A pattern is wrong, I should be upset. But my boy has got a you-know-what in Korea, I shouldn't be upset. What should I be?"

"Well, we got to think," Karp says. "Figure out something."

"What? He'll bring her here, raise a family? Can you picture this? My sister Bessie?"

So Karp gives a groan now, even he could see now I got a real problem.

"Listen," Rosenzweig says, "after all, it's ten thousand miles away——"

"So this is your solution?" I say. "To turn the back? Let her suffer there, poor girl, with a child? Maybe kill herself altogether?"

After a minute Karp says, "Well, first thing, I guess you got to have a heart-to-heart talk with the boy."

"You think this is so easy?" I say. "What am I going to say to him? 'I went to your room, Harold, I picked up a letter there, it was none of my business but I read it anyway, like a spy, congratulations you made me a grandfather.' You don't realize what it is with these boys now, Sam. How touchy. I heard a case, just today, a boy was stealing, I don't know, pocketbooks, something crazy, the parents found out, they tried to talk to the boy, reasonable, just to find out, to reason with him—so he ran out of the house like a wild Indian and finished. Disappeared. Maybe they'll find him in the river yet."

So they both sit for a minute, worried like me, then Karp says, "You going to tell your wife?"

"Sure," I say. "This is all I need. What should I tell her, she shouldn't go out of her mind? I got to try to figure out something first, at least. A solution." And then I say, "You dassent say a word, boys. Nobody. You got to promise me."

So Karp says, "You know me nearly twenty years. All of a sudden I became a blabbermouth? Talk to Rosie."

"Never mind, talk to Rosie," Rosenzweig says. "You just see you don't get confidential with your pinochle pals from the Lodge. Mr. Honorary Pallbearer."

Well, I get home, it's late, I figure everybody will be asleep, but Harold is in the kitchen with Sophie, she fixed him a couple sandwiches and he's eating them with a glass of milk. Isn't it funny, you see a boy drinking a glass of milk, you couldn't imagine such a boy could ever get into any real trouble?

"Hello," he says to me, very nicely. I look at him, it's like a dream. It's just a few years ago I was helping this boy with his homework.

"How about a sandwich, Pop," he says.

"No thank you," I say. "I got no appetite." I'm wondering a little how *he* can sit and eat so fine. So I see Sophie is looking at me a little funny, she says, "Have something, Morris. You didn't eat all night," but I don't answer, I go out of the kitchen and I go upstairs, I'm outside Harold's room, I listen for a minute, then quick I go into the room again, I look for the letter, it's gone. He came back, he put it away. Hidden. . . .

four

Well, this night you can believe me I didn't sleep so good. The next day I'm walking around in the shop, my mind is in a turmoil. Should I talk to Harold? Should I not talk to him? Is it right for me to interfere? After all, it's not so long ago I made a big speech to Sophie about his being now a citizen, with his own responsibilities, his own future to decide. I made a resolution with myself not to mix in. And suppose I *would* mix in? What kind of an advice should I give him? Do I know better than him what he should do?

And Sophie? This is paralyzing me altogether. Just picture I should say to her, "Sophie, dear, I got a little problem to discuss with you. Our Harold has got a Madame Butterfly in Korea."

That evening, at dinner, Jenny is all wound up, she's talking a blue streak. In school she saw a picture, visual education, about the birth of a baby. Gladys is serving the soup, as usual she's got to put her two cents in. "I don't know what the world's coming to," she says, "showing pictures like that to children. In public school."

"I'm not children," Jenny says. "I'm old enough to have a baby myself."

"Hush your mouth, child," Gladys says. "You want to give your parents heart failure?"

"Well, why be square about it?" Jenny says. "You might just as well make a fuss about breathing. Or metabolism. It's all part of the same process. Circulation of the blood, gestation, sexual intercourse——"

"And jacks," Harold says. "Don't forget."

"You're so cute," Jenny says.

It's ironic, you know, the children sitting and talking like this, my girl fifteen, she saw a movie and she thinks she knows now the whole story, the biggest mystery in the world, and Harold, making jokes, God knows what he's really got in his mind, a boy twenty-one, already with a family ten thousand miles away in Korea, and he's got to keep it a secret.

"What about this Marvin Block you've been dating?" Harold says. "Did you talk over this metabolism routine with him?"

So Jenny gets pink in the face now and she says, "All right, be ignorant."

"No, I want to learn," Harold says. "After all, I've been away for a while, I haven't kept up with the latest in smooching."

"Harold, be quiet," I say. "And you too, Jenny. You're talking too much already."

126

"Well, it's a perfectly natural thing," she says, "and I'm not going to be shushed about it. I'm not going to get any complexes or neuroses. You fall in love and this thing happens and you have a baby. I'm just not going to get excited about it."

"When are you planning this?" Sophie says. "Don't forget you've still got to finish straightening your teeth."

"Oh, come on, Mom," Jenny says. "Don't you be square about it too."

"Well, I don't know," Sophie says, "I guess I'm not very modern. To me it was always very exciting, the whole thing."

"Well, I don't mean exciting," Jenny says. "I guess I'd be excited too. I mean, scared. You know."

I'm looking at Harold, to see does his face show something, some kind of a reaction, but from his expression I can't tell a thing. What's going on inside, that's something else again. I don't know, and I realize now I'm not going to know. Father and son. Dumb, like strangers.

Afterwards, Sophie goes out, she's got some kind of a meeting with her ladies, Jenny goes to her room to do homework, I go into the living room, I'm sitting there with the paper, it could just as well be a cave. After a while Harold comes out of his room, he's walking up and down, I see he wants to talk and would you believe it, now I'm scared he should begin? Maybe because I figure he'll want from me an advice and, frankly, I don't know what to tell him. What am I going to do, start to holler on him that he should have known better, now he's spoiled his whole life? How do I know I would have known better in the same circumstances?

127

Finally he says, "Anything wrong, Pop?"

"Wrong? What should be wrong?" Sure. What should be wrong. We are living all together, happy, singing, like birds in a tree.

"You were so quiet at the table tonight," he says, "I thought maybe you're worried about business."

I put down the paper. "You want to know?" I say. "I'm worried about you, Harold. I've been worried about you ever since you came home. It's true you're a man now, you told me off practically the first day you were back. But you're not in a position to be independent yet. If you got some kind of problem, you're in trouble of some kind, I want you to know, whatever it is, I'm not a policeman and I'm not a judge. I'm still your father. I want to help you."

So he puts out a hand on my arm and he says, "You're the best there is, Pop. I didn't mean to fob you off—but I guess I am kind of preoccupied these days . . ."

"I understand," I say, "I would be preoccupied too. But one thing, Harold. Take my word. Whatever you do in this life, you got to take the consequences. You can't run away from it."

"Sure, Pop," he says, and he looks at me, like he don't understand a word I'm saying. "I didn't realize I was giving you so much occasion to worry about me."

"How much occasion does a parent need?" I say. "You realize how peculiar you've been acting lately? Your old friends you're not interested to see. All the time in your room, keeping to yourself, writing, reading. But about going back to school you don't have a word to say——"

"Well, like I told you, I don't know about school," he says. "It seems late in the day. I mean—well, it's such a long haul, six or eight more years before I could become a lawyer or a doctor——"

"And you're thinking maybe you want to settle down soon, raise a family?" Family. Kim Sung. Mei Ling. Fan Tan.

"Well, it's not that so much," he says. "I'm just not sure that being a doctor or a lawyer is what I want any more. I've been thinking in a different direction. It started while I was in the army, in Korea. I've been working at it too. But I'm not getting very far, very fast."

"You want to tell me?" I say. He don't answer me right away. "This is maybe the letters you are getting?" I ask him. "They make your face look like a funeral parlor."

So he gives now a smile, like his lips are chapped, and he says, "I suppose you may as well know, Pop. They're rejection slips."

"Rejection slips?" My heart is going down a little further in my shoes. "You want to go back in the army?"

"Army?" He laughs now. "God, no. They're from magazines, publishers. I've written some stories."

"Stories?" I say. I'm really surprised. "That's what you've been doing? So why are you making such a secret, like you were putting together bombs in your room?"

"Well, everybody writes stories," he says, looking like he's ashamed. "I was hoping I could get one or two of them accepted, published, before I said anything about it. But it's rough, with the magazines. I can't get past those printed rejection slips. Not even a personal note. Except from one magazine in Idaho." He gives me now the crooked smile. "They wanted me to take a year's subscription, for five dollars."

"How many you got?" I ask him. "Stories? Enough for a book?"

"I imagine," he says. "I've been writing them for a couple of years. In Korea. And Japan."

"So I'll tell you what we're going to do," I say. I'm glad I got something definite to think about, to take off my mind from the other problem. "We'll make from the stories a book and we'll publish it. What do we need? A printer I've got——"

"No, Pop," he says. "That's not the way I want to do it. Either the stories have got something to say or not. I want them to be brought out in the regular way——"

"So you'll wait maybe a year, five years for a regular publisher to make up their mind. What do they know? You know what they told Ernest Hemingway, he won the Nobel Prize lately? I read the other day that his first story he sent in, the editor wrote him a letter he should stop wasting time and go into some other business. So you'll sit and wait for these high-class clerks to make up their mind if you're good enough? I say you're good enough."

"But how do you know, Pop? You haven't seen any of the stuff——"

"I don't have to see it. I'm your father. I know. Look, Harold, a book is a book. Printing is printing. You're a writer, you need a publisher, you got one. M. Seidman, 267 Seventh Avenue. A good address, believe me. There's people coming to it from all over the world. Substantial people, they read, they know what's going on and they can sign checks that don't come back from the bank. So you need Knopf, Simon and Schuster? You got people to read your book, you're a writer. It lays on a shelf and it could be the greatest book in the world. You're nobody. I got thousands of customers all over the country. In Europe too. South America. Believe me, they'll buy your books or they don't get from me another dress."

So he laughs, kind of a laugh, and he says, "No, Pop, that's just what I don't want. I've got to stand on my own feet. Either the stuff's good enough to be published or it isn't. I've got to find out the hard way."

"You don't want to give your father the pleasure? In his old age to be a publisher? Of his son's book?"

"It's not that. You might not even like the stuff, yourself. They're not the kind of stories everybody will like."

"Am I everybody? Listen, Harold. You were born in this country, you don't understand how it is. People like me, immigrants, we always got to prove something. You understand what I'm saying? I'm not saying it's right or wrong, I'm not blaming anybody particular, but a couple thousand years we don't belong anywhere in the world, pushed around, here, there, for us it's important to have something people will respect, *got* to respect. That's why you hear a Jewish family making such a fuss about a son, a lawyer, a doctor, it's maybe funny to you, you maybe feel a little embarrassed even, but that's what it's all about, for the respect. And the same with writing. For me, it's always a wonderful thing, a person puts words on paper and they make people laugh, cry, or only to think, understand things a little better. And my own son should be an author? A book? And I can help him to put it together, to publish it? Why should you deny me this pleasure, Harold?"

"You make it tough, Pop," he says, and I see his face is pale. "Okay. I hope you won't be sorry."

Well, now I got this settled, I figure I can wait with the rest till later. We'll see what happens with the book. Maybe he'll get from it some satisfaction, the feeling he accomplished something, it will help him make up his mind, what he's got to do.

And me, I got in the place other problems to occupy my mind. I got in some bids for redecorating the showroom I got to consider, I'm getting out the invitations to my Style Show, already the bills for it are coming in, in advance—only one thing I haven't got yet. Styles. My designer, Miss Youssem, is brooding. The models we bought in Paris don't inspire her any more. God is on vacation with her. He's visiting by Henry Rosenstein Frocks, two floors below.

It's always like this when I got to get out a new line. Everything is going wrong. I'm supposed to get some embroidered material from India, you know they're making there these beautiful saris, I'm putting it in the line this season, so the material doesn't come, week after week, I'm cabling, calling, nothing. In Italy, the fall before this, I ordered tie silk, so it comes in finally but in the wrong widths. So I'm trying on the telephone, long-distance to Milan, and now comes in the designer, Miss Youssem— yes, it's an odd name, I don't know what nationality, maybe Russian, Jugoslav, maybe a new nationality altogether, from Mars. Actually she is a very high type woman, talented, and attractive too. But such tempera-

132

ment. When she is angry, she is angry all over, her knees, her elbows, her hair, sparks are coming from her. And after her is coming in Larry Kogen, the expert with the needle, and in between they got Marie, my favorite model, she's got on one of the new styles, it's not finished, you know only pinned, and mostly in the bust.

"Will you look at this, Morris?" Larry says. "Where am I supposed to sell this dress? Ancient Egypt? Look at it. What is this business here? Geometry? What do we call this? The Square Look? If God intended a woman's chest to look like that, He would have built them that way."

"You and God," I say. "Since when did you become with Him so confidential?"

Meantime Miss Youssem is looking at him, she's holding in her hand a scissors, I'm afraid she'll stab him with it.

"*Mister* Seidman," she says, and when she says like this Mister, it's like somebody else is saying to you about what your grandma did with the iceman. "*Mr.* Seidman, I am not going to have an itinerant peddler with rocks in his head passing judgment on my work. You can make up your mind right now, either he goes or I go."

So I say, "Miss Youssem, he's not going and you're not going. You got with me a contract and if you break it, I'll throw you in jail. I'm sick and tired your coming in here and having tantrums. When you got the style finished, I'll come in and look. If I like it, okay. And if not, I'll throw it out. And you, Larry, get back in the showroom and stay there. Go, play gin, break your head, wait until somebody asks you an opinion. When the line comes out

133

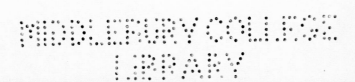

you'll sell it. And if you can't sell it, you'll go somewhere else where they make better styles. Now get out from here, both of you. What do you think I am, some kind of a Jewish teddy bear, you can throw me around, play games? Get out."

"And you, Marie," I say to the model, "get me an aspirin, like a good girl. It's ten-thirty in the morning and already my head is busting."

So she gives me a smile, and she makes with her hand on the lips, you know, like blowing a kiss, this is already as good as an aspirin, such a beautiful girl, a doll—— Can you meet her sometime? Of course, why not? I want you should meet her, and my Sophie, and Harold and Jenny—but we got time for this. You got to hear the story first. You got me started, you can't stop me now.

So in the middle of everything, comes a call now from the printer. "Seidman," he says, "I got here your son with a bundle manuscript." It's like he was, I don't know, a doctor and he's saying, "I got here your son with a bad case of typhoid." This is also a character, this Hungarian.

"So," I say, "I got here a designer with hysterics. What's the problem?"

"This is a serious proposition," he asks me. "You going to pay for this?"

"You done printing for me before," I say. "Do I owe you something?"

"I know," he says. "But a whole book? It weighs maybe two pounds."

"You're a critic from books now, Mr. Ferentzy? How much should a good book weigh?" I ask him. "A pound and three-quarters maybe?"

"Don't get insulted," he says. "I only want to know the score. This is for the family, this book? How many copies you want?"

"You got to know this now? First you got to set up the type, no?"

"Yeah, but if it's fifty copies, it's a different proposition than for a thousand. Then I got to job it. I ain't got the equipment here."

"All right," I say. "Figure for a thousand. Maybe it'll be five thousand. That's like the regular publishers, no?"

"Okay," he says. "It's going to cost plenty. It ain't letterheads, you know."

"I didn't ask you the price," I say. "Just do a good job. Like the boy wants. He's there? Put him on."

In a minute I hear Harold say, "Hello, Pop." His voice is shaking a little on the phone.

"You're excited, hah?" I say. "More than in the old days a dog, or a new bicycle? You're going to be an author, with a book, you can hold it in your hand, regular printing——"

"Pop," he says, "are you sure you want to do this? It's going to cost a lot of money. Maybe you ought to think it over. Maybe it's not just the editors. Maybe the stories are no good."

"You wrote them," I say. "I know they're good."

"But maybe you ought to read some of them, first."

"No," I say, "let me have a little pleasure in my life. Birthdays is no celebration for me any more, my age, Hanukkah is for the kids, Christmas is for the Gentiles, I want to have once in my life a surprise, a present. I want to lay down in bed, turn on the light, open up the

135

book, see my son's name, a published author. Just see that Hungarian should do a good job, good paper, big letters, you look on a page it should be like an honest face."

"You're a wonder, Pop," he says, "you deserve a book all to yourself."

So I'm embarrassed and I say, "This is what Larry Kogen told me also. Only he says, a comic book. Morris Seidman in the Twenty-First Century." I don't want to tell him what Larry really said, about the models. It's not nice and, besides, I seen Marie come in with the aspirin and a glass of water. She's waiting I should take them and she's got on her face a smile, listening.

"Wait a minute, Harold," I say, "I'm having here a Seventh Avenue cocktail." I take from Marie the aspirin, with the water, and she says, "Wish him good luck with the book, for me."

Harold says on the phone, "What's a Seventh Avenue cocktail, Pop? Have I missed out on something?"

"Another few years, maybe," I say into the phone. "But your name is Seidman, you'll get around to it in time. Listen. There's a beautiful girl in my office who is wishing you good luck with the book."

"Who—Mom?" he says.

"Marie," I say, "Marie Anderson."

"Oh," he says. "Let me talk to her."

So I give her the phone and I hear now a conversation, something exceptional. "Of course," she says. "Oh yes, a likely story. . . . Have you tried long walks and a hot martini at bedtime? . . . Well, naturally. . . . The most —— Oh yes, crazy. . . . I'd love to sometime. . . . Must

136

I answer that?"—and all the time she is looking at me over the phone and smiling, like I would know exactly what she's talking about. Finally she says, "Well, natch . . . one o'clock then," and she hands me back the phone, she's pink like a carnation, I know it's not stylish nowadays with the modern girls, blushing, but to me this is so appealing, I can't tell you. I say on the phone to Harold, "You know, you were talking not only to a beautiful girl, but she speaks a marvelous Greek, too, I couldn't understand a single word." And then, like a fool, I ask him, "You want to come for lunch?"

"Thanks, Pop," he says, "but I just made a date. I'm taking Marie to lunch."

"Good, good, fine," I say. "You should both eat in the best of health." Why not? He's on top of the world. A book. Lunch with a beautiful girl. And all of a sudden I'm getting a little sick in the stomach, I'm thinking about the one in Korea, with the beautiful handwriting, sitting in a garden, waiting, waiting. And the little boy, too, with the big, sad eyes. Forgotten. It's like a stone in my heart.

Well, the next days I'm busy in the place, morning till night, getting ready the line, figuring, figuring, all the time arguments, fights, heartburn, sometimes I'm thinking it would be a better business selling bicarbonate of soda on Seventh Avenue than dresses altogether. It's maybe a week, maybe two weeks later, I ain't keeping track, I come home, I find Harold all excited, he's got the galleys from his book. Two copies, one for him, one for me. You know what are galleys? You're getting them from the magazine too, I suppose . . . So I don't have to tell you.

Well, Sophie's not home, she's attending at the Brooklyn Museum a lecture, Harold didn't say anything to her about the book, me neither, I figure let it be a big surprise for her too. The whole family. Surprise. Me, I'm lucky I didn't get from the whole business a heart attack.

I don't know why, all along I had an idea this would be a certain kind of book, a love story, sad-sweet, about an American boy, a soldier, and a Korean girl, or a Japanese, or maybe a Eurasian, from an aristocratic family, you know a modern type Madame Butterfly. What should a boy like Harold write about? Something he knows, he's been through the experience. No? This is what the biggest authors are doing, especially when they are young. Like Goethe, with the *Sorrows of Werther*. So this could be the Sorrows of Harold and the same time he's writing, he would maybe get for himself a clearer picture of the situation, what he's got to do.

Well, this is what I had all the time in my mind and now I'm settling myself down to read. You know, all my life I've been reading, sets, Dickens, O. Henry, Balzac, it's a little funny for me, these galleys, long, like reading from a drapery or something. From the title I can't tell anything. *Stars in the Purple Dusk*. It's pretty but what does it mean? You got to find out. Underneath, where the title is, I see it's from a poet named Conrad Aiken, there is a piece of the poem, also very pretty, very nice, I don't understand it entirely, it's something about a man named Senlin, I guess he is maybe a Chinese or some kind of Asiatic, it says in the poem how he is getting up in the morning and facing the sunrise, and he says—this I remember—"On a swiftly tilting planet, I stand before a glass and tie my tie."

So I begin already to get the idea. The world is cock-eyed, tilted, it's racing away maybe to an explosion, and this Senlin, this Chinese philosopher, is standing by a mirror and tying his tie. You know, fiddling while Rome burns, the same idea. This is irony and it's a department, I figure, is better from a fifty-year-old man than a boy, twenty-one going on twenty-two. But who knows, maybe we got in the family a philosopher, a Maimonides, he was born fifty years old. It can happen.

I start in to read the first story, it's about a soldier in the war, he's helping with the wounded, in a hospital, and he finds out a colonel doctor is stealing from the supplies narcotics because he is a dope fiend. Why is he a dope fiend? Because he can't stand the misery, the suffering he sees all around. So the boy says to the doctor, "Why don't you try better to fight the system that is making all the misery in the world, instead of stealing morphine from patients who are in pain and need it, and shooting it in your arm you should forget the whole thing?" So what's the answer? The doctor is afraid the boy will tell and he makes up a case against him, that *he* is stealing the morphine, and the boy goes away to jail for seven years.

Well it's not a very cheerful story. But life sometimes ain't so cheerful. And Dostoevski is not so cheerful neither. So, number two. A boy from a fine family, he's in the war, in Korea, and a soldier, a Negro, saves his life. When he comes home, he wants his father, a big corporation lawyer, to give the Negro a job in the law office. So the father would maybe do it already, but his partners talk him out of it, they got big clients in the South, it's not a good idea. So the boy is disgusted, he goes away from home, he joins a union, becomes an organizer, the first time he goes out on a strike with the men, he gets hit on the head with a baseball bat and killed.

Well, by now it's getting a little dark in front of my eyes. But I'm going on reading, four, five more stories, always the same, a young man, full of ideals, he bumps his head against the system and he goes either to jail, or he loses the girl, or he is starving, or he is killed entirely. So finally, I know Harold is waiting, I got to face him sooner or later, I go into his room, he's sitting with a pencil, marking on the pages, he looks up at me and it's heavy in my heart. He's expecting from me a hooray, compliments, and I got to throw on him a pail of cold water.

"Well, Pop?" he says.

"Well, Harold," I say, "I'm not a critic but I think you are writing very fine, sometimes the descriptions are very strong, the people are talking very good, honest, like people, only one thing I don't know. To whom are we going to send the books? Seems to me like you didn't leave out anybody. In the North the industrialists are robbers, in the South the textile manufacturers are vampires, in the West the citrus growers are gangsters, in the East the whole government are crooks, the unions they're corrupt, the workers got no courage, the teachers are scared. So who's left? The hero and he always ends up in the soup, in jail, in a flophouse, or dead. Tell me, the system

140

he is always knocking his head against, what is it? Capitalism?"

"It's got a lot of names," he says. "Greed, indifference, selfishness, whatever it is that keeps people from being decent and kind instead of murderous and mean."

"Tell the truth, Harold," I say. "The young man in your stories, he believes in communism, no?"

"Call it what you want," he says. "He believes in the dignity of the individual. In brotherhood. In a fair shake for everybody."

"For everybody?" I ask him. "But bosses he don't like, generals he don't like, policemen he don't like, politicians he don't like, union officials he don't like——"

"It's not the individuals," he says. "It's what they represent; power, greed——"

"I'm sorry, Harold," I say. "People who read this book are going to call you a Red."

"So let them. Names don't scare me. Red. Purple. Green. I've got something to say and I'm going to say it."

"But you got to have some consideration for other people's feelings. Tell me, why are you so much against the system? You've had such a hard time in your life? Your father did pretty good with this system. You got a good home from it, an education. Why have you got such a hate on it? Where can you find a better system?"

"Right here," he says, excited. "We can make this system work for everybody, everybody in the world, not just you and me and a few fortunate others. The world doesn't begin and end in Great Neck, Pop. Just because you did all right doesn't mean we can sit around now and say everything's fine. It isn't."

141

"Sit around?" I say. "Einstein sat around? Eisenhower is sitting around? General Motors sits around? Your father sits around? How many American boys sat around in Korea, they got killed, or they wasted like you precious years of their lives. We're spending billions of dollars. This is sitting around? You're talking like a child."

"I'm sorry, Pop," he says. "We're not talking about the same thing. You just don't know what's going on in the world."

"What do you mean I don't know?" I'm getting now a little exasperated. "Last year I was in Paris, Italy, Austria, I get goods from India, a whole factory is working there, turning out goods for me, what do you mean I don't know what's going on in the world?"

He starts now to shout a little too. "I mean it's not enough to go to these places and stop in fancy hotels and talk to people with money in the bank and goods to sell. There are other people. A billion and a half of them. With nothing to sell. And nothing to eat. And nothing to hope for. I've seen them. Koreans. Indochinese. Japanese. Do you know what's going on? Do you know how many people are hungry and hopeless in the world? You think it can go on like that forever, while you go down to your office every day and manufacture dresses? For a profit?"

"Ah ha," I say. "Profit. That's the dirty word, hah? So if I sold my dresses and lost money, it would be better. If I went bankrupt, in Indochina there would be a celebration? Firecrackers, hooray. Seidman is broke, we can eat."

"Pop, please. All I'm trying to say is that you've got to have a social conscience today. It's not optional any more.

142

People can't go on living for themselves alone. It's not just that it's a sin against other people. It's a sin against yourself. Because if people go on not caring, the world's just going to blow up. It's got to. That's what I've tried to say in the stories."

"Social conscience," I say to him. "You just woke up? Listen, my fine philosopher. From what do you think you're eating, sitting without headaches in your room, writing? This house? Everything? From a social conscience, how do you like that? Because when I worked myself up from a shipping clerk in a stationery business, ten dollars a week, to a cutter in a dress factory, I was seeing how the material goes into dresses for four hundred dollars, for Bergdorf Goodman, Henri Bendel, for the fancy ladies, and I thought, my mother—she should rest in peace—my sisters, why shouldn't they look nice too, haven't they got a right, haven't they got men they want to please? And for years I was saving and figuring and planning, how I'm going to take the four-hundred-dollar dresses and I'm going to make from them the same styles, dresses I can sell for thirteen seventy-five, a girl could buy it in the store for nineteen dollars. So everybody says I'm crazy, I'll ruin the whole business and myself into the bargain and I'll be broke in six months. So I'm not broke and today, a girl in an office or a shop, she dresses up in the morning, a waitress she dresses up at night for a party or a dance, you can't tell the difference, is she from the Blue Book or not. Go, my traveler, over the whole world. Go look on Fifth Avenue sometime, pick me out who is the rich girl and who is the poor one. Social conscience, he tells me."

143

Well, one word and another. Finally I say to him, "It's no use talking, Harold. I got my business to protect. And I got you to protect. This book you're not going to publish. Not with my money."

So he throws down the whole thing on the floor and he jumps up. "All right," he hollers. "I knew this would happen. Why did you get me started? Build up my hopes? I didn't want you to do it in the first place. I knew you'd be afraid."

We're so busy hollering, we don't hear Sophie, she comes in now, she is home from the lecture. "What's going on?" she says. "Who's making a revolution?"

"Don't bust in in the middle," I say. "We are having a discussion."

"Some discussion," she says. "They can hear you in Connecticut." She looks in my face, then in Harold's, and she says, "I want to know what's going on, a father and son got to holler on each other you can hear it all the way down the block."

"You want to know," I say, "I'll tell you. Your son wants I should throw away my business because in Indochina there's people who are hungry."

"Oh, for Pete's sake," Harold yells. "There's no use talking to you. You twist everything I say to make a joke, or make me sound stupid. We just don't talk the same language any more."

"Then I'll tell you something, my boy." I'm getting good and mad now, he's standing there, hollering at me. If his mother wouldn't be there, believe me I would tell him once and for all what's in my heart, what he did to that poor girl in Korea with his big social conscience.

"If we're not talking the same language," I say, "you better learn another language. Because around here you are going to talk *my* language."

"No, I'm not," he says. "I'm not going to be around here. You can go on living in your plush-lined vacuum. In your ivory tower with central heating. Not me."

And before I know what he's doing, he runs out of the house. Sophie is standing there, we're looking at each other, I don't know what to say, it's like somebody just hit me on the head with a hammer. "I don't know," Sophie says, "I go out of the house for five minutes, to a lecture——"

"You were out of the house three hours," I told her. "And if you stayed home and didn't go so much to lectures to find out how other people's children are behaving, you would maybe know what's going on in your own house, with your own son."

"What did you do to him?" she says. "What did you say to him?"

"I said to him what a father would say who's worried about his boy. He's got in his head a lot of nonsense, he thinks from a good heart, from feeling sorry, you can make over the whole world. He could get into plenty trouble, believe me. It's not for a nickel firecrackers he's going to put under a streetcar."

"Maybe you'll tell me what you're talking about," Sophie says. "The boy didn't run out of the house for nothing. Did you insult him, what? Tell me what you said to him."

"I'll tell you." And now I'm hollering on her, I'll tell you the truth, I don't know who I'm hollering on any

145

more, maybe myself. "And I'll tell him. Plenty. When I was sixteen, I was a Socialist too. For six months I went around, hollering Debs, Norman Thomas, Workers Unite. Then it was finished. I settled down and got a job and made my ten dollars a week. Young is young. He's nearly twenty-two years old. I got enough already."

So now she starts to cry. "What are you carrying on?" I say. "He went out for a walk, he'll cool off, he'll come back." But I'm sick in the stomach, I'm telling you. Maybe some people they can stand big emotions. I'm a quiet man. I like scenes but they should be on the stage, in the movies, opera, with singing. Not in my own house, with my own boy, and my wife should stand crying. "Stop the faucet," I said to her. "He'll be back."

But ten times during the night I'm getting up to look out the window. And he don't come back.

Next morning, first thing, he calls up. Sophie is on the phone with him for half an hour. She comes back to the table, her face is white.

"Where is he, Ma?" Jenny says. "Did he elope?"

Gladys is standing by the buffet, listening, her face is white too. Nearly.

"He's in a hotel," Sophie says to me. "He's not coming home."

"What hotel?" I ask.

"He wouldn't tell me. He says it's a nice room, I shouldn't worry. I can imagine."

"Did he tell you what he is going to use for money? Or this is a hotel that's maybe run by an idealist who don't want money for the rooms."

"He's got a job," Sophie says. "In an all-night garage."
She looks now like she's going to cry so I say quick, "Did
you find out the address of the garage, at least? I could
give him some of my business." She gives me a look now,
believe me, not very friendly, and from a graduate psychologist yet. But at least she's not going to cry. "Well," I
say, "I'm glad he picked out something with a future. If
he works hard, applies himself, they'll maybe promote
him to daytime."

"Will you stop with the jokes," Sophie says. "Fine time
for jokes." She's telling me. From all my hopes for him,
he's got now a job in an all-night garage.

"He wants to know," Sophie says, "can he come sometime and get his things."

"What do you mean, can he come?" I say. "What are
you asking? Who's going to stop him?"

"Do I know what's going on around here?" she says. "I
turn my back for five minutes and my boy is out of the
house, in some horrible hotel."

Again with the five minutes. "How do you know it's
horrible?" I say. "Could maybe be a very nice hotel." But
I see she's not looking at me. I look at Jenny, she's also
got something in her plate she is studying, like homework.
I look at Gladys, she turns away, she can't stand the sight
of me neither. So I throw down my napkin. "All right," I
say, "the monster. Simon Legree. Ivan the Terrible. Tell
him I'm not going to be in the house all day, or tonight
either. He can come and move out whatever he wants. He
wants some furniture, he can have that too."

So now Sophie looks at me. "What's tonight?" she

147

says. "You're going to a hotel too, maybe? Maybe I should call in a real estate agent, sell the house, nobody's going to need it any more?"

"I'm going to be in the shop," I say. "Attending to my business, for a change. Instead of worrying about your son. So he don't have to worry I'll shoot him with a shotgun if he comes to get his clothes."

"Some house," Jenny says. "Harold comes back after three years in the army, living in swamps and on potato peel, and now he's got to stay in a crummy hotel."

"Listen, young lady," I say, "maybe you would like to pack your clothes too and join him in the hotel? Some house. What's the matter with the house? You got some fault to find with it? Your mother is already calling in a real estate agent——"

"Leave her alone," Sophie says. "You've done enough already. Go. Go to your business."

Well? You think I had enough already that morning? I get down to the place I get right away a call from my sister Bessie, in Flushing. "I just talked to Sophie," she says. "What's the matter with you? You lost your mind or something?"

"Listen, Bessie," I say, "don't jump in like a chicken with its head cut off. You don't know anything about it."

"I know that Harold is in a Bowery flophouse," she says, "he could get a disease altogether. What's the matter with you, Morris? You made a little money so you got to act like a Boston blueblood?"

"For heaven's sake," I yell, "what are you talking about?"

"What am I talking about? I'm talking about a father and son, that's what I'm talking about."

"So what can I do if he runs out of the house like a wild Indian?"

"For no reason," she says. "He runs out of the house for no reason."

"We were having a discussion," I say.

"A discussion," she says. "I know your discussions. A person could get from them an apoplexy."

"We were having a discussion," I say. I'm trying to keep patient. "I didn't say anything to him. A father can give an advice to his son, no? And he gave me such an argument——"

"So now from an argument," she says, "you got to send him away from the house? Tell me, it's got something to do with a girl?"

"No, it's nothing to do with a girl. I wish it was. I was better off with only a Korean grandchild."

"What?" she says. "What did you say?"

"Never mind," I tell her.

"Listen," she says, "it ain't enough you're driving your only son out of the house? You got to make a fool of your sister too?"

"Bessie," I say, "you'll do me a favor, call up the rest of the family, the cousins too, and tell them I got leprosy, nobody should come near me until further notice from the health department. You'll save me a lot of time and you'll have a good time yourself. Okay?"

And I bang up the receiver, I'm so mad I wish it was somebody's head. Whose, I don't know. I turn around and

Larry Kogen is standing there, with an order pad in his hand, he's waiting to see me.

"I got a call from Silverstein in Jersey," he says. "He wants an exclusive on number 612."

For a minute I can't think even what is 612. "That's the print with the pleated bodice?"

"Yeah. He says he'll take six dozen now and six dozen in two weeks. But he wants exclusive for Newark."

"And what's with Bamberger when they call up for reorder?"

"That's what I was thinking. But maybe you better talk to him. You know how he is."

"I don't want to talk to him now. I got too much on my mind."

"Having a little trouble with the pride and joy?" he says.

"Larry," I say, "no remarks. Please. I'm not in the mood."

He picks up from my desk the picture I got there of Harold. "Why don't you get him down here? I could make a topnotch salesman out of that boy in six months."

"And a topnotch bum, too," I say.

"No fooling," he says. "He's got a terrific personality. The girls in the showroom are still talking about him."

"Some fan club," I say. "His mother will be tickled to hear it."

"I'll bet he'd be a real fireball in this business. It's time he latched onto something——"

"He's got his own ideas. He wants to work in a garage and reform the world."

"Ah, that's just newspaper talk. Listen, Morris, you haven't got any problem with this boy. If he was on the junk, with a monkey on his back, you'd have something to worry. But this? So he's got a few nutty ideas. He'll get straightened out. He's been cooped up in the army, over there with those slant-eyed——"

"Larry, do me a favor. Keep your advice for somebody that wants it."

"All right," he says, "make a federal case out of it if you want. But I'm telling you. You give me the green light, I'll turn him over to Agnes or Shelley or Doreen——"

"The green light you want? You mean the red light."

"All right. But I'll guarantee you, in one week he won't want to reform the world, he won't even want to reform Pinsky's Poolroom. He'll be lucky if he's got enough energy left to comb his hair in the morning."

"All right, Larry," I say. "You said enough. Go away already."

So he makes with his shoulders, what can you do with an old duddy fuddy like me, and he says, "What'll I do about Silverstein? You want to give him an exclusive?"

"Don't bother me with Silverstein," I say. "He wants to buy like everybody else, okay. No exclusives. And take care of it yourself. You got charge of the account, no? Everybody's got to come running to me with everything. I haven't got a business here, I got an albacore around my neck. I'm getting sick and tired already. When am I going to have a little peace, a little relaxation? Every day a million problems, my head is splitting already."

Well, you know, my mother—she should rest in peace—if you complained to her you got a headache, she would say it's a lucky thing you haven't got a backache too. If you told her you also got a backache, she would say it's lucky you got something to take your mind off the headache. So, lucky for me, this morning I got coming in an interior decorator, he's got the plans for me for remodeling the showroom. Why do I have to remodel the showroom? Chairs I got for the customers, very comfortable, space I got, mirrors I got, tables I got, ash trays—I did plenty of business here, nobody ever complained it wasn't fancy enough. So why must I change everything? Don't ask me. Maybe it's somewhere a big secret I'm sharing with General Motors, every year changing the models and I got yet to hear the new ones are going sideways, or up, or even that they're using less gasoline.

I'm looking over the plans, Sophie went over with the decorator, it's her taste, going to be all new furniture, stylish, modern, blond wood—trees got nowadays styles too, blond, brunette—fixtures from black onyx, travertine floors, very handsome, it's going to cost a little something too, maybe fifteen, twenty thousand dollars. But from this Sophie doesn't want to know. Money, this is not her department. So I got enough aggravation for a couple hours, thank God, to take off my mind from other problems.

Lunchtime, I'm not feeling very hungry, you understand, but I got to have a little nourishment to keep up the struggle, so I go down to Ephraim's Hi-Lo Restaurant for a bite. I meet there my friend, Joe Wachtel, he's also in the rag business but a different kind, cloaks and suits.

"Look who's here," he says, "Mr. Gotrocks. Sit down, take a load off the feet. Have some protose steak, it's very good today, Ephraim is mixing in a new kind of floor polish, very tasty."

"So if you don't like it," I say, "why are you always eating it?"

"Who said I don't like it?" he says. "I'm crazy for floor polish. At home I can't get my wife to make it for me. She uses only Chlorox in the cooking."

"You are feeling exceptional cheerful today, I see. What's this Mr. Gotrocks business?"

"Nothing. I heard in the street today you made last season half a million dollars."

"Who told you? The halvah man on the corner?"

"What's the difference? I heard it. A rumor like this couldn't do you no harm."

"From Dun and Bradstreet, especially not. But why should I lie to you, an old friend? It's true. Not exactly. But the general idea. It wasn't last season, it's this season, and I didn't make half a million, I'm going to lose twenty thousand dollars. The reason I'm not going to lose twenty-five, is I haven't got twenty-five."

"Congratulations," he says. "The look on your face, I thought you really got troubles."

"What look on my face?"

"I don't know. Worried."

"Worried? Why should I be worried?"

"What are you asking me? Do I know? You look worried, that's all. How's business? Without the kibitzing."

"Business is fine," I say. "Fine? It's pretty good. I mean, it don't get any worse I won't kill myself."

"So what are you worried?"

"Well, I got a little trouble with Harold." And I tell him now the story. Not the whole story. Only about the book. He listens, doesn't say anything. "So how do you like it?" I ask him finally. "You didn't know your old friend is a monster? I'm living in a plush-lined vacuum?"

"I don't know," he says, "you went so far, you got the

printing from the book, why didn't you finish already? Let him have his book?"

"Are you crazy?" I say. "Everybody will call him a radical, a Communist, he wants to make a revolution in the country, throw over the system, he'll be investigated, I'll be investigated, God know what! Who needs it, such nonsense? You think I'm going to let him make such a rope to hang himself?"

"I don't know," he says, "a boy's got ideas, you should let him alone with them."

"All right," I say, "but he should let me alone with mine too, no?"

"He didn't ask you," he says. "It was your idea, the book."

"Listen," I say, "for this advice I didn't have to talk to you. I could go to the office of the *New Masses* and do just as good."

"Don't get excited," he says. "You're asking from me an opinion, I'm giving it to you. This is still a free country."

"So what's with the Communists who are sitting now in jail?" I ask him. "For them it's also a free country?" Free country, he tells me. I know what is Joe's problem. With a wife like he's got, revolution wouldn't scare me neither. I would maybe look for a little excitement too. Only somebody else's Harold should start it. Not mine.

I'm back in the place an hour, Sophie calls me up from the house, Harold is there. "He's really going," she tells me. "He's really moving out. I can't believe it."

"Where is he now?" I say. "He can hear you?"

"No. He's in his room, packing his clothes."

"He's still mad on me?"

"I don't think so. But his mind is made up. I never saw him like this. So stubborn."

"Ask him if he'll talk to me on the phone?"

In a minute he comes on the phone. "Hello, Dad," he says.

Dad! Some word to hear from a boy you spent practically a whole lifetime together in the same house. "From last night to now I turned into a Dad?" I say. "Pop isn't good enough any more?"

He doesn't answer me.

"Harold," I say, "last night was last night. Today is today. I want you should wait home for me, we'll have a talk."

"There's nothing more to talk about," he says. "We don't talk the same language."

I'm holding myself in but inside I feel like I'm going to bust. "You're starting again with the language business? Twenty-one years I talked a language you could understand. You'll strain yourself a little, maybe you'll be able to understand me a little longer. Long enough to hear what I got to say."

"There's no point in it," he says. "It's not going to change anything. I've decided it's better for me to be by myself."

So I see it's no use, he's calling me Dad, pretty soon if we go on talking I'll answer him back with an insult too, better I should let be the whole thing. "All right, Harold," I say, "do whatever you want. Be independent. Leave at least your address, we can send you a post card, you'll maybe want to hear if there is sometimes a crisis in the family, your sister is getting married, or Samson needs maybe some shots—supposed to be your animal, you know. Unless maybe you are figuring to throw away your family entirely. And now, if you'll please, put back your mother on the phone."

In a minute I hear Sophie's voice again, it's coming up like from a cellar. "What did he say?" she asks me. "He won't change his mind?"

"What did he say? He wants to be independent."

"I can't stand it," she says.

"Listen, Sophie," I say. "Listen to me a minute and don't turn on the faucet. When I was Harold's age I was already a married man."

"It's true," she says. For a minute she don't speak. I know exactly what she's thinking, she's thinking how many years went by since we got married. A dream. "Isn't it fantastic," she says. "You were twenty-one. Harold's age. He seems like such a baby in comparison."

"Maybe my mother thought I was also a baby."

"But it's different," she says. "If he was going away to be married I would be the happiest person in the world. But like this, leaving home for what, to go live in a hotel, with bedbugs."

"How do you know there's bedbugs, for God's sake? You been there?" I'm hollering now. I don't want to but I'm hollering. It's so foolish. Bedbugs. "All right, Sophie," I say, "I don't want to have with *you* an argument now. Find out better where is the garage where he's working. Maybe we can send him sometime a corned beef sandwich, some fruit, he should have at least a balanced diet while he is making his war of independence." And I give a laugh but I'll tell you the truth, if I heard it myself on the phone I

156

would think somebody is trying hard not to make a noise from a toothache.

I put down the receiver now and I see Marie is standing in the door, she doesn't know should she come in or go out. "Excuse me," she says, "but Miss Youssem wanted you to see this dress on."

"Come in, come in," I say. "You'll give me just a minute, Marie. I got to put myself together."

"Is anything wrong, Mr. Seidman?"

"No, I'm a little upset. We got in the house a domestic situation. Family business."

"I know," she says, and she takes toward me two steps. "Don't worry about Harold, Mr. Seidman. He'll be all right."

"You saw him? Since he left the house?"

"I talked to him last night. He called me."

"Did he tell you what happened?"

"He said he'd decided to live by himself for a while."

"You think this is a good idea?"

"Mr. Seidman," she says, "I'm sure you don't want me to take sides in a situation like this——"

"You're right," I say, "you're absolutely right. I'm putting you in a bad position, between the family. I'm sorry. So show me the dress."

She walks for me up and down with the dress and I see it's a good number, simple, very classic lines. You think I know what I'm saying, classic lines? It sounds good. A lady in Ottumwa, Iowa, she hears a saleslady say "classic lines," she right away thinks she'll put it on, she'll look a statue in a museum in Paris, France.

"You like it?" I ask Marie.

"I think it's stunning."

"It's a funny thing, some dresses," I say. "On the hanger they don't look like anything. You try them on, it's a different story altogether."

"That's true," she says, "some of the best styles are that way."

She's looking at me very straight and I realize we're not talking about dresses entirely. "Depends also," I say, "who's trying them on. For instance, this number. You'll tell Miss Youssem, please, before I decide, I would like to see it on one of the other girls. Because on you, Marie, I can't be sure. It could be a burlap bag, it would still look good."

"Thank you," she says and she gives me now a smile, with the side of her mouth, it's so sweet you could eat her up. "Could I paraphrase that just a bit for Miss Youssem? I think she's feeling a little fragile today. Burlap bag might upset her."

"Yes, paraphrase," I say. "And I'll tell you something I don't have to paraphrase. It's a pleasure to talk to you, a girl like you."

"The feeling is mutual, I assure you."

"You don't think I'm a monster? With central heating?"

"You know what I think," she says. "I'm president of your fan club."

"Maybe I should send you to talk to Harold. I just lost him as a member of my fan club. Permanent."

"I don't think so, Mr. Seidman. You should hear him talk about you sometime."

"Like last night?"

"Well, he was upset."

"He told you about the book?"

"Yes."

"What did he say?"

"He said you'd both changed your minds about having the book privately printed. A book ought to stand or fall on its own merits. And he thought it would be better to wait until some regular publisher——"

"Marie, tell me, who's being the gentleman? Him or you?"

"No, really, Mr. Seidman. That's what he said."

"Listen. We had a big fight. By him I'm a big reactionary, I'm living in a plush-lined vacuum, I don't know what's going on in the world, I got no heart, I don't care for nothing but a dollar. This is because I don't like the book. You could take my word for it, Marie, the only people who could get pleasure from this book are living in the Kremlin."

"Is it really that bad?"

"I would like you should read it. I'd like from an intelligent young person an opinion."

"Well, I'm not sure my opinion would mean very much. The point is, he feels very strongly about it——"

"All right. This I understand. But why don't he understand I feel strongly too? And I'm the father. A father is not just a machine for giving out bicycles and chocolate bars. He's entitled to a little consideration. After all, I got the responsibility, I got to make the decision, even if it hurts him. So we got different ideas. So the only solution then is he's got to run away from the house?"

She looks at me very serious and she says, "Sometimes young people have to get away from their families, get off by themselves, to find out what they're all about, who they are, what they really want."

159

"And you think it's right," I ask her, "he should go now and work in an all-night garage? This is how he's going to find out what he is all about?"

"I don't know," she says. "I don't think I should be making judgments about this."

"But you met the boy. You talked to him. He belongs in a garage, with his talent, his personality, his education? It don't make any sense."

So she says, "I'm sure neither of my parents thinks it makes any sense that I'm working as a model. I don't expect it to be my life's work either. But I know I've found out more about myself, and people, and what living is all about, in the year I've been here than I would have otherwise in ten. Or maybe a lifetime."

This is for me very interesting and I say, "What does he do, your father, if you don't mind my asking."

"Well right now he's probably golfing in Scotland, or maybe shooting ducks in the Adriatic. My mother is in Reno, arranging about her third divorce. My father was number one."

"*You* are from a broken home?" I say. "I got to introduce you to my wife. You will bust up all her theories."

"Don't be too sure," and she gives me now that smile, with one side of her mouth, you could fall in love with her from this alone. "I'm probably riddled with complexes that'll all rise up to smite me the first time I've got to face a real crisis in my life."

"I would bet on this a lot of money," I say, and she comes over, bends down quick, gives me a kiss on the cheek and runs out. And I'm sitting and thinking. Democracy. People are fighting for this, dying. Harold is willing to make a mishmash from his own life because he's worried about all the people in the world who aren't getting their fair share. And what about God? Is He worried? Look how many girls, lemons, in the world. No looks, no personality, no brains, nothing. Only wishes. Hopes. And here is one girl, so much beauty, so much sweetness—and so much sense besides. This is democracy? Equality? Go tell this to my cousin Fanny, she's sitting there in Perth Amboy with her two prize packages, waiting, waiting somebody should come along, he could have a wooden head, or a wooden leg, only he should take them off her hands. Or my friend Joe Wachtel, he is chained to that Maggie Dooley of his twenty years. Where are the equal rights?

Well, in the middle of this philosophy, steps in my accountant, Applebaum, with a long face. He's got for me some figures. It's a breakdown of the expenses for the last Style Show, the room, the *décor* like they call it in French so it should cost twice as much, the champagne to put the customers in a good mood, an orchestra, a few thousand hors d'oeuvres, also for the mood, sometimes I'm wondering, you know, what is it all about, every year spending a fortune for a showing, new styles, a new line, and if I break my head and everything comes out fine and the prima donnas like the champagne and also the styles, maybe I'll sell enough dresses to make back the expenses and pay for what I got to spend now remodeling the showroom, because the old one isn't good enough for customers I'm training to drink champagne while they are looking at the styles. I'm telling you. Crazy.

I look at the figures and I say to the accountant, "You're

sure you added it up right, Applebaum? You haven't got in here also the mayor's salary?"

"Mr. Seidman," he says, "I ran this up on the adding machine. It's made by IBM, a very reliable concern."

"What's the matter you're so sarcastic?" I say. "You had a bad breakfast? You got a heartburn?"

"Mr. Seidman," he says, "I went four years to accounting school, to learn figures. You hired me to give you figures. I give you figures. They are the right figures. What else do you want from my life?"

Has he got a sense of humor, this Applebaum. He could be a Turk altogether.

"You want to know what's on my mind?" he says. "I'll tell you. I just talked to my wife on the phone. My boy, Michael, smashed up his whole bicycle I got him for his birthday last week."

"My goodness," I say, "he hurt himself?"

"Himself, no. For this he's got sense. But the bicycle—smashed. To pieces. You know how? A plate glass window ran into him."

"Well, Applebaum," I say, "a bicycle is a bicycle. You can get him another one. Thank God the boy isn't hurt."

"I would like," he says, "to thank God already the boy should look where he's going and not be such a dope, thirteen years old, all the time dreaming, except when it comes time to sleep."

I'm telling you. Wherever you'll find a father, with a son —problems. Big. Little. But always problems.

Well, one thing and another, I'm late in the shop that evening, I get home around midnight, Sophie is still up, reading the paper.

"It's late," she says.

162

"So it's late," I say. I'm feeling very irritable all of a sudden, like she would be accusing me.

"What did you have to do so late?"

"I had things to do," I say. "I don't keep a diary."

"Why are you raising your voice?" she says. "You'll wake Jenny."

"You mean we got left in the house a child," I say, "she didn't run off yet to the Bowery to lead a fuller life? She's home sleeping, not working in an all-night drive-in, a taxi dance hall, practising up to call me Dad——"

"Oh, Morris, don't," she says and she starts in to cry.

Well, this always makes me feel helpless and guilty, the same time. "Sophie, don't turn on the faucet," I say. "What is it? Somebody died? Went to jail?"

"I can't help it," she says. "I feel just awful."

"Tell me," I say, "all those lectures you're going to, they don't teach you anything? Here is a psychological situation. Didn't you learn from them not to go to pieces?"

"That's just the trouble," she says, "I keep thinking that we've failed Harold in some way."

"Why is it always a one-way street with psychology? It's always the parents who are failing the children. Couldn't it be sometimes the other way around? Maybe they are failing us a little too?"

"Maybe you should have let him alone, with the book?"

"Sophie, if I came into his room and I found him there, with a revolver, playing Russian roulette, I should also let him alone? I explained it to you already."

"I don't know," she says. "I don't know. I just feel awful. Like we drove him away."

I put my arm around her and she lets fall her head on

163

my shoulder but she's still crying. "Sophie, be sensible," I say. "Stop already. It's no tragedy."

But I'm not feeling so good in the stomach myself, believe me. What would be if she knew the whole story with Harold? Unbelievable. Our son. Who would dream he could get into a situation like this? This fine, honest boy—to turn into such a hypocrite. Only hollering about the world, the world, it's full of sin and in his own heart—well, I could only tell you, I thought this boy, if he made a mistake in his life, would be man enough to do the right thing. I wouldn't deny it, it's a big heartache to me, how he is behaving.

Next morning, at breakfast, there's more of the same. Sophie starts now with the business of his being bottled up, the emotions, none of this would have happened if he was interested in a girl, then he wouldn't worry so much about social conditions, he would be writing love letters, not tracts, he would have an outlet, and so on and so on. Is this an irony? Love letters. She don't know he wrote a whole opera over there in Korea!

And what's the conclusion, when she's finished talking? It's somehow my fault. Something I should have done I didn't do, or something I shouldn't have done I did do, or something I should have told him I didn't tell him, or something.

And I'll tell you the truth, she's got me so nervous, I'm starting to think maybe she's right, maybe it's my fault, the whole thing. Maybe I should have given him some lectures, warned him. Or maybe just the opposite, it was too free always, the talk in the house. Maybe I should have been more strict. But what do I know about this whole subject, after all? My daughter, Jenny, is always saying I am a square from Delaware. And it's true. When I was a child, who spoke to you about such things? If the older people would want to talk sometimes about someone in the family who was in confinement, for instance, the children would have to go out of the house. My father—he should rest in peace—if he would hear sometimes the conversation that is going on at the table in my house, between the children, he would die all over again.

Well, I'm driving to the place, between these thoughts and the traffic together I'm getting pretty aggravated, I decide it's better for me to stop off in Turkish bath before I go to the place. I'll take a little steam, sometimes when I got things on my mind this is calming me down a little. So my man there, Hymie, he's rubbed me down now for fifteen years, he is very smart with the fingers and he knows besides all the arias from the operas, he starts to dig around in the shoulders and the neck and the same time he is singing from *Boris Godunov* the "Song of the Flea" and throwing himself around a little bit. So I say, "Hymie, control yourself, my back is not the Metropolitan Opera House and besides, for the neck you picked out the wrong music. How's about from *Traviata* a little and, please, not so much force, you'll put me yet in the hospital."

So he says, "Mr. Seidman, you are tense."

"I know," I say, "past tense."

"No joke," he says. "I ain't seen your trapezius like this since the time you had the strike."

"Well, I got also now a little strike on my hands," I say. "Tell me, Hymie, maybe you know why with me the tension goes always in the neck? You think this is maybe because my emotions are bottled up and this is the narrowest place?"

Well, naturally, he hasn't got an answer for this. When I get to the place I find there a message from my sister Bessie in Flushing I should call her. Well, this is a woman not too smart, even if she's my sister I got to say it, and her husband is altogether an idiot, I did for him some financial favors from time to time, so I got to be extra careful with Bessie she shouldn't get insulted. So I call her back and first thing she says, "I heard about Harold. I feel terrible."

"So what else is new?" I ask her.

"I had a feeling when I was over the house the other night," she says. "I don't know, something about him, I said to Sophie, Sophie, I said——"

"Bessie," I say, "I would like to discuss the whole thing with you, I'm sure you got a lot of valuable ideas, and you wouldn't keep a single one of them a secret from me, but I got lots of things to do this morning."

"You got nothing more important to do than your son's welfare," she says. "You know that he is working in a garage on Twenty-third Street?"

"I heard it was Twenty-first Street."

"Myron stopped there this morning, it's near his office, he just called me. You know what Harold was doing? Washing cars."

"So what do you expect him to do in a garage? Paint pictures?"

"This is what you want, Morris? Your son should go on washing cars for a living?"

"And if I don't want it, what can I do about it?"

"You got to do something," she says. "You got to control

166

that temper of yours and talk some sense into the boy. Why does he have to work in a garage, his father is rolling in money? You could at least give him a job in your place, he can wear a suit like a person, not overalls."

"All right, Bessie," I say, "don't get so excited. You were living in chicken feathers until you were sixteen years old and there were plenty times in my life I was lucky if I had a pair of overalls to put on. It didn't kill us. I haven't had a chance yet to think over what I should do. But I got it on my mind, I assure you. And before I cut him out of my will, I promise I'll call you."

So I hang up and I try to think, what should I do. Should I go down to this garage, try to have a talk with him? If I know the boy, it will only make him embarrassed and I'm liable to get mad altogether and then he'll get stubborn and what will I accomplish? Sure, to blow off some steam, make speeches, this you can do in a garage too. But if I want to accomplish something with the boy, it's a ticklish situation, the whole future is mixed in here, I have to go another way, I got to beat around the bush a little.

I call in Marie to my office. "Can I have a talk with you, personal?" I ask her. "Man to man?"

"Certainly, Mr. Seidman," she says.

"You know my Harold," I say, "I want to ask you an opinion. His mother has an idea the reason for his entire behavior, the writing, his leaving the house, everything, is a revolt against the father and it comes because his emotions are bottled up, he don't know enough about girls, he didn't have enough experience with them, he's too shy. It's maybe a funny question to ask you. But I'm asking. What do you think?"

167

"Still man to man?" She's smiling but serious too.

"Man to man," I say.

"Well, you can tell Mrs. Seidman to stop worrying. Harold knows everything he's supposed to know. And he's not one bit shy." And now I see her face is getting pink but she's looking me straight in the eyes. "I mean," she says, "he's very sweet and idealistic, but—well——"

"I know what you mean," I say. "All right, this is one question. Number two. You don't mind?"

"No. I'm interested in Harold. I mean, I think he's quite an unusual person——"

"I think so too. So tell me. You know he is living by himself now and working in a garage. You think this is such a hot idea? Excuse me. Such a cool idea?"

"Well, it's what he wants to do, apparently."

"You think it's what he wants to do, really? You don't think it's for spite?"

"I'd be surprised if Harold did anything for spite. But if it is, I'm afraid he'll have to find it out for himself."

"But when? By the time he finds out, his whole life could be wasted."

So she hasn't got for this an answer and I say, "All right, he doesn't want to go back to school. This would be the best thing, but he doesn't want it. The only other thing is a garage? He wants to be a worker, with his hands? Well, I got here a factory, with proletarian jobs. So the boss is not a stranger, it's his father. But he can have here the same independence. If he wants, I could call him George or Mike, I'll even get him a spittoon he can practise on it. But at least, the same time, he'll be learning a business from

168

which he could sometime make a decent living. Live like a person. Not washing cars."

"I don't know what to say, Mr. Seidman," she says.

"Tell the truth, Marie. If this was your young man, if you were interested in him, I mean serious, would you want him to be a car washer? This is a career?"

"I'd want him to do what he feels he must do, to realize himself. I'm sure he doesn't intend to wash cars the rest of his life. It's just until he finds himself."

"So couldn't he find himself here, just as well? I'll ask you a favor, Marie. You'll see him sometime, ask him to come up at least and have a talk with me. He don't have to change his ideas. I'm not going to put a gun to his head. I just want to have a talk with him."

"Man to man," she says, and again she smiles, but with a little pleat in the forehead, and all of a sudden I see this girl is not on my side, she's not my enemy neither, but I am the parent, the older generation, no matter how much respect we got for each other, how much we like each other, still when it comes to a crucial thing, we are against each other. Got to be this way in life, I guess. Unless the parent wants always to give in. But he's a person too, no? He's got a right to an opinion, a point of view, himself?

So I say, "All right, Marie. I see we got different ideas about this situation. I don't want to influence you. Forget it."

"I hope you're not angry with me now, Mr. Seidman," she says. "I just don't feel that I've the right——"

"I understand, Marie," I tell her. "You don't have to explain any more. And to show you I'm not angry, I'll let you bring me please two aspirins, with some water."

169

five

So, naturally, I don't expect anything will happen from this talk, anyway not so quick, but next morning I come into my office, who's there waiting? Harold. My heart gives such a jump in my chest, you wouldn't believe it.

"Hello, Dad," he says.

I could see he's not feeling friendly. Very strict. "Hello, Harold," I say. "What brings you to Seventh Avenue?"

"I thought maybe you might tell me," he says. "Mom suggested yesterday that I should come down and have a talk with you. And I got the same suggestion from Uncle Myron in the morning and from Aunt Bessie, twice, once in the morning and once in the afternoon. And Marie last night. I haven't heard from the mayor yet but everyone else in town seems to think I ought to talk to you."

170

So, he's making with the sarcasm. I'm going to have here a little contest. "First of all," I say, "you're not going to hear from the mayor because the pipeline I got to his office got busted this season. He is off my payroll. The second thing, facts. Your mother said you should come talk to me, this is her idea, not mine. Your Aunt Bessie said so, this is also her idea, not mine. Uncle Myron said so, this is your Aunt Bessie's idea, not mine. Marie says so, this is something different. I had with her a talk yesterday, not only about you, general things. I like to talk to this girl. She's very intelligent. When a homely girl has got some sense, this is already a tonic. But when a beautiful girl's got also brains, this is an inspiration. Do you agree?"

"I agree," he says. "So?"

"So. It's encouraging we should agree on something. To start."

"So," he says. "We agree."

"So fine. I just want you to know it's not a plot, to bring you down here. I was talking yesterday to Marie and I told her if she would see you sometime she should mention I would like to have a talk with you."

"Well, she mentioned it."

"Where? In the garage?"

"I don't live in the garage. I just work there. We had dinner last night."

"And she mentioned I wanted to talk to you?"

"Yes. For about two hours. She also mentioned the idea of my working here, instead of the garage. I suppose you had nothing to do with that?"

"That's right. Nothing. Could be, you know, this was her own idea. We agreed she is an intelligent girl. And even," I say, "if she was less intelligent, it could still seem pretty funny to her that a boy like you, in your position, has got to work in an all-night garage. What's the next step? Dishwashing, I suppose. Or you could maybe take a course in a correspondence school and become a short-order cook in a hamburger joint. Starting out like this, you got unlimited possibilities for your future."

I'm letting myself go a little, giving him what's in my heart. After all, he's not the only one who can use a little sarcasm.

"Okay," he says, stiff, like a rooster, looking at me. "Is that what you wanted to say to me? Have you covered everything?"

I'm holding myself in now. I could say plenty more, believe me, a boy, twenty-one, he messed up already two lives in Korea, and he's still going strong. But I got something to accomplish, if I don't want to lose the opportunity, I got to keep my temper. So I say, "You want something? A cup of coffee, a sandwich, a drink, something? I'll send down."

He shakes his head. He don't want no favors from me. Not even a cup of coffee. Whatever he needs, he could get it in his garage.

"When did you have breakfast?" I say.

"I stopped at the Automat on my way up here."

"You still like it, the Automat?"

"I like the price."

"We had some good times at the Automat, the family," I say. He gives me for a second, a look, I think, maybe, maybe, it could turn into a real smile. "I had a little more of your confidence those days, I think," I tell him.

So the smile is gone again, he looks at me, very strict. "Look, Dad, what's on your mind? Can we get to the point?"

"All right," I say, "you prepared to listen to me, like a stranger? No emotion? Just plain facts?"

"I can try."

"All right. Try. First thing. Forget about me, I'm your father. I'm a monster. I'm living in a plush-lined vacuum. I don't understand anything. Forget about me."

"I see," he says. "No emotion. Just plain facts."

"You got to excuse me," I say. "I been thinking so long like a father, it's hard for me now to stop, even if I want to. You'll excuse me."

"Look," he says, "we're not going to get anywhere talking like this. I've got to get some sleep. I've got a date with a publisher this afternoon."

"With a publisher? I'm glad to hear it. Just so long it's not with the FBI."

"You're awful worried about the FBI."

"No," I say, "I'm worried about you. Listen. You want to be independent, your own ideas, publish your own books, take your own consequences. Okay. But this garage business. This is a help to you in your plan?"

"It's a job," he says. "I've got to have something to do."

"I got here a factory with a couple hundred employees. Why couldn't you find something to do here?"

"First of all, I don't want to put anybody out of a job, to make room for me. Second of all, I don't know anything about the dress business."

"You could learn. You're not going to put anybody out

173

of a job. I'm not going to fire anybody. I need somebody to look after my interests. I can't be everywhere at once. In the spring, I got to put on a Style Show, an annual affair, for this I'm always hiring a firm to do the publicity for me. They send out the announcements, they make the advertisements, they get space in the newspapers, whatever publicity people are doing. If you want, you could do this job for me."

"But I don't know the first thing about it," he says.

"You got brains. That's all you need. The rest you can learn. You'll come into the place, eight o'clock every morning, like a regular employee, you'll punch a clock, you'll work for a while in the shipping department if you want, in the piece goods, you'll see what's going on, the whole operation, next week I'm starting to remodel the showroom, I'm spending there a small fortune, you could supervise, you'll keep your eyes open, you could save me a lot of money there. More than your salary."

"I could save you a lot of money on *that* operation right now," he says.

"I know," I say, it's like I could read what's in his mind, "I don't have to remodel at all. And I could use the money for a settlement house, for the Porto Ricans. Look," I say quick, "I'm not asking you to change your ideas. I'm doing business with plenty of people, I don't like their ideas, they don't like mine. Think what you want. You only got to do your job, like any other employee."

"Aren't you afraid I'll infect your other employees with my ideas?" he says. "That's the nature of ideas, you know. They're contagious."

"You think they've been waiting just for you for the

revolution? If they haven't been infected until now, you wouldn't infect them."

"But you wouldn't be figuring to muzzle me by giving me a job? That wouldn't be what's in your mind?"

"What is it, Harold?" I say. "You want to be like the hero in one of your stories? You *want* to get your head broken? This will make you happy?"

"I want to speak out against what I think is wrong and rotten in this world," he says. "However and wherever I can."

"All right, speak," I say. "But I want *you* should remember. I read somewhere about speaking, Justice Holmes, I think. All right, free speech, he says, but this is not the right to holler 'Fire' in a crowded theater. You understand? For me the system's been very good. From fourteen dollars a week when I was your age, I got now my own business, my own home, I could stop altogether now if I want, I'll have enough to live the rest of my life. Other people haven't been so lucky, I'm sorry. But for myself I can be glad, no?"

"I guess that's the difference between us," Harold says. "For me the answer is no."

"All right, then show me something better. Not just talk. From ideals alone you can't run a business, you can't make a world, you can't even get books published. You saw this already. I'll tell you something else. You got here a business. Two hundred employees. You think you can take it over, run it better than me, for the employees, for everybody, I'm willing you should do that too. Only you got to show me you know what you're doing. You got to learn the business first."

175

He looks at me a minute, he's thinking it over, to see if I got mixed in here some kind of a scheme, then he says, "Well, it's a fair proposition. I'll think about it."

"Fine," I say. "Think about it. And I'll expect you when? Tomorrow morning? Wednesday?"

He gives me now a smile, crooked, like he copied it from Marie. "Proposition X," he says. "Vote yes or yes." He goes to the door and he stands there for a minute, then he turns around and he's got on his face a big smile now, all over, not just the side. "I just voted," he says. "I'll be in tomorrow morning."

Well, you wouldn't believe it maybe but I'm feeling weak in the knees, like I just nearly had an accident with the car, or I climbed up a big flight of stairs. It's a funny thing, the whole time with Harold, everything that's happening has got always this kind of mixed-up emotion in it, I'm only worried about the boy, his happiness, his future —and the same time it's always like it would be some kind of a contest between us, who's going to win. Can you explain this?

Well, anyway, it's settled he's coming to work in the place tomorrow, and naturally, the first chance I get, I call up Sophie to tell her and all afternoon the telephone is ringing in my office, naturally Sophie called up right away Bessie, to tell her, and naturally Bessie called up Myron, and naturally they all got to call me, to tell me thank God I came to my senses finally, if only now I shouldn't lose them again.

I go home a little early that evening and Sophie is already making plans to furnish over Harold's room, nicer, and she's going to make for him a big party, look up his old friends to invite.

"It's going to be a different story around here now," she says. "I'm not going to listen to you any more. A boy needs some direction in his life, even if he is twenty-one."

"And don't forget," I say, "he needs also devil's food cake, and afterwards you should tuck him in."

"Why are you so mean?" she says. "Why do you have to spoil everything?"

"I'm only telling you," I say. "Seems to me, Sophie, not only Harold and Jenny got to grow up in this family. Don't you see what's going on?" You know what's on my mind. When am I going to tell her the real score with Harold, if she's acting like this? "Don't make arrangements for him," I say, "like he was still tied to the house. He's got his own ideas. I'm warning you."

Well, sure enough, he calls up later and she says, on the phone, "When are you coming home, you want us to come down in the car and help you with your things?" And I see on her face, printed, the answer. He's not coming home, he's going to stay in the hotel.

"Maybe it's better for him," I say to her afterwards. "He's his own boss, he can stay up as late as he wants, come in when he wants, without disturbing anybody."

"Why does he have to stay up late nights?" she says.

"I don't know," I say. "Sometimes a boy has got to stay up late nights. Could be he's explaining something to a girl and she doesn't understand it. So he's got to go over it again a couple times——"

"You're so smart," she says. "What I know, I'm only a

stupid mother, a boy works all day, he's supposed to sleep at night."

"If you'll keep a secret," I say, "I'll tell you another reason. Harold is no fool and I think I made him realize it's silly for him to keep working in a garage when he can have with me a better job, there's pretty girls in the place, and so on. But the dress business doesn't really interest him, Sophie. He wants to be an author."

"Nonsense," she says. "This is just a phase."

"Okay," I say. "Have it your way. Maybe it's because he's bottled up. Who knows? Maybe Tolstoi was bottled up too. Maybe this is how it is with authors. They come in bottles."

"You and your jokes," she says. "Once you get hold of a thing you could drive a person crazy with it. I suppose I'll never hear the end of it now? Bottles!"

"Sophie," I say, "maybe you think you are the only one who is worried about Harold. I worry plenty, maybe I made mistakes, maybe after all I haven't been a good father—anyway, not good for the boy. The only thing, you don't seem to realize. Harold came home from the army a couple months ago. Not from summer camp."

"Never mind about my realizing," she says. "If you would realize a little more, yourself, and control that temper of yours, you wouldn't have to worry so much about him. Harold's going to make a big success of himself in business. With his personality he'll turn the dress business upside down. Wait and see."

Well, you know, she's right. Not just the way she means, but the general principle. Next morning I come down to the office early, I want to be there when Harold comes in, explain him a few things, plan a campaign, like they say in the army. He's there ahead of me and what do you think he's doing? He's got from the porter a broom and he's sweeping the place.

"Harold," I say, "for God's sake, what are you doing?"

"I'm starting from the ground up," he says. He's got on his face a smile but I see he's not joking.

"Listen," I say, "this is not a Horatio Alger story. You know, for an intelligent boy you are acting very peculiar sometimes. Put away the broom and come in the office. I want to show you the setup, the bookkeeping system, the inventory, piece goods, you got to start to learn these things. I want you should spend some time with Larry in the showroom, make the acquaintance of the customers. This is what you got to do, not push a broom around the floor."

Well, I'm watching him the next days and I see that he picks up things very quick, it's really a pleasure, you know, the mind of an intelligent boy. I hear nice remarks from the customers in the showroom, they like him, he's polite, enthusiastic, not a smart aleck, the same with the people in the office, they could be a little touchy, you know, with the boss's son. And with Miss Youssem it's altogether a love affair between them, I'm thinking it wouldn't be so bad he should know already the ins and outs of the business, I wouldn't mind he should deal with her entirely and leave me out of it, I'm tired of her problems and her temperament.

This is a new idea for me, you know. I'm not a man who was all the time dreaming that my son should come into the business and take it over, I would have been happier he should become a doctor or a lawyer or an architect, something in the professions. The same time I realize his mother is right, if he would want it, the business, he's got a terrific personality for it.

The very first opportunity, I send him out with Larry on the road, to see how does he take to it, the selling. It's only for a few days, to call on a few key accounts. They come back the end of the week, they got some very nice orders, and Larry says to me, "Like I told you, Morris, the kid's a fireball. He's got the makings of a great salesman. Great personality. But I wish he'd learn to keep his nose out of the customer's business and stick to our own. I had quite a thing with him at Magnuson's."

"Magnuson's? In Detroit?" I say. "What happened?"

"Well, before we go in I tell him this is one of the biggest accounts in the country and we had a run-in with them last season and it's going to be a little ticklish getting them straightened out because Magnuson is such a bastard. This don't faze the kid a bit. I'm nervous, but he, you'd think we were going into a candy store for two cents plain. He's got the relaxed approach, *nichevo*, it's only an order after all. And so far it's worked out fine, everybody likes the kid, he's Peter Pan among the pirates. Somebody else, they could maybe think he's a dummy, he's the boss's son, he's just along for the ride, but for Harold it works like a charm. So I'm in a hassle with Magnuson and the basement buyer, Miss McCarthy, you know she's the one got me in dutch in the first place, she said I promised her an exclusive on 314, a bitch on wheels, and she's putting me through the wringer, and Magnuson just stands there like a flounder, giving me the dead eye, and meanwhile this

McCarthy is flipping through the samples like they were past-due gas bills and out of the corner of her mouth she asks about number 711, you know, the cocktail dress—she wants to know does it come also in peau de soie as well as bengaline.

"Before I got a chance to say anything, Harold gives her a big smile and he says, 'I'm sorry, I don't know one material from another, all I know is my father is a genius and you can't go wrong with anything he'll send you.' So she looks at Magnuson and starts to laugh——"

"He really said that?" I ask. "His father is a genius?"

"Yep. Just like I'm telling you. So then Harold says, 'What is peau de soie,' and she shows him, there's a dress hanging there, she starts to explain him the difference— well, in two minutes this Irish icicle is melting all over the kid, she's ready to teach him the business from the ground up, all he has to do is move in, and even Magnuson is mesmerized, you can imagine, this is on his time yet and pretty soon he's got an arm around the kid's shoulder and he wants us to come out to the house for dinner, he wants Harold to meet his daughter, I'm telling you, we're in like Flynn. A picnic. So I'm writing up an order, all is forgiven, and I'm laying it in, a dozen of this, two dozen of that, black, brown, navy, you saw the order, telephone numbers. And all of a sudden I hear the kid say, 'What kind of pension plan do you have for your employees, Mr. Magnuson?' Can you imagine? I almost went through the floor. You know Magnuson. He still hasn't heard about Lincoln. He taught school for Simon Legree. He thinks when employees get old they should drop dead quietly and not bother anybody. I was sweating blood before I got the kid out of there. I tried to talk to him afterward, explain to him he's got to keep his mouth shut about this kind of stuff. You know what he says? 'If I got to keep my mouth shut about this kind of stuff, I'll go into some other kind of business.' What's with him anyway? He's really hipped."

"He's got ideals," I say. "Maybe it's not such a bad thing. Even in the dress business."

"Ideals," Larry says. "I know what's ailing this kid. And so do you. I'm telling you, you let me fix him up with Agnes or Doreen——"

"Go fix yourself up," I say. "He doesn't need you to fix him up with anything."

"Well, at least, have a talk with him, Morris," he says. "He's got to get hep. This is kid stuff. He can queer a lot of business for us with that Commie routine."

"All right," I say. "He's got to learn. It'll take a little time. We got to be patient."

Patient. A couple days later, my senior presser comes into the office, Simon Karp, he's been with me a good many years, a little bit of a sourpuss but a very capable man, from the old-time good workers and an old friend besides. I give him a cigar, he puts it in his pocket and I say to him, "Well, Simon, I see on your face we got problems. So start hollering. But don't shout."

"I'm not going to holler," he says. "I just came in to tell you. I think I'm going to retire."

Well, I heard from him this talk before. I don't take it too serious. "What's the matter?" I ask him. "You had an argument with the designer?"

"No."

"The production man?"

"No. No arguments. I just got enough already."

"Listen," I say. "You don't want to talk to me, we'll call in the Grievance Committee——"

"Leave them alone on their golf course," he says. "I got no grievance. I just want to stop and leave me alone. I had enough already. Thirty-five years. I got sixteen units in Jackson Heights——"

"Tell the truth," I say, "you got an offer somewhere else? More money?"

"Did you hear me complain about money?"

"What then? You're working too long hours?"

"Too long hours? I got more time on my hands than I know what to do with. My daughter-in-law wants I should take up a course in the New School for Social Research. A business for me in the old age. To become a schoolboy."

"So what then?" I say. "A man like you can't stop working, just like this. No rhyme. No reason. You'll go crazy."

"So what's the difference?" he says. "If I stay here I'll go crazy."

"For God's sake, Simon," I say. "Don't tell me you are getting a neurosis from pressing."

"I better just go," he says. "We've been friends a good many years, why should we have now hard feelings, I know how you are with your family, thank you very much for the cigar." And he starts to walk out.

"What's my family got to do with this?" I say, and then I realize. "You mean Harold?"

"Yes, Harold," he says.

"What happened?"

"I'm warning you. You'll get mad."

"I won't get mad. What did he do to you?"

"He makes me terrible nervous."

"How, nervous?"

"Every day in the shop, he's asking me questions."

"For instance."

"For instance, how do I feel?"

"So you are such a goddam sourpuss," I say, "you can't stand it somebody asks you a polite question?"

"I told you," he says. "You'll get mad."

"I'm not mad," I say. "But this is a crime, a boy wants to know how you are feeling? He's interested in your welfare? If this is making you nervous, Karp, you really got to get your head examined."

"Wait until I finish," he says. "Welfare, shmelfare. The very next thing, he wants to know how many years am I working on the pressing machine. So I tell him, twenty, twenty-two years. I don't know exactly myself. And how many hours a day am I working, he wants to know. So I tell him, in the beginning it was ten, twelve, now it's eight, slack season less, sometimes there's overtime, it's more. 'So why all the questions,' I ask him. 'You want to know about the hours, the machine, ask your father. The machines belong to him.' 'Oh no,' he says. 'This machine belongs to you. You put in so many years of your life, your labor, this machine is part of you, you're part of it, it belongs to you.' 'I'm sorry,' I say to him, 'you'll excuse me, this reasoning I don't understand, this machine is your father's property.' 'So what is property,' he says, 'if it's not the sum of a man's time, and sweat, and labor.'

"How do you like this? Such a lecture. What is property? he asks me. So I tell him, property is what I got in Long

184

Island, in Jackson Heights, sixteen units, I didn't put any sweat in it, and no labor, this was for the carpenters and the plasterers, they got paid plenty, what I put in was my hard-earned cash, with a mortgage it's paying off, and that's property. Next thing he's going to tell me that because the tenants are living in the apartments all day and night, and they're dreaming there too, it really belongs to them, not me."

"Simon," I say, "from this nonsense you are leaving the shop? My son's going to take away your apartment house?"

"Listen," he says, "this boy could drive you crazy with his arguments. This morning, Rosie is telling me what he wants with a certain garment, number 517, you know, with the pleats—well I don't have to tell you, Rosenzweig with his temper, so he's hollering and I'm hollering too, I guess, a little, and afterwards your boy comes up to me and he says I shouldn't let the production man holler on me like this. 'Do I let him?' I say. 'He hollers. This is his nature.' So then starts in another lecture. Dignity of the individual. So I stop him off in the middle, I tell him the production man ain't interested in my dignity, he only wants I should press out the pleats a certain way which for me ain't practical, and this is the whole argument, it's got nothing to do with dignity. And besides, I tell him, I got to listen to the production man, even if I don't like his ideas, because he is the representative of the boss in the shop, and if I don't like how he is conducting himself, we got a Grievance Committee I can complain to them, it'll be a cold day in July before I would ever go to them.

"So you know what he says to me next? He says it's not just the hollering, the production man shouldn't give me orders. He should consult with me, man to man. I'm working twenty years or more, I know my business, I'm entitled to respect. I'm entitled to a voice in the conduct of the business. I earned it. My labor, he says to me, built this business and I should have something to say about the operation. So I'm getting sick and tired already and I say to him, 'Listen, Mr. Junior, I'm nearly sixty years old, I got three grown children, married, I got five grandchildren, I got a property in Long Island, I got along all these years without dignity of the individual, I'll get along the rest of my life without it too.' Did you ever hear such a thing? A voice in the operation of the business, he tells me. This I need like a hole in the head. 'Let your father,' I say to him, 'have the voice, and the dignity, and the headaches. Who needs it? Who wants it?'

"So then he says, 'I know it's a revolutionary idea, Mr. Karp. But think it over,' and he goes away finally and I'm thinking to myself, this cockeyed philosopher, you'll excuse me the expression, he's going to be in the shop, I'm going to hear every day a lecture like this, sooner or later I'm going to have with him a real argument, then he'll go to you and I'll have with you a fight, what do I need such aggravation? Better I should quit now altogether."

So I say to him, "Simon, you know what is the trouble with you, you're not keeping up with the times. You think all a man has got to do is stand behind his machine and do an honest day's work and have a family and save up for a property in Jackson Heights for the old age. But don't worry your head. You don't have to quit. Go home to your grandchildren, have a nice week end fighting with your

186

tenants, come back here Monday morning, everything will be all right. No dignity. No voice. No more lectures. I promise you."

Well, you know, from a thing like this, a person could either die laughing, or else he could bust a blood vessel, and I got to think it over a little, I can't decide which. When I tell Sophie about it that evening, she says, "Well, you made an agreement with Harold, you wouldn't interfere with his ideas. You've got to stick to your bargain."

"This means I'm supposed to let him turn the shop into a lecture hall for communism?"

"What are you talking about communism?" she says. "You and your Seventh Avenue bunch. Every time somebody opens his mouth, he's maybe a little liberal, right away he's a Communist. What's Harold got to do with communism?"

"That's what I would like to know," I say. "This is a question I've been asking myself many times."

"Don't talk such nonsense," she says. "What's going on in your mind, Morris? Just because a boy is interested in the working conditions in the shop? What has this got to do with communism, for God's sake?"

"So what has it got to do with?" I ask her. "Psychology? I suppose it's because he's bottled up, the emotions? Excuse me. I forgot this is a closed subject."

"Believe me," she says, "I know what I'm talking about. If only he would get interested in a girl."

"It's a funny thing," I say, "how you and Larry got exactly the same idea. What I heard, Stalin was interested in quite a number of girls, and Hitler too, and Mussolini, and Napoleon, and Alexander the Great, and Genghis Khan was also not a virgin, so why did they turn the world upside down besides?"

"I don't care about Genghis Khan," she says. "All I know, I'd like to see Harold married already, settled, we should have a grandchild . . ."

So I'm thinking, if only she would know. How happy this would make her! And sooner or later she's got to know. I got to tell her. But from where should I get the nerve? How do you say to your wife, "We got a grandchild. In Korea. His name is Kim Sung."

Well, there's other things, I'm hearing from Rosenzweig and Larry, they're having arguments account of Harold, they're threatening to quit, also, I forget exactly what day, it's not even a week later, comes for me the last straw with Harold. Marie comes into my office and I see from the expression on her face something is not kosher. This is not my regular friendly Marie, with the sunny smile. Seems like my Harold, lately, he's got a real talent to make the sun go down. I want to pass it off, make a joke, so I say, "You know, Marie, I noticed, ever since you got acquainted with my son, things ain't the same between us. What's going on? You want I should get jealous?"

So she don't answer, no smile, nothing, she sees on the desk a bottle of aspirin and she says, "Could I have one of these, Mr. Seidman?"

"You?" I say. "You joined the club?" And she gives me now a look, with a kind of smile you are giving maybe to a doctor, he's just going to operate on you. "You're not joking?" I say, and she shakes her head, so I tell her to help herself and she swallows down an aspirin and then she says, "I guess I better just give you this," and she hands me a paper rolled up.

"What is it?" I ask her, and she says, "It's a petition of grievances from the models."

"Grievances?" I say. "What kind of grievances?"

"You'd better read it, Mr. Seidman," she says.

So I open it up, it's rolled up like in the movies one of those proclamations, it goes with two ushers who are blowing first a horn, and I read, I can't believe my eyes:

> *"We, the undersigned, wish to present the following points for consideration by the management:*
>
> *"1. No model is obliged to submit, without protest, to unseemly advances by the customers, indecent jokes, propositions, pinching, etc.*
>
> *"2. No model shall be expected to work longer than two hours on any shift, without a fifteen-minute coffee break.*
>
> *"3. Some place in the factory, apart from the dressing rooms, should be set aside as a rest and recreation room where the models can relax. It should be outfitted with a small library, record player, with a supply of classical records if desired, etc.*
>
> *"4. No model shall be expected to go out with any buyer whose cultural or political views are repugnant to her."*

And there's more of the same. I look at the bottom, I see it's signed by all the models, Doreen, Agnes, Shelley, Arlene, Marie, and I say, "Marie, this is a beautiful piece of work, it's maybe a historical document, I want you should go out and buy a frame for it."

"You're angry," she says, "I knew you would be," and I hear her voice is shaking a little, another time I would maybe feel sorry but now I'm mad, my head feels like it's going to fly off my neck.

"You'll get a frame," I say, "and you'll put this in and afterwards you'll call me up and I'll tell you what to do with it."

"I don't know what you mean," she says and she looks like she's going to cry.

"What I mean," I say, "is your boss has got political ideas that are repugnant to you and you are fired. And the rest of the girls too. You'll please tell them they should take this petition down to City Hall, or the union, or to Henry Rosenstein downstairs, you can explain him your whole idea. Maybe he will play games with you. I'm not in the mood. I'm running a business here. Not a kinder-garten."

So she starts in to cry now. "It's not my idea," she says. "If you want to know, I'm sorry about the whole thing."

"So why are you doing it then?" I ask her. "This non-sense, it fits for the worst crackpots I got in the place."

"It was Doreen's idea in the first place," she says. "I didn't even think she was serious. I'm not sure she was. But Harold helped her write it up and he thought I should be the one to present it."

"Harold thought?" I say. "Harold is the boss around here now? You got to do what Harold thinks? You haven't got a mind of your own?"

"I told him I didn't want to hurt your feelings," she

190

says. "It's the last thing in the world I wanted to do," and she's crying louder. "But he said it's a matter of principle and I love him and what can I do?"

Well, I look at her, this fine lovely girl all broken up and all of a sudden I got enough, I don't want to be patient any more, reasonable, nothing. I switch on the buzzer and I tell the girl she should call Harold right away, I want him in my office. In a minute he comes in, he sees Marie sitting on the chair, she's wiping her eyes with a handkerchief and her face is white. He looks at me, I'm walking up and down, I feel as if I'm going to explode.

"What is it, Dad?" he says, real strict, like it was me made Marie cry.

"I'll tell you what is it," I say. "This is your idea, this petition?"

"Well, it came out in discussion with the girls. Most of them seemed to think it was a good idea."

"You're sure?" I say. "You're sure they don't think you're an idiot?" He starts to say something but I stop him.

"Who asked you to discuss with the girls? Did I hire you to have discussions with the girls?"

"I thought we had an understanding about that," he says, very stiff. "I made it clear——"

"Shut up," I say, so loud I'm scaring even myself. "You and your cockeyed ideas. Maybe you learned these tricks from your Communist friends. You didn't have nerve enough to bring it in yourself, this stupid paper, you got to send this girl to do your dirty work for you. Next thing you'll be sending in the shipping clerks with an ultimatum

I should get oil paintings for the toilet and a Turkish bath maybe so they can spend there four hours a day, smoking, instead of only two."

"You think that's all the responsibility you've got as an employer," he says, "to provide toilets for your employees?"

"What am I running here, a sweatshop?" I holler. "I got to have petitions for special quarters for my models, recreation halls? Listen to me, young man. Another thing. I had here a couple days ago a delegation from your fan club. Rosenzweig, Karp and Larry. Practically my whole organization. They wanted to quit."

"Quit? Why?"

"Because they are grown men and they got a living to make. That's why. They're sick and tired of your discussions and your cockamaney ideas. And it's time you grew up and remembered you got some responsibilities too. Not just to shoot off your mouth. You're working here, after all, you're an employee——"

"You mean all's right with Seidman and Company," he says. "I should stop trying to improve things, put on a muzzle——"

"Muzzle shmuzzle," I say. "I want you should stop the nonsense and the people in the shop would like it also. You want to work here, behave yourself. Improve yourself. Otherwise you could go back to your all-night garage and lecture there to the Cadillacs."

So just now Karp opens the door, he's holding a dress, he's got a long face, down to here. "You're busy?" he says. "Can I see you a minute?"

192

"You can see me more than a minute," I say. And to Harold I say, "Okay. I said what I got to say. Plain talk. Make up your mind."

"I don't have to," he says. "You just made it up for me." And he goes out of the office, Marie with him, and I don't have to tell you how I'm feeling in the stomach.

"So what is it, Simon?" I say. "You got for me some more problems?"

"I burned a dress," he says, like he would be telling me he burned Brooklyn Bridge.

"What dress?" I say. To me, just then, it's not so important that he burned a dress.

"Number 720," he says. "It's a sample."

"Number 720." I can't help myself, I'm starting to raise my voice. So much aggravation already in one morning. "It's supposed to be at the embroiderer's this afternoon. I got a Style Show coming up—how could such a thing happen? You're sick, you're tired, what?"

So he says, "I would like to tell you how it happened. But I know how you are with your family."

"Again with my family?" I holler. "What has my family got to do with your burning a dress?"

"You know what I'm talking about," he says.

"You got more complaints against my son? What did he do to you now? He held your hand down on the iron?"

"I wish you would be with me on the machine," he says. "All day long you got to listen to this cockeyed philosopher, you would know what it's got to do with it."

"Keep your remarks to yourself," I say.

"Don't shout," he says. "Please."

193

"What's the matter you're so tender all of a sudden?" I say. "Twenty years Rosenzweig's been shouting at you, it's all right. Me, the boss, I can't raise my voice."

"Rosenzweig, I don't care," he says. "Rosenzweig is Rosenzweig. I've been with you more than twenty years, you never shouted at me before, you never told me you were the boss——"

"So maybe it's time, it's more than twenty years," I say, "you should learn. I'm your employer and I want from you a little respect. Plain talk."

"Plain talk," he says. "Respect. When we were together in the shop on Bleecker Street, you didn't have money to pay your bills, you needed somebody to stay till two, three in the morning to get out an order, to catch three hours' sleep on the cutting table and again in the morning, first thing, on the pressing machine—then you didn't want from me respect. Eight months during the depression I didn't draw from you a cent salary, I lent you yet money for lunch, you didn't want from me respect. Now you're the Boss. You want from me respect. All right. Ring there that fancy buzzer and tell the accounting department. You owe me for one week's wages. Take off for the dress I burned. And don't cheat yourself."

And now I hear his voice breaks altogether, he runs out of the office and I realize what I did to this man, loyal, fine, a real gentleman believe me, even if he's not educated. I get sick in my stomach when I realize how I was talking to him, like out of my mind. So I run after him into the shop, he's standing by a rack of dresses, crying. "Simon," I say, "listen to me. I'm sorry the way I talked to you. You know what a temper I got. I didn't mean anything. I got things on my mind now—you know what I'm talking about. Please, Simon."

But he turns away from me, he's sobbing, it's a terrible thing to see a man like this, you know he's ashamed, besides everything else.

"Simon," I beg him, "you think I care that you burned a dress? You could burn fifty dresses. Come on, come back to my office. I'll send down, we'll have a cup of coffee."

So he says now, I can hardly hear him, "Not now. Just let me alone. Please. I'm ashamed. Let me put myself together. I'll go away in a minute."

"Simon," I say. "Please. Don't go away. Don't make me feel like a criminal."

So he wipes his face now with his sleeve, he looks at me a second, then he takes a dress from the rack. "You're going back to the machine?" I say.

"Where else should I go?" he says. "To play tennis maybe? Sit in the park the whole day, playing pinochle with Coxey's Army?"

"All right, Simon," I say. "I'll talk to you later. Maybe tonight we'll go out, the three of us, Rosenzweig too, we'll have a little steam, hah?"

So he gives me now a smile, it's like a piece of tinfoil floating in a puddle, but it's a smile and it's like he would make me the biggest present. I'm feeling so relieved, I couldn't tell you. I turn around to go back to my office, Harold is there with Marie. He looks pale but I'll tell you the truth, for once in my life, I don't care. I'm sick and disgusted with him.

"What is it?" he says. "What's wrong? Is there anything I can do?"

"Do? You still want to do something?" I say. "You haven't done enough already?"

"What is it?" he says. "What's wrong with Mr. Karp?"

"You are a magician," I say. "Twenty-odd years I know this man, never a word between us. You're here three weeks and I just nearly broke his heart, that's all."

I see now he's got his hat and coat on. "Listen," I say, "you're dressed already to go? Go. Before I really give you what's in my heart."

"Mr. Seidman," Marie puts in now. "Please don't let Harold go like this. Please talk to him."

"What do you want me to say to him, Marie? What?"

They are both following me into my office and Marie closes the door.

"Look," Harold says, "if this is my fault——"

"Whose fault is it Karp burned a dress?"

"But what did I do?" he says. "Just because I can't stand it that Rosenzweig yells at him as if he were dirt? I talk to him about his self-respect——"

"Self-respect," I say. "Why don't you worry about your own self-respect. A fine picture you are giving—and if people would only know the whole story——"

All of a sudden I got to let go. "I don't know," I say, fast, all in a rush, "I gave you a chance to come in here, learn something, make something of yourself, instead you're turning my shop into a lecture hall for your social philosophy. Twenty years, my presser, my trusted friend, and you got me so upset, the mess you made of your life, I turn on him like a snake. My production man, he's been with me also twenty years, you make him so crazy he wants to quit. My star salesman wants to quit. The family is in

196

a turmoil, every other night your mother is crying about you, she don't even know yet the whole story—and this is from your big heart, your big social conscience. You got nothing but rocks to throw at all the villains in the world. Well, let me tell you something, my boy. Let him who is without sin throw the first stone."

"What is my big sin?" he says. "You keep hinting all the time. What is it? Once and for all?"

"Look at you," I say. "Putting on such an innocent face. I could stand it that you make a fool of yourself, you're going to reform the whole world. Tell everybody what's wrong, how to fix up their lives. Only your own life you can't fix. Everything I could stand. But that you lie, you're a hypocrite to this girl, she thinks you're a holy wonder—this I can't stand."

Marie says, "He's not a hypocrite, Mr. Seidman."

"All right, you're loyal," I say. "This is a fine quality. I'm sorry I got to break your heart. But I got toward you a responsibility too." I turn to Harold. "This wonderful girl loves you," I say. "Don't ask me why. To me you don't seem so lovable right now. But this is how it is. What have you got to say about it?"

He looks at Marie and he says, "Quite a lot. But do you mind if I say it to her? Privately?"

"Yes, I mind," I say, and you can believe me I'm not whispering. "You told her maybe about your responsibilities in the Orient? You were there with your big heart, spreading the brotherhood of man?" And I see he's giving me now a very fishy look, so I say, "All right, you know already I'm a monster, I'm living in a plush-lined vacuum, chewing up the workers, so I'm also a spy for the capitalists. I saw the picture, with the letter. I went into your room and spied on you. Sue me. What I want to say, until now this was your own business, you could break your own head with it. I didn't say a word, not to you, not to your mother. She's got yet a beautiful surprise coming to her. I was waiting to see, maybe you got a little spark of decency left inside you, you'll do something about it yourself. But no, you got speeches to make. Dignity of the individual. Voice in the operation of the business. Political ideas which are repugnant, shmugnant. The whole world to reform. Only not yourself."

"Seems to me," he says, "you're making a pretty big speech yourself. If you're through, I'd like to go."

"I'm not through," I say, "and you'll kindly wait until I am. Before you are getting this girl involved with you any deeper, you are going to tell her about the whole business in Korea, everything. Afterward, she can make up her own mind. But she's going to have from you the truth. You understand?"

"I'll leave that to you," he says. "You seem to have it all figured out, so you tell her." He turns now to Marie and says, "I'm going back to my place. I'll talk to you later." And he goes out.

Well, I don't feel so good now. Like I told you, I don't like big emotional scenes. I'm sweating, shaking, hot, cold, and now I got to tell Marie the story, it's also some picnic. She's watching me, what am I going to say, and I can't even look her straight in the eyes.

"What is it you think you have to tell me, Mr. Seidman?" she says.

198

"It's not easy, Marie," I say. "I suppose with you too I'm now a monster."

"Of course not," she says. "I understand your position. It's just that Harold—well, he's almost too noble for this world, Mr. Seidman."

Yeah, noble. "Marie," I say, "he talked to you sometimes about Korea?"

"Yes. A good deal." She's looking at me, wondering, I suppose, what I've got to tell her. "It's done things to him," she says. "The war and all. He's so filled with all the troubles of the world. For instance, you know that tenement where he's living now——"

"He's living in a tenement?" I say. This is news to me.

"Yes, he moved from the hotel."

Fine thing. I worked, struggled, to get my family out of a tenement. Now my son is back in.

"Well, there's a family there," she says. "The Sowolskis, there's eight of them living in one tiny apartment, five children and three adults—you know what Harold's been doing?"

"Better don't tell me," I say.

"No, seriously," she says. "He's terribly upset about it. He's been after the landlord—he's called up the Health Department——"

"So what will he accomplish?" I say. "The landlord will get mad, he'll take it out on the tenants. Listen, Marie, I got something to tell you. How noble Harold is. It's going to hurt you."

So she's got her big eyes on me, she's waiting for me to tell her what is the score. I pull in my breath and start.

199

"You say you are in love with Harold, Marie. If this is serious you got already problems. He's Jewish, you're not, what his mother will say I don't know. Or your mother, for that matter. But the first thing, you got to know what is the situation with Harold. Marie, Harold is a father."

She opens wide her big blue eyes and I turn away, I don't want to see them getting filled with tears. "Yes," I say, "he's got a little boy in Korea. I saw the picture. And not an American child. A native. I'm sorry, Marie. But you got to know."

And I sit down now because if I wait another second I'll fall down, I'm so nervous.

"Are you talking about Kim Sung?" she says.

I look at her now, I can't believe I heard right. "You mean," I say, "you know already? Harold told you?"

"Of course," she says. "Why not?"

"I see," I say. Like a blind man, I see. This is for me too modern already. "Well," I say, "I'm glad you can be calm. I suppose we got to make allowances. A young man, alone, in a foreign country, lonesome——"

"Mr. Seidman," she says, "I can't understand why this upsets you so much. Is it because it's a Korean child?"

"You mean *you* are not upset? It doesn't bother you, Harold's got a Madame Butterfly in Korea?"

So I hear now she starts to laugh, I wonder am I dreaming, or maybe I lost my mind altogether. Too much emotion, you know. "This is a joke?" I ask her. "I don't see the humor."

"I'm sorry," she says. "I was just trying to visualize Mrs. Wethering as Madame Butterfly."

"Who's Mrs. Wethering?"

"She's an English woman about sixty years old," Marie says and I see she's looking at me very funny. "She runs this home in Seoul for orphaned Korean children."

"An orphanage?" I say, and it's getting dark in front of my eyes.

"Yes—you must have known about that—if you knew about Kim Sung."

"I didn't hear anything about a home, or a Mrs. Wethering," I say.

"Didn't Harold tell you?"

"I'll tell you the truth," I say, "I didn't ask him."

"Well, he wouldn't volunteer it," she says. "He's like that, I suppose you know, always embarrassed about the good things he does." She looks down at her hands. "I think that's why I fell in love with him, more than anything else. And why, in the end, I'd always forgive him anything else, I guess." She looks up at me now and she gives me a smile and the same time she's twisting her hands together, and I try to smile back but it feels like I got leather on my mouth.

"I'm afraid you've jumped to some wild conclusions, Mr. Seidman," she says. "From what Harold told me, he met this Mrs. Wethering in Korea, she's a friend of his commanding officer and he went to visit the orphanage and then he got some of the boys in his company to agree to adopt a number of the children, you know, sort of a foster-parent arrangement, they send clothes and toys and money when they can, and Harold's been acting as a kind of secretary for the group, to see that they don't fall be-

201

hind. And he adopted Kim Sung himself. He's going to see that he's taken care of until he gets through school. And I'm going to help him."

She gets up now. "I'm sorry about what happened," she says. "About the petition, I mean. It's silly—you've always been more than fair with us. But Harold says it's not a personal thing against you. It's a matter of keeping up the fight for the rights of the individual against entrenched wealth and power."

"That's me?" I say. "Entrenched wealth and power? I'm glad to hear it, I got to go count my money again, I made somewhere a mistake. Listen, Marie, I'm the boy's father, I only want to help him, he should get over his crazy ideas and get started in life, not going around all the time in circles."

"I know," she says. "And I know how much he respects and loves you. That's what makes it so—difficult—and, well, I better go," and she starts to go out.

"Marie," I say, "you'll tell him I'm sorry. About the Madame Butterfly business."

"I'll tell him," she says.

"But not about the petition," I say. "I got principles too. With my entrenched wealth and power."

"I understand," she says. "Good-by, Mr. Seidman."

"Good-by."

Well, good-by, Marie. And good-by, Harold. And good-by, Charlie.

six

So what are you going to do in a situation like this? Only one thing. You could get drunk. I got a couple bottles in the place, I keep them for the customers, so I open up one and I take a drink, feels kind of funny, I'm not a drinking man, you know. But I put it down like medicine and, naturally, it don't make me feel better, only worse. How could I build up such a fantasy against my own son? I could have settled the whole thing with a simple question. Why did I jump right away to such a conclusion? After all, even a criminal gets the benefit of the doubt. I know this boy, he's not a stranger, I lived with him in the same house for years, I saw him grow up, a person doesn't change, the basic thing, the character. Only an old fool who gets dust in his eyes, maybe like my sister Bessie says, I'm making too much money, I'm getting soft in the head, I don't know what. I can see in my mind the picture of that Korean boy, the little face with the big eyes, so much sorrow there already, and I'm thinking: It's only yesterday, last week, Harold was a kid himself, and I remember how when he was little and he would see on the street a beggar or a blind man or a cripple he would come home crying, you couldn't make him stop. Once, in the neighborhood, there was a boy with a big head, you know, foolish, and all the kids would make fun of him. My Harold would take him in the house and read with him the comics and on Saturdays he would take him to the movies, and Christmas time he gives him his bicycle for a present. I remember one time, he was maybe seven years old, a man comes to the door, he's selling matches and pins from a satchel and he faints there in the hall, falls down, he's got, I don't know what, heart trouble, T.B., all kinds of troubles, and Harold takes him in the house, gives him milk to drink and food from the icebox. For two weeks the man comes every day, he eats, drinks, he takes pieces of jewelry Harold finds for him in his mother's jewelry box, money. And then I find out from my cousin, Max Ellenstein, who runs an insurance and escrow business in the neighborhood, that the man only owns two apartment houses, with maybe fifteen units. I didn't tell Harold about it. I didn't want he should feel bad.

Now I'm thinking, maybe I should have told him. It's a wonderful thing in this world for a person to have a heart. But it's a good thing also to have a head with some sense in it. With all heart you can make as big a mishmash from your life as with no heart at all. You got to have a sense of proportion in life.

And then I realize. I'm only saying this to myself for an excuse I shouldn't feel so bad. What my Sophie calls a rationalization. You know what is the hope of this world? Not old fools like me, they got everything figured out, take it easy, don't rush in, don't go overboard, think it over, yes but also no, make here a little compromise, there a little compromise. No. It's young people like Harold, they're in a big hurry to make the world better, not next year, or a hundred years, but tomorrow morning, they got no time to be careful, to figure out the angles, they only got a heart and a dream of how they would like things to be and they're not afraid to make fools of themselves for it, or to get a bloody nose, or to starve. This is the hope of the world and God bless them for it, my Harold with the rest.

So I got to make this toast to Harold, sitting in my office, and I guess I made it too many times because I'm getting dizzy, things are going around in my head, I could see Mrs. Wethering, she looks in my mind like a certain movie actress, maybe you remember her, Edna May Oliver, this is some Madame Butterfly, so I start to laugh, thinking about it, and then I think about the orphanage and those little brown kids, sitting, with their big eyes and I remember what Harold said to me the day I was taking him to Rogers Peet for some suits, how the little kids and their mothers would be fighting for the garbage that fell in the road from the trucks, and one thing and another, I start to cry and I'm getting disgusted with myself, so I leave the shop and I'm driving home finally, I get a ticket for going through a red light. Then I get home, Sophie is waiting up for me, the face is again with cold cream and she says to me, "Good morning."

"Good morning?" I say. "What happened to good evening?"

"Look at the time," she says.

I look but I'm not sure what's there on the clock. Five after six or half-past one, I don't know. I bend over to kiss her, she pushes me away.

"You smell like a brewery," she says.

"So?" I say. "You married me for better or for worse, no?"

"Who do you think you are," she says, "coming home at this hour, drunk? A Polish landlord? An Irish cop?"

"I'm a Jewish fool," I say. "An old Jewish fool. And if you'll pardon me, I'm not drunk. I'm only a little intoxicated, a man is entitled once in a while, and don't give me a big argument, Sophie, I won't stand it." So she doesn't say anything, and I say, "I had a couple drinks in the shop, that's all."

"And what's the occasion, may I ask?"

"I'm starting up a foundation for orphans," I say. "You want to hear about it?"

"I want to hear about Harold," she says.

"Harold will be vice president," I say. "He will help me give away all the money. Then everybody will be happy."

"Stop talking like an idiot," she says. "What happened between you and Harold today?"

"You talked to him? What did he tell you?"

"Nothing. But I could tell from his voice that something must have happened at the shop between you. I want to know, Morris. You lost your temper again, I suppose."

206

"It's a long story, Sophie," I say. "Have we got some brandy in the house?"

"You don't need any more brandy. I don't know what's going on with you. What are you celebrating, for heaven's sake? You got something to celebrate?"

"Maybe," I say. "Maybe I'm going to be a father-in-law. Who can tell?"

I realize all of a sudden, I can talk about this now like a regular father, without my heart feeling heavy as lead. I feel like dancing suddenly.

But Sophie, it's another story. "What's this nonsense you're talking now?" she says.

"You were worried Harold doesn't pay enough attention to girls," I say. "He's paying attention. I think he's in love."

"What makes you think so? Did he tell you?"

"A little bird told me," I say. "He talks to you on the phone every day. Didn't he say anything to you about it, the whole time?"

"He said there was a girl he wanted me to meet sometime. But I didn't think for a minute it was serious."

"Well, it's serious." I look at her now, she's folding the paper, unfolding it. "I don't notice you are jumping for joy," I say.

"How can I jump for joy?" she says. "I haven't seen her yet."

"You're afraid?" I say. "You're afraid maybe you'll like her."

"Don't be such a psychoanalyst," she says.

"I know how it is with you, Sophie," I say. "You want

Harold should meet a girl and get married, in the worst way. You are dying for this to happen. It don't matter who the girl is, so long as she's from a good family, beautiful, intelligent, educated, rich, and you pick her out, and then it should happen tomorrow, not today."

So I see she puts away the paper now and takes her handkerchief. "Sophie," I say, "you're going to turn on the faucet now?"

She don't answer me.

"Sophie," I say, "I was only making a joke."

"I know," she says. "You were only making a joke. Somebody else is only making a hatchet. With a rusty edge."

"Please, Sophie. What did I say, you should start crying?"

"Well, what do you think?" she says. "All of a sudden, out of a clear blue sky, I hear my son is practically married. I'm glad you decided to take me into your confidence finally."

"I didn't know myself until now."

"Well, who is she? How did he meet her?"

"She works for me. In the place. Marie Anderson."

"Oh my God," she says, and she slaps a hand on her head, it makes a sound like a pistol.

"You want some brandy now?" I ask her. "You'll join me?"

"A model," she says. "And a Gentile."

"She's a wonderful girl," I tell her. "A prize. You'll be proud to have her for a daughter-in-law."

"Over my dead body," she says.

"All right, Sophie," I say. "You want to make a fool of

yourself now, go ahead. It's your turn. But you'll take my advice, better get a little drunk now, instead of later. And make up your mind. Some other woman is going to make him devil's food cake and tuck him in at night, and you can take this to your psychology teacher and have him make you a *tsimmess* from it. Because this is how it's going to be. And you'd better like it. Otherwise you won't even have him for a visitor in your house."

Well, after a while I go to bed but I can't sleep. Maybe it's the liquor, maybe something else. Finally I get up, quiet, not to wake Sophie, I put on my clothes but the minute I'm by the door, she's sitting up in bed, it's always like this, like we would operate on one motor.

"What's the matter?" she says. "Why are you dressed? Where are you going?"

"Nothing," I say, "go to sleep. I'm going out in the car for a ride."

"This time of night? Are you crazy?"

"Sophie," I say. "Please. I'm not a child. I want to go out a little, for some fresh air. It won't kill me to be up for a couple hours at night."

I get out the car and I drive into New York, to Twenty-first Street, to the garage where Harold was working. I go in, you know how a big garage looks at night, there's a bulb hanging from the ceiling, without a shade, the light is so strong it hurts the eyes, and I see Harold is standing there under the light, with a hose, he's washing a car. And it's a funny effect, on the cars the light makes them look very shiny but on the boy he looks dark, and the whole place, it's so empty and sad, I don't know, my stomach is turning over inside. It's not what he's doing, I did plenty things when I was young, delivering, packing, washing, running—but it was always for something, for the future, and this is not for the future, what he's doing, it's got no direction to it, it's just because he's angry with me, with the world, I don't know what. I know it's not good, that's all, and I'm sorry, and I want to ask him he should excuse me, come back to the place, he can do what he wants, say what he wants, he can have the whole business if he wants . . .

So I walk over and say, "Harold," and he turns around and I see it's not Harold, it's a colored boy standing there, he's got on big yellow boots, to the hips, shiny now with water.

"Excuse me," I say, "I'm looking for a boy, Harold Seidman."

"Oh, yeah, Harold," he says.

"I understand he was working here," I say.

"Yeah," he says, "he was. But he ain't here now." He looks at me like he thought I was maybe a detective or something. "What you want him for?" he asks me.

"I'm his father."

"Oh, you're Harold's father," he says. "I'm glad to meet you. You got a fine son, Mr. Seidman. He's a fine man, that boy."

"Yes," I say, "a fine man. If you'll see him you'll tell him please I was here, and he should call me. I'm very anxious to talk to him."

"I'll do that, Mr. Seidman," he says. "Sure will. I hope he shows up, myself. I owe him some money he lent me. And a couple of books he gave me to read."

"Books," I say.

"Yeah. Guess he thought they'd improve my mind.

Must be kind of hopeless. They just give me a headache." He gives me a big smile; you know, with all the problems they got, I think the colored people got the greatest smile in the world.

Well, I don't want to make a long story, I didn't sleep no more that night. He put something in my mind, that boy in the garage, and the next morning, on the way to my office, I stop off by Ferentzy, the printer.

"You still got the plates from the book?" I say. "The one you were making for my boy?"

"You told me to break them up and send you the bill," he says.

"I know what I told you," I say. "I'm asking you if you still got the plates."

"Yes. I still got them."

"All right. I want you should run off enough for a hundred books, fix them up, with the bindings, covers, everything. You got somebody who can design a nice jacket?"

"I can get somebody. It's going to cost money."

"You don't say. I thought maybe you became such an art lover, you would do it for free. When can I have them?"

"I don't know. I got to see. It's a lot of work."

"All right, so strain yourself a little. And when you get somebody to make the design for the jacket, I want to talk to him, give him my ideas. I want something real nice."

In the afternoon, Sophie calls, she's very upset, she didn't hear from Harold all day, so she called up the hotel where he is living and he's not there any more, he checked out.

"I'm worried," she says, "I knew yesterday, when I was talking to him on the phone, something was wrong. And he always calls me before this. It's four-thirty and I haven't heard from him."

"For heaven's sake, Sophie," I say, "he's not a baby you got to keep tabs on him every minute. You've got to get used to the idea he can skip a day without calling you."

"When I have to I'll get used to it," she says. "Why did he move away from the hotel without letting us know? Where is he? I'm terribly worried, Morris."

Tell you the truth, I'm worried too. So I call up the garage and talk to the boss. He says, "You're Harold's father, he told me he was going to work for you, in the dress business."

"It didn't work out," I say.

"I know," he says. "It never works out. I got a boy too, I wanted him to come in with me here, he doesn't want it. He wants to be a golf instructor altogether. So let him be a golf instructor."

"I thought maybe Harold would go back to you to work," I say.

"Any time he wants," he says, "he's got a job here. But I'll tell you the truth, between you and me, I don't see the sense, a high type boy like this."

"Well, anyway, you haven't seen him," I say, "he hasn't been there?"

"No," he says. "You want I should tell him something in case he comes in?"

"Please," I say. "Just that he should call me up, or his mother, we should know he's all right."

Well, I'm wondering now, how am I going to get in touch with the boy? Imagine this situation now, my son is in the same city, I don't even know an address where I could go see him, call him on the phone, tell him I'm sorry what happened. I'm debating with myself should I call Marie at her home, find out from her Harold's address. I feel a little funny about it. Well, before I could make up my mind, yes or no, I get a buzz from my reception girl, Marie is on the phone.

"Marie," I say, "I'm glad you called up. I want to get from you the address of the tenement you said Harold was living."

"That's what I'm calling about," she says, I hear now her voice is kind of shaky. "I'm down there now. There's some trouble, Mr. Seidman. Could you possibly come down? Maybe you could help."

So I don't ask her what kind of trouble, I get from her the address, on Christopher Street, I run out and get a taxi. Well, what should I tell you, when I get there? Some mishmash. That poor family, you know, the Sowolskis, they got five kids and the old grandmother, besides the Mister and Missus, and they're living all together in three rooms, the father can't make a living, he's some kind of a peddler, neckties or something, so naturally this is for Harold a federal case against the system, he made a big fuss with the landlord, like it would be his fault altogether, he demanded for them more room, better living conditions, and the landlord told him probably to go you-know-where, so Harold got in touch with the Health Department, they should put some pressure on the landlord, they came and looked and it's true, the conditions were unhealthy, too many people living in the three rooms and, like Harold wanted, they put pressure on the landlord. So what does he do? He sends over a dispossess, the Sowolskis

213

should move and find themselves better conditions. And now they are on the street, the whole family, with the furniture together.

Well, this I didn't find out until later. But meantime, it gives me a funny feeling, I can tell you, when I get out of the cab, to see this scene. Like a bad dream from my youth. How many times I seen it, on the East Side. What family didn't live there always with this nightmare in the mind, they should be on the street, with the furniture? And in this day and age, the same thing should be going on. It's making me hot and cold.

There's a lot of people on the street, arguing, hollering, Harold and Marie are in the middle and a woman, she looks like a janitor, is standing, shaking her fist in Harold's face. "What business is it of yours, how many people live in an apartment?" she hollers. "You had to stick your nose in. Make trouble. Buttinsky."

"Dirty stool pigeon," another woman says. She's got a breath like a distillery. So I step in the middle, Marie is saying, "But he was just trying to help, don't you understand?" And the same woman says now, "Dirty capitalist," and she spits on Harold. I'm asking you. Is this an irony, or not?

So I say, "Wait a minute, everybody, please. Take it easy."

"Sure, take it easy," says the janitor lady, some kind of an Irish accent I guess. "You and your flannel suit. These people got no place to sleep tonight. They're going to be on the street."

"They wouldn't be on the street," I say. "Where is Mr. Sowolski?"

214

Somebody points him out to me, a poor *shnook*, he don't know what hit him, he's standing by the furniture and children are hanging from him in bunches, like grapes. So I go over, I say, "Listen, here is some money. Take your family to a hotel tonight to sleep. Here is my card, you'll call me in the morning I'll see what I could do to find you a place. And don't worry. I'll fix up with the janitor she should look after the furniture till you are settled somewhere."

All right, I got this out of the way. Now I want to get hold of Harold finally, ask him to come back with me to the place, so now there is a siren going, comes up a police wagon, two policemen get out, they don't want to know nothing, the landlord signed some kind of a complaint against Harold, he was interfering with the dispossess, he made an assault and battery on one of the movers—a likely story, you ever seen a New York mover?—but anyway, Harold has got to go to the police station and the Sowolskis too.

Well, before, when I was talking to him, Mr. Sowolski looked as big as a minute but now, he sees the policeman, he turns green like a herring and you would think he'll shrink away altogether. And just now, a woman leans out from a window upstairs, she hollers out to Harold, "Hey, Mr. Social Service. Compliments of the Health Department." And she spills out a whole pail of garbage, very democratic, it falls on everybody, the policemen, Harold, me, Marie.

Well, the policemen are now good and angry, one of them grabs Harold by the arm, he says, "Come on, buddy, no arguments," and Harold makes a fist and punches him in the face. So what's the next installment? Naturally we are in a police station, waiting. I got my lawyer there, he tries everything, but the sergeant is mad, he don't like civilians should hit policemen, and he's right, you know, it's a bad precedent. But the upshot is, Harold's got to stay overnight in jail, he can talk to the judge in the morning.

And Marie keeps saying, "But he only wanted to help. Don't they understand?" It's pitiful.

I say to her, Harold should hear also, I want at least he should learn a lesson from this experience. "Marie, if you want to help people, you got to *be* somebody. You got to have some influence, some position, and money don't hurt neither. Just from making speeches to landlords you couldn't accomplish anything. They got problems too, you know. Bills to pay. Mortgages——"

So Harold says, "I might have known you'd be on the landlord's side."

Well, what should I say to him? He's sitting there with his black eye, he looks already like one of the characters in his stories. I tell the lawyer to be there first thing in the morning and to Marie I say I'll take her home but she wants to stay there, maybe there is something she can do.

Quite a little situation, hah? Naturally, when I get home I don't say anything to Sophie, she's already upset she didn't hear from Harold for two days. Next morning, in the shop, I get a call from the lawyer, he's sweating there, in court. He was arranging with the judge the papers, whatever it is, and Harold decides this is the time to give the judge a lecture about social justice. He wants to know why doesn't the judge put the landlord in jail? Why isn't there some recourse for people like the Sowolskis?

Well, the lawyer had a time, you can imagine, but finally he paid a fine, I don't know, contempt of court, or what, and Harold went away.

"He didn't say he was coming here, to see me?" I ask on the phone.

"No," the lawyer says. "He just went out with the girl."

"She waited there the whole night?"

"I guess so," he says.

Well, it's again a picture. The poor girl sitting there the whole night. I'm telling you. Anyway, I figure Harold will surely come now to see me, I know he's worried what's going to be with the Sowolskis, so I call in Karp, I ask him about a place for the Sowolskis in his apartment house in Jackson Heights. He hasn't got a vacancy but we're talking about the possibilities, he says he's got a place in the basement, it's got windows, could be remodeled for an apartment. I tell him to go ahead, get a contractor and remodel, I'll pay for it.

After this I'm waiting the whole day to hear from Harold. Nothing. When I get home Sophie is a little frantic, she didn't hear from Harold now three days. I tell her I saw him, he's all right but she don't believe me, she thinks I'm saying it so she shouldn't worry. She's positive something terrible happened to the boy. I decide to go down to the tenement, see if I could get hold of him, at least have him call his mother.

So I drive down again to Christopher Street, Harold is not there, the janitor says he packed up his things and went away, she doesn't know where, and good riddance. Well, I don't want to make a production but it's kind of nerve-racking, you know, the whole thing. You could understand Mrs. Seidman's reaction. We had such a time during the Korean business, it's like there would be an alarm system set up, whenever something like this happens it starts the whole mechanism shaking in the nerves.

Next morning I'm in the shop, I can't concentrate on anything, I got such a peculiar feeling in my stomach. Thank God, about ten o'clock Marie comes in. I look up, she's standing by the door of my office, she looks nervous, like a child in front of a strange schoolroom.

"Marie," I say, "come in. Why are you standing there by the door, like a stranger?"

She gives a laugh, embarrassed, and she says, "I didn't know how you'd feel about seeing me, after what happened."

"Don't be a child," I say. "Come in, sit down," and I take her by the hands and pull her into the office. "You want something? A drink? A cup of coffee? I'll send down."

She shakes her head and I say, "So. What's with Harold? I didn't hear from him all day yesterday——"

She says, "I think he's gone away."

"You mean, away from New York?"

"I think so," she says.

"Where?" I ask her. "You got any idea?"

"He said something about San Francisco. He said he might try for a job on the docks there."

"Is he crazy, or what?" I say. "He's going to become a stevedore now?"

"Well, you know his ideas. He wants to be part of—I don't know—the great proletariat, I guess, that works with its hands."

"So for this he has to go to San Francisco? There's not enough docks here?"

"I think he wanted to get away for a while. Think things over. That's what he said. He wanted to get away from everybody and everything he knows. I guess that includes me too." She tries to smile but I see her face is real pale and there's circles under her eyes.

"Tell me the truth, Marie," I say, "you had some trouble at home, on account of Harold?"

"Trouble at home?" she says and she twists up her mouth on the side, I never saw before this expression on her face. Or the tone of her voice. Bitter. "I haven't had a home since I was eight years old. And it looks to me," she says, "with your son, I won't do any better. A hall bedroom some day, maybe, or a trailer. Next to a wharf or an all-night garage."

"So tell me already, Marie. What happened?" It's got me very nervous, how she sounds.

"Well, Harold was terribly upset, naturally, about the Sowolskis. Whatever he says, I know he feels guilty about having caused the whole mess, and not being able to do anything about it." She looks down at her hands. "I guess maybe I picked the wrong time to lecture him but I couldn't help it. I was getting a little fed up too. You have to live in the world too, be a little practical, not out on Cloud Nine all the time.

"The truth is, I don't know what Harold wants, really. We'd been talking about the future, what he's going to do. I've read some of the things he's written and I wish I could feel he's the new Hemingway, but I can't. I don't even think he wants to be a writer, really. Writing's not important, he says. What's important is to keep pounding away at people for their greed and cruelty and indifference. But, Mr. Seidman, if you expect people to read your books and pay money for them, it's got to be something more than that. You can't expect them to put their heads in a hoop and have you throw tomatoes at them all day long. It's unrealistic."

What a sensible girl this is. A pleasure, I'm telling you. But is she happy from it? She's miserable, only fighting to keep away the tears.

"So you quarreled," I say.

"You don't quarrel with Harold," she says. "I don't know if you know it about your son, but he can be quite a tyrant in his own quiet way. If you disagree with him about his view of the world, it can't be because you have an honest difference of opinion, it can only be because you're selfish and greedy and don't care about what happens to other people."

"And you're a monster," I say. "Living in a plush-lined vacuum. I know. Poor Marie."

So she flares up now. "I don't intend to be poor Marie," she says. "I told him just that. I don't intend to be miserable and deprived because others are that way. Not if I can help it. I'm not going to spend my life feeling guilty every time I draw a happy breath."

"And this he didn't like?"

" 'Well, what do you want me to do?' he said. 'Crawl back to my father's place, beg him to take me back?' I told him I didn't know, that was something he'd have to decide for himself. I just said I knew you were sorry about having misjudged him and I also said I thought you had reason to be annoyed—about the petition. Principles and ideals are fine but an employer has a right to expect a certain amount of loyalty from his employees, especially if they've been as well treated as we have. It's not just a contest about who can gouge more out of whom."

"So?"

"So he said that was just a lot of talk, all I was really interested in was that he could make more money working in the dress business. So I said frankly I was, and I didn't think it was a sin either. I was worried about his going on, so unrealistically, working nights in a garage or whatever, someone with his capabilities, it's ridiculous. So then he said I was just like all the rest, only interested in money and comfort, those were the only gods a woman ever served, the minute a woman gets hold of a man she goes to work changing him, squeezing out all his ideas and ideals, turning him into a domestic animal."

"That's what he said? To you?"

"He said a lot more. And so did I. I wasn't particularly tactful either." She takes out now a handkerchief. "He knows as well as I do that I'd do anything, live in a tent, starve if necessary, if it was a question of helping him with his career, or with something he really wanted to do that made some sense. But just to go around in a cramp of pity all the time, feeling responsible for every poor, downtrodden person in the world—or making up idiotic petitions for girls who haven't a thing in the world to complain about, really—" She stops, and she pinches her nose with the handkerchief, like she would be angry with it.

"So what happened, finally?" I ask her.

"Well, we agreed to break up and he said he was going

away and that's all, I guess," and she starts to cry now. I put my arms around her and she puts her head on my chest and sobs like a child and she says, "I don't know what to do. I love him so much. I could die."

Well, she stops crying in a minute and blows her nose. And she says, "I'd better go," and I say, "Where are you going now?" and she says, "I've got to make some kind of sense out of my life again, first of all I've got to get a job——"

"You got a job," I say, and she looks at me and shakes her head and I say, "Marie, don't be a fool. Go back in the showroom, whatever happened got nothing to do with your working here. Miss Youssem has been bothering me every day, when are you coming back, she can't pin together a dress, the other girls either they stick out too much or they fall in in the wrong place, or something."

So she begins to smile, not the old-time sunny smile but better than nothing, a beginning. She goes to the door and Karp comes in. "Marie," he says. He is a big fan of hers. "Where were you? You been sick?"

"No," she says. "I'm fine."

He shakes a finger at her. "Don't go away from here," he says. "If you leave, I retire."

"You," she says. "You're just a young man. I'll probably retire before you do."

"Stop the mutual admiration society," I say. "What is it, Simon?"

"I talked to the contractor," he says. "He gave me some figures. He could break out the partitions, and this and that, it would come out a five-room apartment. But it'll be quite a job."

222

So Marie is listening, she says now, "Is this for the Sowolskis, by any chance, Mr. Seidman?"

"Yes," I tell her and to Karp I say, "Tell him to go ahead. I'll pay for whatever it costs."

"You don't have to pay," Karp says. "It's my property. I'm improving it."

"All right, we'll figure out something, let's not argue. I don't know if they could afford the rent, even. You think they could move in now?"

"Wouldn't be very comfortable for them—with the hammering and plastering——"

"Better than to be on the street," I say.

So he says, "All right. Let them move in whenever they want."

He goes out, Marie looks at me a minute, she comes over and gives me a kiss. "That's for Harold too," she says.

"Sure, Harold," I say. "He would do it with a hatchet. Don't you realize yet, Marie? I'm the enemy."

"If that's true," she says, "then he's really in trouble. Because he loves his enemy very much."

I got to turn away from her. I feel like breaking down altogether. My boy has run away, I don't know how but it's my fault. God knows when I will see him again. And I never even had a chance to say to him, "I'm sorry, Harold, how I misjudged you."

Well, it's about a week later, there's the first postcards from Harold, Marie got one and Sophie got one. From somewhere in Iowa. He stopped off and he's got a job on a farm, working on a combine, he says. It don't take two hours, I get a call from my sister Bessie in Flushing.

"So you accomplished finally," she says. "You turned your son into a real bum."

"What number do you want?" I say.

"I got the right number," she says. "It's you who's got the wrong number. Oh, have you got a wrong number, Morris. I never thought when we were living with Mama, in Delancey Street——"

"Look, Bessie," I say, "maybe you got nothing else to do today but write a Memoirs from Delancey Street but I got plenty here to attend to——"

"I'm your sister, no?" she says. "I'm still part of your family, no? Even if my husband ain't rated in Dun and Bradstreet. I want to know what's going on. I talked to Sophie before, she said you got a card from Harold, from Iowa. What kind of a state is Iowa?"

"That's what Harold's trying to find out," I say. "Maybe if he likes it, he'll buy it."

"Sophie says, in the postcard, he's working with a combine there. What is it, a combine? Bookmakers? Race track?"

"It's a machine for harvesting wheat," I say.

"Wheat?" she says. "What does a boy like Harold know about harvesting wheat?"

"Maybe this is something he wants to find out too," I say.

"Some profession," she says. "All the time he was growing up, I only heard lawyer, doctor, engineer, architect. Now all of a sudden he's harvesting wheat. In Iowa."

"Don't worry," I say, "this is just a temporary thing. He's got bigger ideas. He's going to San Francisco to work there on the docks."

"Oh, my God," she says. "Morris, you got to do something. He'll get killed. I saw a picture, what goes on there, on the docks. Morris—they murder people. They hang them up on butcher hooks. Morris, you got to go out and rescue the boy. You hear me?"

"He's not there yet," I tell her. "As soon as I hear he's arrived there, I'll communicate with you and ask your advice. And meanwhile, do me a favor, Bessie. You got something to say, write to the *Times*. Please. I got a business to run."

Well, you know how things are happening in life, ironic, now in the middle of everything comes in a big package of books from Ferentzy and they're sitting in my office, I don't know what to do with them. I call in Marie and I give her one and Miss Youssem comes in one day, she sees me looking at the jackets, they came out very nice, she wants to know what is it. So I tell her it's a book of stories Harold wrote and she's very much interested, she's an intelligent woman, very fine education, Wellesley, I think, and Europe too—well, she wants to read the book, she says she knew all the time Harold must have creative talent, a boy like that in the dress business, it's like a unicorn lost in the jungle.

So I give her one of the books, I'm curious to know what she's got to say about it. I see next morning she is not rushing into my office with her reaction, so I'm pretty sure she don't think we had here in the shop for a time another Shakespeare. But I still want to know so I go to her in the designing room and I ask her if she read the book.

Yes, she read it, she says.

225

"Well," I say. "What do you think? I got a young Maupassant in the family? Or just O. Henry?"

"It's a very confusing book," she says, wrinkling up the forehead. "It's not exactly easy reading, is it?"

"For me certainly not," I say. "Tell me, you think the boy could go to jail for this?"

"Oh, that's silly," she says. "People don't go to jail for writing books. But—I'd like to do something, Mr. Seidman," she says. "With your permission—since Harold's not here. I've got a friend who reviews books for the *Retail Bookseller*. I'd like to have him read the book. It wouldn't be conclusive, of course, one way or the other, but it would be interesting to get a professional reaction."

"I would be very happy," I say, "I would like myself to hear from a professional critic, what he thinks."

Well, a few weeks go by, I almost forgot about it, in the house Sophie is going around kind of sad, but she's getting used already to the idea Harold should be away again, like in Korea, every once in a while a postcard, one morning Miss Youssem comes in the office, she's holding in her hand a little magazine and she says, "I hope you won't be angry, Mr. Seidman, I don't know how it happened, I sent the book over to my friend with a note saying I'd appreciate an off-the-cuff reaction, and I didn't hear from him, and now I got a copy of the magazine in the mail, there must have been a misunderstanding of some kind, because there's a review of Harold's book in it."

"You mean, printed?" and I take the magazine, sure enough it's there, just like it would be a book by a regular author, a best seller even. I got here the clipping, in my wallet, you could read it if you want . . .

STARS IN THE PURPLE DUSK, by Harold Seidman. Published by M. Seidman and Co., New York. (No price)

This is one of those literary oddities which, due to the high cost of publishing, come less and less often to a reviewer's attention. It is difficult to categorize this book. In the presence of youth and talent one has a wish to do more than simply dismiss as hopelessly amateurish, a work which has obviously exacted much time, thought and dedication from its creator. One is reminded of Chekov's reply to a literary aspirant who sent him a ms., begging for his comment: "Your work, my dear," he replied in part, "shows undoubted talent and freshness, but, alas, talent and freshness are not enough."

One might say to the author of these angry, confused and compassionate stories—plainly a young man of great sensibility—alas, anger and pity are not enough. Essential to an author is an awareness of his public and, beyond that, an awareness that reading is an exercise in empathy. Without that, one is merely a visitor at a waxworks, a locale more suitable for the emotion of horror—and of ultimate boredom—than the pleasures and pangs of recognition.

Certainly as a commercial item, assuming that it sells at around the minimum price of $2.75, it would be surprising if this book brought back the price of its attractive dust jacket.

Well, it could be worse, I suppose. He could have said, for instance, the book is an attack on the government and the FBI should investigate, which frankly I wouldn't have been surprised, neither. You know my opinion about this book, I made no bones about it. But even so, from this review, I'm getting a little nauseous, for the boy. It's a terrible thing, you know, to be a writer. Well, I don't have to tell you. But like you would be taking an examination all the time, to join a club or something, you are waiting with your heart in your mouth to find out did you pass, did you flunk, were you accepted. Work, break your head, lose sleep—and then somebody writes for you an obituary notice. It's no good. Go kill yourself. I'm telling you, with all the aggravations, the dress business is a picnic by comparison.

Anyway I figure Marie got an interest in this too, so I call her in and show her the article and I see her face is getting a little green, reading.

"It's not exactly a rave," she says, "is it?"

"Not exactly," I say. "But one good thing. Harold don't have to read it, at least."

"I'm not so sure of that," she says, and I see she gets the little pleat in her forehead, thinking. "I wonder if I can buy a copy of this magazine."

"Ask Miss Youssem," I tell her, "it's her friend, the critic."

Well, I didn't figure what she is going to do. It's maybe a week, ten days later, I'm in the shop, I hear on the public address I got a long distance call. Omaha, Nebraska. I go in my office and pick up the phone, I think it must be a customer of mine there, the Bon Ton Store, what do I

228

hear, a voice is saying, "Hello," I almost fall over. "How are you, Pop?" he says.

How am I? I hear "Pop," from this already a person could get strong and healthy. But it's such a surprise, for a couple seconds I can't get my voice. "Pop," he says, "are you there?"

"I'm here, son," I say. "You're in Omaha? I thought you would be by now in San Francisco."

"I didn't make it," he says. "How's Mom? Jenny? Samson?"

"Everybody's fine. You need something? Money?"

"No, I'm all right," he says. "Pop, I've got something here. From Marie. It's a review of my book."

"She sent it to you?"

"Yeah. She wrote that there's a whole slew of my books in your office. What made you change your mind? About having them printed?"

"Well, I was wrong about one thing," I say. "You know what I mean. So I figured I could be wrong about this too. After all, I don't want to be like those editors. I could maybe be squashing down a masterpiece."

"Some masterpiece," he says. "Did you read this notice?"

"Well, he could be wrong too, the critic," I say. "It wouldn't be the first time."

"He's not wrong," Harold says. "But it's not important any more. The book, I mean. What's important to me is that you went ahead and had it printed. Knowing how you feel about it."

"I wanted to surprise you," I say. "So you surprised me instead. You went away."

"I'm not sorry," he says. "It's been quite an experience, Pop. Quite an experience."

"How did you travel?" I say. "Without any money——"

"I had some," he says. "And I stopped, places. Worked a while, hitchhiked. Rode the freights——"

"Freight trains," I say. "Like the hoboes?"

"Yup," he says. "And I can whip up a pretty fair mulligan too."

"Mulligan. What is mulligan?"

"You've heard of prairie oysters? Well, this is prairie borscht."

"All right," I say, "you're making jokes, long distance. But just don't tell your Aunt Bessie about the freight trains. She'll have a heart attack."

So he laughs, then he says, serious, "Pop, Marie wrote me what you did for the Sowolskis."

"Yeah, you should see. Looks like a new man, Mr. Sowolski. I'm giving his wife some work now too. I think in a few months I could maybe get her in the union."

"That's wonderful of you, Pop," he says.

"What's wonderful?" I say. "If you got a chance to do something for a person, why not? It's a world, after all. People got to act like people."

"I know," he says. "But it's swell of you, just the same." So he stops now and all of a sudden I got nothing to say either and my heart is in my mouth. I want to ask him something and I don't want to. "So now?" I say finally. "You going on from Omaha to San Francisco?" He don't answer me right away and, over a thousand miles away, I can see his face, exactly like when he was a little boy and he tried out for the first time his two-wheeler bike and he fell off, how he jumped up, real fast, he didn't want to show me he hurt himself.

"I wasn't planning to go on," he says. "I wanted to tell you I stopped in to see a man named Kittner at the Emporium here, in Omaha. I remember Larry talked to me about him, we were thinking about flying out here to see him, that time we went on a trip. Mr. Kittner says he knows you from way back——"

"Yes, and he's a chiseler from way back too," I say. "This, I suppose, he didn't tell you."

"Well, he said you'd had some kind of a run-in, a long time ago. But we had a nice talk and I think we can do business with him. He uses a lot of merchandise."

"Harold," I say, "I heard something just now. A little word. *We* can do business with him, you said?"

So he doesn't say anything for a minute. "That's what I said, Pop. I'd like to come back. Really go to work and learn the business. How about it?"

How about it, he says. "So come, already," I say. "What are you wasting my time on the phone? You'll be very welcome." It's like I would be asking him for Friday night dinner but I can feel my hand is wet around the phone. I'm telling you, it's a peculiar thing, so much emotion, with a son.

Next day, seems fantastic, Omaha, Nebraska, and already he's in the office. I'm expecting he'll be pale, skinny, run down, rings under the eyes—what should I tell you, he looks wonderful, sunburned, filled out, he even looks again taller than the last time I saw him.

231

"Listen," I say, "I didn't know exactly the plane you would be coming in on, so I didn't say anything to your mother. Call her up now, the first thing."

Well, what should I tell you, I'm pretty excited, you understand, I don't remember exactly what he said but I could give you an idea, what he told me about his experiences. Certain places where he was traveling he looked up some of the boys who were in the army with him together, in Korea.

"You know," he says, "you meet these fellows in an army barracks, outside the country, you never really get to know them. Who they are, what they're really like. You've got to see them where they belong, among the things they know and care about. It's a great country, Pop. I don't want to sound corny, but it came rushing at me like a dozen symphonies busting loose, all at once. It gave me a feeling I never had before in my life. I was proud, and I felt like a fool, too. I know what that reviewer meant when he said you can't make a book out of anger and pity alone. You can't make a life out of it either. Not unless you want to live it in a psychopathic ward. I want to build, Pop. Whatever it is. A business. A dress. I want to work. I want to belong. I want to raise some kids and teach them that they live in the most blessed country on earth. I don't want to throw rocks any more. I've had all I want of that."

I start to say something but he rushes right on. I let him. Let him get it all off the chest. "Like with the Sowolskis," he says. "I shot my face off and got them nothing but trouble. You stepped in and did something for them, with a wallet, not noise. You said it once. It's registered, finally. If you want to help people, you've got to *be* somebody yourself. You can't help anything or change anything by joining up with the misfits yourself. I found out something else, Pop. Hitting the jungles and the flophouses. The outcasts, the lost ones of the world—they used to break my heart. Thinking about them. I mean, for a while there, there wasn't room for anything else. Marie and I had a big quarrel about that before I left. I thought she was heartless, selfish. Well, I was wrong about that too. You can't give all your heart to pity. Maybe, if you're a saint, or a misfit yourself. But if you want to go on, as a creative person, to breathe, to grow, you can't lock yourself up in that tunnel forever, you've got to come up for air. I'll tell you something I found out, that kind of rocked me. They're not very interesting, the misfits of the world. As people. They're all wrapped up in themselves, in their own peculiar ideas, or their own bitterness. You very seldom run into one that's interested in other misfits, in helping them, or worrying about what happens to them. You realize there's something more that's involved in human unhappiness than the system. Anyway, what I thought was the system. There's all kinds of reasons, personal reasons that have nothing to do with the system.

"You know when you really learn something about people," he says, "what really goes on? When you sit down to a meal—on a farm—oh boy, those farm breakfasts, they're something, Pop—or you stop for a hamburger somewhere, or cop a ride with a truck driver. You know what? This is a capitalist country. Not just Wall Street or Pittsburgh. You want to talk to a real capitalist, it's

233

the fellow who owns his own two-ton truck and does hauling for the township, or he's got a tractor, or a bulldozer, or a combine, or a lathe, or a fix-it shop. Are they capitalists! They give the Wall Street guys cards and spades."

Well, it's kind of cute, you know, how he's discovered America and he's explaining me about it now. He could have found out the same thing here, in the shop, in the street downstairs, in the subway, in any electrical appliance store. But I don't say anything, everybody's got to find out things in his own way and in the time that is right for that person. The main thing is you should find out *some* time, they shouldn't lay you away in the cemetery the same ignoramus as you started out.

"Well, Harold," I say, "I'm glad you've had a chance to talk to people, this is an education in itself. I only want to say two things to you. And then enough talking. First of all, I want to apologize about the Madame Butterfly business."

"Don't even talk about it, Pop," he says. "It's a big laugh. It's my fault, really. I shouldn't have been so damn close-mouthed."

"All right," I say. "You want to be easygoing about it, fine. But I was a big fool. It was a very insulting thing. I'm sorry. Now the other thing. About the book. I don't want you should forget this book, Harold."

He looks at me now, he don't understand.

"I'm not talking about the writing," I say. "Something else. What you had in your heart, when you were writing these stories. Anger and pity, like the critic said. Maybe it's not enough for literature. But for a person, it's something different. What you wanted to say—people got to have some feelings, they got to care what happens to each other, they got to remember things—for a young man to believe in this, to be willing to fight with his father about it—this is a fine thing, Harold. I learned something from you too, the last few months. Boys coming home from the army, not thinking about hot rods, where is the first dame they can pick up—but what's going on in the world—misery, hunger, orphans in Korea —well, I'm proud you're one of these boys, and you're my son. This is what I got to say, and I said it and now I'll call in Marie."

So I call her, on the public address, she comes in, in a new little number, 864, a street dress with a sheath skirt and a bolero jacket, we're going to feature it in the line, and she looks in this, I'm telling you, a dream. She stands in the door a minute, she says, "Yes, Mr. Seidman," then she sees Harold and she looks for a minute as if she's going to faint. Then she runs over to him and she says, "Darling, darling," I don't know is she laughing or crying and both of them are saying, "Darling, darling," I got enough already, this is a conversation it's better in the movies, or private altogether.

Yes, he is with me now in the place. I'm just now getting printed up new stationery, Seidman and Son. How does it feel? Well, like I told you, I'm not a man who was all the time dreaming his son would take over the business. Ever since he was a kid I had always the idea he would be a big doctor, or lawyer—still and all, feels pretty good. Seidman and Son. Got a nice sound to it, somehow.

Marie and Harold? Of course they are married. What do you think, we're living like gypsies, the Seidmans?

They got a very nice apartment—no, it's not near us. They are living in Manhattan, in the Village. I don't want to start up the business of the children living on top of us, or vice versa. They got their own lives, their own friends. Yes, if they want to come sometimes for a dinner, Friday night, or brunch on Sunday, fine. They are very welcome. But no possessive business. No Momism. No Popism. No sir.

You know something? Just between us? It's very fine, what I just said. I would get an A from any psychologist. And I would like to throw away the book and the kids should be over to the house seven times a week. Sophie? Reconciled? You mean, on account of the religion? Listen, every Jewish family should only have in it a few Gentiles like Marie, they would be very lucky. Did you ever see a Presbyterian Jew? I would like to be one. And my Sophie, she is so crazy about this girl, I'm only worried our Jenny shouldn't get jealous.

Well, so again I chewed your ear off a whole afternoon. It's a ridiculous situation, you are the writer and I'm always telling you stories. So we'll get down to business. You want I should tell you something for this article you're going to write. All right, so where should I begin?

seven

I'm glad you could join me here for lunch.
How do you like this setup? Pretty fancy, no? I tell you,
in America anything can happen. A haberdasher becomes
President. A general becomes a typewriter salesman. My
wife becomes a professor of psychology. You made me a
Dior to the Masses. And now I am a member of a country
club. Morris Seidman from Delancey Street. You should
hear my sister Bessie on this subject. Only one thing I
could guarantee you. I am not trading-in Samson for a
Dalmatian or a Boxer. And a golfer they wouldn't make
from me neither. Chairman of the Social Committee, okay.
But this is as far as I will go.

So, my writer friend, what brings you East this time
of year, you could be sitting there in the sun by a swimming pool with Darryl Zanuck and Marilyn Monroe?

You just escaped from a producer's basement? Never mind, this suntan you didn't get in a producer's basement.

Me? What should be with me? You want a dress manufacturer should be a hero in a scenario? Styles and more styles, this is the big adventure in my life. The family is fine, fine, couldn't be better. The only thing, I'm getting complaints from my daughter-in-law, Harold isn't home with her enough. You know, since I made him a partner, this boy takes everything so serious, he is on the road practically all the time. He wants to meet every one of the accounts, personal.

Pension plans? You remember with Mr. Magnuson, hah? Well, I'll tell you a funny thing. With the customers, he stopped giving them arguments. But *we* got now a pension plan in the shop. Looks like I will be the first beneficiary. How? Well, let's face it, he's pushing me out, little by little. Of course he is diplomatic about it. He tells everybody I am a genius, the business couldn't run without me. But me, he's always asking why I don't go to Florida, take my wife for a vacation in Hawaii. Why do you think I joined a country club? He insists I need more rest and exercise. Wait, I'll be out there in California yet, with a yachting cap and a flitgun, spraying my oranges. You know something, a little secret? I'm not looking forward.

Yes, yes, got to be careful these coming years. The Dangerous Age. My friend, Joe Wachtel, is already recommending me an analyst. If you would know why, you would laugh. You want to hear? It's again a long story, you sure you got time? You don't have to go do a little research in the Stork Club? Twenty One? All right so I'll tell you.

238

You remember you met my designer here last time, Miss Youssem? You said she reminded you of Katharine Hepburn, a little? The same type? And I mentioned to you also my star salesman, Larry Kogen? Well, a shop like mine, gets to be a little bit like a family. Closed in, every day you got to be in contact, you couldn't stay impersonal. Nilly-willy, you are getting involved. And with this you lose the perspective, like with children. Sometimes things could be going on right under your nose, you are like blind, you can't see them. On the other hand, sometimes from the smallest thing comes an explosion. Me, I'm not a very observant person, actually. Something touches me, interests me, yes. But usually I got a lot on my mind and I got my private family life, it's very important to me too, so it's got to be something special in the shop for me to pay attention.

Well, Larry and Miss Youssem, this is something special. First of all, they are both strong personalities. How should I describe you Larry? Handsome he is, no question. The character, well he's a goodhearted boy, he's got a soft spot for horses and slot machines, girls he's very considerate, he likes to give everybody a chance and he's got a very long list. He plays a fine game of gin and the last time he read a book, was by that big literary man, Bob Hope. He is still quoting from it. But go fight City Hall, the buyers are crazy for him and I'll tell you the truth, I'm fond of him too, even though I can't take him serious.

Miss Youssem is another story. This is a high type woman, educated, talented, she speaks fluently three languages. Why is it like cats and dogs between her and

Larry? Maybe this is the reason, he thinks she is snooty or something. But whatever it is, it's like there would be a devil in him and she's got just the right powder, she sprinkles a little and it comes dancing up in his eyes. He is all the time teasing her and a woman like this, creative, there's always big tensions anyway, with the temperament. So you can imagine.

I'll give you a scene. It's the time when we are changing the line, preparing for next season the new styles. My production man, Rosenzweig, is hollering at the pressers, the pressers are hollering at the finishers, the head operator is running after the cutter with a scissors to stab him, the models are getting temperamental too, quitting, the union delegate is looking on every stitch, figuring out how he can squeeze from me another drop of blood. A regular circus.

So, in the middle of everything I got to answer the telephone, it's my sister Bessie from Flushing. Well, this morning she's got big news for me. She's got a new doctor for her headaches and he's got a new theory. It's not an allergy, it's tension and she's giving me a whole conducted tour of her sinuses, so I cut her off in the middle, I say, "Bessie, you've got a new doctor? Congratulations. Use him in the best of health. The details you could tell to Sophie. I've got a lot of things to do in the shop this morning."

"Always too busy," she says, "I want to come in this afternoon, try on my dress."

"It's not ready," I tell her.

"So when will it be ready?" she says. "I'm waiting two weeks already."

240

"Bessie, yours is not the only dress I got to worry about. I got a new line to get out."

"I see. A sister in your life is nothing any more. You became too important——"

"Listen, Bessie," I say, "you got complaints to make, write to the *Times*. I'm busy. Good-by already."

This woman, you know, she's been making me nervous nearly fifty years, since we were kids on Delancey Street. Now she's really got time to concentrate. Her kids are married, one is away in school, so she's got nothing to do all day but sit by the television, or figure out what I did, she should be insulted. Well, anyway, I hang up the receiver, I'm a little aggravated. Harold comes in, he's getting ready to go on the road for a week, we're talking this and that, business things, but I could see he's upset about something, so I ask him and he tells me it's nothing, he had a little discussion with Marie this morning.

"So what was she crying about?" I say.

He looks at me, shakes his head. "Pop," he says, "I've known you for a long time and I still underestimate you."

"Listen," I say, "in the first place I'm a married man myself a good many years and besides, between a father and son, radar is not a new invention. So I could guess what is the problem but maybe you would like to tell me."

"It's no problem," he says, "really. Marie is a wonderful girl but—women are so unreasonable."

"She thinks maybe you are working too hard," I say. "You don't spend enough time at home?"

"Yes. Can you imagine? I told her. If a person wants to take hold of a new business, really learn it, get to know what goes on, it takes time. Naturally I'm preoccupied. So you'd think 'preoccupied' was a dirty word or something. Like adultery. She starts to cry and she says before we were married I was preoccupied with the state of the world, and now I'm preoccupied with business and she'd like me to be preoccupied with her for a change, before she's too old to care. So what's the answer to that one, for Pete's sake?"

"Well," I say, "I'm an old-fashioned man and from me you could only get old-fashioned answers. You got a career in the business, keeps you busy all day long, and week ends and nights too sometimes—a woman's career is a family. She's entitled."

"Well, good Lord, Pop," he says, "we've been married six months. I want to have a family but I want to get established, get my feet on the ground, know where I'm going——"

"Harold," I say, "I said all I'm going to say on this subject. I don't want to mix in in your personal affairs. You'll work things out for yourself. All I could tell you, this girl you got is a jewel. But if you'll try to keep her in a case, like a jewel, you got trouble. Now tell me. You're going to be in Dallas, you'll see McKittrick there, I want you should straighten out with him once and for all. We are not running a consignment business here. We don't send out merchandise on approval. Next season, let him order what he can use and keep it. If he's going to keep on with the returns the same way as before, it's finished. There's other accounts in Dallas. If he wants our line this is the way it's got to be."

"Okay, Pop," he says. "I agree with you. I'll lay it right

on the line. And maybe, while I'm gone, you'll take Marie out to lunch sometime——"

"I took her out to lunch last week," I say. "This wouldn't solve your problem, Harold."

So now the buzzer sounds, I answer. Very urgent. Miss Youssem wants to see me right away.

"Fireworks," says Harold. "That's your department. I'm leaving."

"Never mind," I say. "You got a half interest too. You stay right here."

So Miss Youssem comes in, with Larry together, and Doreen, a model, she's got on a new number, pinned, looks very striking but a little extreme. Right away Larry starts in.

"Look at this garment, will you, Morris? What's going on here with the new line? We're going to have some season."

"Wait a minute, Larry," I say, "don't go off always half-crocked. What is the problem?"

"Well, look at it," he says. "I would like to get across to Miss Youssem one very simple idea. Plumage was intended by Nature as a mating device. Not a disguise."

"Mr. Seidman," Miss Youssem says, "I understood I was hired to design a line of dresses for smart modern women. Mr. Kogen's concept of style seems to have congealed around Minsky's Burlesque."

"Modern women," Larry says. "This is for the stratosphere. Be great on the first spaceship to Mars. I can just see the stewardess beaming over it. With her aluminum head."

"Larry, stop with the remarks," I say. "Mr. Star Salesman."

243

"Well, look at it, Morris. It's a libel on the female form. What are we here, an annex of the Modern Museum of Art? You want to win the Cannes Festival Award for cockeyed designs? Or you want to sell dresses?"

"Larry, I want to sell dresses," I say, "and I want to have a normal blood pressure. And I would like to have a business where there isn't fights and arguments all day long."

"I'm sorry," Miss Youssem says, "but I'm sick of this constant heckling and interference. Let's throw the dress out of the line——"

"I'm not throwing it out of the line. Don't be in such a hurry," I say.

"Pop," Harold says, "if you don't need me I'll run along home for a few hours. I'm catching the five o'clock plane to Dallas."

"When you see McKittrick down there," Larry says, "tell him we're whipping up a new line based on themes from the *Architectural Digest*."

"I think you're wrong, Larry," Harold says, "I think the dress is stunning." He gives Miss Youssem a big smile. "As a matter of fact, I'm putting in an order for one for Marie right now. I'll call you tomorrow from Dallas, Pop," he says and he goes out.

"Mr. Seidman," Miss Youssem says, "I'd like to have your decision on this number." She's twisting the scissors in her hand, and I know I jut got to say one word, the wrong one, and I got no more designer.

"My decision, Miss Youssem," I say, "is I hired you to design the dresses here and Mr. Kogen to sell them. Larry,

244

I want you should keep your nose out, from now on, of the designing room."

"I'm only trying to co-operate," he says, sour cream wouldn't melt in his mouth. "After all, I ought to have some idea of what the customers want."

"Yes, and you got a little address book to give it to them. Go, Miss Youssem," I say. "Create. I got complete confidence in you."

"Thank you, Mr. Seidman," she says, and she gives Larry a look, he is canceled, like a stamp, and she goes out.

"You know," Larry says, "there's nothing wrong with that dame that a week end in Atlantic City wouldn't fix."

"This is your cure for everything," I say. "If only Congress would spend every week end in Atlantic City we would have in Washington a paradise."

"You said it," Larry says. "What do you say, Doreen?" And he gives the model a pinch, you know where. She slaps his hand, like she would be patting a baby's behind, and she says, "Mr. Kogen, if you'd keep your hands to yourself, it would be a great relief to all concerned. May I go, Mr. Seidman?"

"Yes, go, Doreen," I say. "Don't pay attention to this bum." She goes to the door, he makes again a grab for her, she screams a little but not so the Police Department should answer, you know what I mean, and she goes out she gives him a big smile, like he done something real cute. You know, with some girls, you don't have to be a Phi Beta Kappa to pass the examinations.

So I say, "Larry, Larry, what am I going to do with you?"

245

"Morris," he says, "let's face it. We're in a business that's just a branch of the world's oldest profession. Who are we kidding?"

"Some philosophy," I say. "Thirty years. This is what I worked myself up to?"

"Well, it's true. Look at the perfume business. They stick to fundamentals and they sell a lot of ambergris. You give me a dress called 'My Sin' and watch me go to town. And I'll tell you something else," he says, "if that dame got herself a man, we'd have a line with some oomph in it."

"Listen, Larry," I say, "there's no customers in the showroom now. Go down to Pinsky's Poolroom, get yourself a *Racing Form* and knock your head together there. When I need your advice how to get out a line, I'll send for you."

A big pleasure he just gave me. Such an idea. A branch of the world's oldest profession. Not even the main entrance. My mother, she should rest in peace, would be very happy to hear this, what I accomplished with my life. She wanted me to be a violinist altogether.

So this will give you an idea what's going on. I could tell you more things—I'm having one time an argument with Larry, I got a rule in my showroom, no dates between the customers and the models. So I just explained this, nicely, to a new customer, I said to him, "Mr. Farber, we got nothing to sell you here but dresses. If you are looking for romance, I could recommend you a couple places on the street, or maybe you should spend a week in Grossinger's altogether, get the whole thing out of your system." So he gets sore, Mr. Farber, and he walks

246

out. A little later, I'm talking to Miss Youssem, Larry comes up.

"What did you say to Farber?" he asks me. "All he wanted was Doreen's telephone number. I spent a solid year, trying to get that guy into the showroom———"

"I don't want such guys in my showroom," I say. "Musketeers. They got an expense account instead of a sword. Let them go somewhere else with their business and their nonsense. Turns my stomach to see how they are carrying on, middle-aged men———"

"Morris," he says, "what are we here, a branch of the YMCA?"

"I know what you think we are a branch of, Larry," I tell him. "But I will run my business my way, and that's final."

Well, anyway, this is how things are going. One evening I got to stay a little late in the office, I go into the shop to close up, everybody is already gone, you know how it is with good union members, comes five o'clock, out, like shot from a gun. I'm walking by the designer's office and I hear, inside, a sound, at first I can't believe it. I go in, I see Miss Youssem is sitting by her table, crying, not like a grown person, like a child, catching the breath real loud, like somebody just grabbed away from her her lollipop.

"Miss Youssem," I say, "what's the matter? Why are you sitting here, crying?"

"Sure," she says. "Why? Does a stone cry? Does a machine cry? Why should I cry? Didn't you feed me my quota of chalk and pins today? Didn't I get screamed at and trampled on by everybody in this establishment, from the production manager down to the pressers? What have I got to cry about?"

"Miss Youssem," I say, "I didn't come in here to have a debate with you why you are crying. I just want to know if I got something to do with it? It's something I said? I'll right away apologize."

"It's not you," she says, "it's just everything at once."

"So come with me downstairs," I say, "we'll have a bite to eat, and you'll tell me."

"I wouldn't know where to start," she says.

"We'll start with a little appetizer," I say, "then some soup——"

She takes away the handkerchief from the eyes and I say, quick, "I'm making a joke. Nothing to get insulted."

"You don't have to humor me," she says. "I'm not a mental case."

"And suppose I'm humoring you a little," I say, "you're entitled. You're working in a business, even when it's going smooth there's enough aggravation to make a person crazy. Come on, you'll have a drink, a little food, you'll feel better."

"I'm sorry to let go like this," she says, "but sometimes it just gets to be too much. Just too much."

"I know," I say. "So powder up the nose a little. The people in Longchamps will see my designer's been crying, they'll figure we got troubles, we can't get out the line, right away will start the rumors, next thing the credit is chopped off, then *I'll* start crying and from this could come a flood altogether."

So she's smiling a little now, already I'm a big success with the diplomacy; she goes to powder her nose and I call the house, I tell the maid, Gladys, I'm staying late in the shop. "We got chicken chockabelli for dinner tonight," she says.

"So eat it in the best of health," I say. "Tell Mrs. Seidman I'll be home later."

First thing in the restaurant, Miss Youssem orders up a stinger, you know what this is, brandy with some crème de menthe, it's a nice drink for a lady, and we start in to talk, she's an educated person, she studied art, music, she was in Italy a few years, she knows a lot about opera, I'm a little bit of a fan myself, so we got things to talk, she orders up another stinger, we discuss a little about pictures, the history, she orders another stinger, about Venice, Rome, another stinger, Michelangelo and Donatello is each one stinger and I'm afraid if we're going to go on like this through the whole Renaissance it could take maybe twenty, thirty stingers and from being such a diplomat I'll end up with her yet in the hospital.

"So tell me," I say, "what happened in the place today that upset you so much?"

"I don't know exactly," she says, "I guess it's an accumulation. But 816 was the last straw."

"That's the Picasso print you copied from Dior? Excuse me," I say, "I don't mean copied. I mean you were inspired by it."

"There you go," she says, "humoring me again." But she gives me now a big smile, then she turns to the waiter, he should take again her glass.

"What's the problem with 816?" I ask her.

She sticks out, all of a sudden, a finger, almost in my eye. "Your production man, Mr. Seidman. He's a sadist."

249

Again psychology. I'm getting it all the time at home, from my wife. "Rosenzweig?" I say. "I think you got a wrong number, Miss Youssem. In the Turkish bath, with the steam, he is maybe a little bit of a masochist——"

"Well he has no more feeling for style," she says, "than Jack the Ripper. You know what he did today? With 816? He took the whole dress apart and he comes in with his insane figures, it takes too much material, the operating costs twice what it should, the finishers can't finish the dress in less than a week, too much this and too much that, the dress can't be made for the price and I can just take it out of the line and hang myself."

"Why didn't you come to me?" I ask her. "I'm still the boss."

"Well, I don't like to come running to you twenty times a day. It's such a constant battle," she says. "All the time. And that Larry Kogen. He's the worst of all. I think he stays up nights figuring out ways to torment me."

"Miss Youssem," I say, "Larry Kogen is staying up nights, yes. But believe me this is not the reason."

"I can't tell you how I detest that man," she says, and she gives herself a shake, like she would see a spider. "It's getting so I can't stand to look at him."

"His looks are so bad?" I ask her. "I thought, the way the models are making a fuss about him, he's a regular Tyrone Power."

"Oh, he's good-looking enough, in a common sort of way," she says, "but he's so infuriating. That deceptively boyish air of his. He must be forty-five——"

"He's thirty-six, going on forty-five. Miss Youssem," I say, I know already the problem, it's not the first time it happened in the place with Larry, "this boy has been working for me six, seven years, I got yet to hear from him three sensible words together. He's a salesman. Maybe at night when he goes home, he turns into a person. But in the place? How can you take him serious?"

So she swallows down the rest of her drink and holds the glass up for me, I should put it under the faucet again. I give it to the waiter and he gives me a look, this is not a Longchamps-type client, it's more for one of the Irish places uptown, and he says, "What's with a little food, you going to eat something too?" So I tell him to bring some chopped liver, with the drink, and she says to me, "You've given me a wonderfully penetrating analysis of the Kogen character."

"I gave you an analysis?" I say. "When?"

"Of course, you know him better than I do," she says. "But I would just love to teach that man a lesson. I really would."

"My dear Miss Youssem," I say, "I want to give you an advice. I know this boy Larry, he plays a fine game of gin, he knows a million jokes, he'll make you a map of the United States, you could go from one end of the country to the other and never be more than two minutes away from a poolroom, a booking parlor, or you should excuse me, some fancier places. A regular barrel of fun. We had in the place, a few years ago, it was before you came, an Italian girl, a model, she had from him so much fun she took one day fifty sleeping pills and then she tried to jump out of a window besides. How much fun can a person stand. You, you're an attractive woman, talented, educated, maybe rich even. You got time, you're looking for a

251

little adventure, excitement, take up parachute jumping, dynamite throwing, shark hunting—something safe. Don't give Larry Kogen lessons. From this you could only get a broken head." I'm saying "head," it's only because it sounds foolish, "broken heart."

So she gives a laugh now, like a high-tone actress. "Please, Mr. Seidman," she says, "I appreciate your concern, I really do, I'm touched, but give me a little credit. Maybe you don't suspect it but I can take care of myself. I can handle a Larry Kogen any day of the week."

Sure. And with seven stingers I could maybe handle Marilyn Monroe. And Joe Louis, the same time.

"Listen," I say, "take it from an old man——"

"Mr. Seidman," she says and she puts a hand on my wrist, it's shaking a little like she would be cold, and it's making me feel—I don't know how to explain you. Just that I haven't got the heart to take away my arm from the table. "Don't say that, Mr. Seidman," she says, "you're still a young, vigorous man, with a great deal of understanding. A great deal."

"So have a little liver," I say, the waiter just put it down. And I make for her a canapé, with a cracker, and she says, "Thank you," she puts it down by her plate, she takes from her pocketbook her handkerchief, a mirror and a lipstick, she makes up the lips, she puts down the mirror by her plate, she takes out a pack of cigarettes, keys and a cigarette lighter, she puts back in her bag the lipstick, the handkerchief, the mirror, the keys and the cracker with the liver, then she lights a cigarette and she drinks down the stinger, the whole thing, one swallow, phwwt. You heard sometimes the expression, career woman? This is a woman she could make a career from stingers.

"But you're right," she says, she sits back and now I'm afraid she's going to cry altogether. "You're absolutely right, of course. I've always had a fatal attraction toward the wrong kind of man and it's about time it stopped. I'm thirty-two, you know."

"You want some coffee?" I say.

"No, thank you," she says. "I'm just right now." And she gives me now a smile on one side of the face, very appealing. "I don't do this very often," she says, "but it's been a great relief to let go. I do appreciate it. But you must be anxious to get home," she says, "and I really should go." I motion the waiter he should bring the check, he's watching her like she would maybe be a fire-cracker, she's going to explode and I'm wondering too, will I maybe have to carry her to the door, but she walks very good, only stepping a little like it would be in feathers. I call a cab and I ask if she wants I should ride with her to the house and she says no, she took up already enough of my time.

"I'll be fine," she says, "I'm feeling much better, really. Thank you, Mr. Seidman, you've been very kind."

"I'm selfish," I say. "I got to look after the best de-signer I ever had."

So again she puts the hand on my arm, thin, like a child's hand. "Mr. Seidman," she says, "I've always known you were a good employer. Fair. Generous. You're one of the few men I know who has real style sense. But for me you have something ever so much more important. An understanding heart. Don't lose it in this cold and crazy world."

She goes off in the cab and I'm standing there, I got all of a sudden a very peculiar feeling. First place, I should have gone with her in the cab. Escort her home, like we used to say in the old days. This is the polite thing, all right she's an employee, she's an elderly girl, she's lived by herself a long time, she knows the way to her apartment—I could give you all the reasons why it's not necessary but still and all, it's not nice, she should go home alone. We had dinner together, even though for her it wasn't much, one cracker with liver, in the pocketbook. But the main thing, this funny feeling, you start out with a woman, she's got a certain form, face, I seen it nearly every day for more than a year, she is sitting there in the restaurant, drinking like a fish, like she would be a drunkard, or a comedienne—all of a sudden she puts her hand on my arm, it's a whole different story. I got an impression of an entirely different woman. I could picture her now in my mind, she's paying off the cab driver, good evening to the doorman, to the elevator boy, she's looking in her pocketbook for the key, maybe she finds there now the cracker, and she feels funny, did she make a fool of herself with the boss, talk too much, and she comes in the dark apartment, she puts on the light, maybe she's got there a cat so she puts down the cracker on the rug and watches the cat eat off the liver, you know how they do, so dainty, with the tongue?

Has she got a cat? Yeah, a Siamese, with blue eyes. Why do you ask? Oh, I see. You're foxy. You want to know was

I ever in her apartment? So I'm going to tell you. Have a little patience. It's not on television, there's no commercial coming. Well, I don't feel like going home right away, I decide to go back to the shop, see what's the problem there with Style 816. Rosenzweig says it takes three and a half yards, he's a good man, but he could be wrong too. This was in the old days my specialty, to lay out a pattern, so I could save some goods. It's not a big trick, like you would paint a picture or write a story. It's just you got an eye to see how you could make a compromise. But you know how it says in the Bible? Whatever comes to your hand to do, do it with all your might? I always believed in this.

But now I got a little bit of a mood when I come into the place, I walk into the shop and I'm thinking, thirty years I've been at this business, building, building, comes six o'clock, turn out the lights—where is it? Where is the worry, the aggravation, the fights, the dreams too—all right, dress manufacturer's dreams, it's not like Da Vinci, Beethoven, but it's also got to do with—I don't know, not just for the family, a living, responsibilities—something else, like you would want to rinse out your name from daytime and hang it on a star, something to be proud, to make a success instead of a failure in the world, to be somebody. You come down to it, everybody is reaching for the same thing, in his own piece of sky, even a shipping clerk. Well, and where is it, the years, the dreams? In the piece goods? In the trimming department? On the shelves? The inventory? The rating by Dun and Bradstreet? In the fancy showroom I fixed up, with travertine floors, onyx fixtures, Danish modern, I spent in advance the

255

money I will maybe make for two seasons if my Style Show is a success?

Well, I come by the cutting tables, I find there a janitor, a new man, he's looking in one of the bins, you know, where the cutters are throwing away the remnants from the piece goods, we are collecting this and selling to the rag dealers. The man hears me now, he didn't realize there was anyone in the shop, he jumps up and he says, some kind of a foreign accent, "I didn't take anything, gentleman, I was just looking." And he looks scared, like I would have found him with his hands in the safe.

So this don't make me feel so fine, neither. Sometimes, you know, the kind of world we live in, it makes you a little sick. I can't even look at him, I say, "You got a little girl home, I suppose, likes to sew. I got two kids myself. When they were little they would come here, a whole Saturday afternoon they could be busy in the bins, dresses for dolls, pennants, I don't know what." And he's still standing there, looking like he is not sure am I going to call his office, or the police, or what. I see on the table a bolt of cloth, I cut him off half a yard and give him. "Take it," I say, "it's from India. Very fashionable now. Tell your girl to make from it a sari for her doll. Like a maharani. And you want, bring her here sometimes, she could look around, take what she wants."

So he gives me now a smile, he says, "Thank you, gentleman," and he goes away and I would be glad to believe him, I'm a gentleman. But what happened tonight, I'm not sure. It's been for me a very peculiar evening.

Anyway, I find the pattern for 816, I lay it out, start to figure, finally I see a way, if I lay on the skirt across the material instead of lengthwise, I can save a quarter-yard of material. This is maybe for you not an important consideration, to save a quarter or a half a yard of goods, but when you're getting out a dress for a price, to sell in quantities, could be the difference whether you make a profit or not. Then I see I can also take out two pleats from the tunic, it won't hurt anything and will also save some material. And also, instead of French piping, it's very nice but expensive, I can make facings on the seams, it will look all right, and one thing and another, the material and I can fight out with the union delegate on the operating and finishing and pressing, I could cut the cost maybe two dollars and at this price, with this much class, it could be a leader in the line.

So I'm driving home, thinking, I got a production man, an assistant production man, a designer, an assistant designer, two cutters, four pressers, architects, interior decorators they can spend for me a fortune for a new showroom—but to figure out how to bring in a dress at a price and the same time the style shouldn't be ruined, for this they still got to come to the old man. Never mind what Miss Youssem said, I'm still a vigorous young man. Sometimes I'm feeling two hundred years old. And it's good I should have the feeling the old boy still knows a little the score, he can still put his shoulder to the wheel and save a buck.

Well, I get home it's nearly one o'clock, Sophie is still up, reading in bed. She's got cold cream on the face and curlers in her hair.

"Where were you?" she says. "It's one o'clock."

So I'm getting a little annoyed, she sounds so strict,

like a district attorney. "I was in the shop," I say, "saving for you a little money you'll inherit when I'm dead from aggravation."

"For an aggravated man," she says, "you look very pleased with yourself. Where did you have dinner?"

"At Longchamps," I say.

"And how many drinks did you have?"

"Listen, Sophie," I say, "what's going on with the questionnaire? If I want to relax a little, dinner time, have a couple of drinks, I got to have an accountant along, he should give you a certified statement?"

"And who was the woman you were relaxing with at Longchamps, may I ask?"

How do you like this? You think the FBI has an organization? "So," I say. "Which one of your private eyes sent you in a report? You're waiting here like a third degree, I should put my foot in it?"

"Stop accusing me," she says, "it happens the Roselles were in Longchamps——"

"So she's got to sit there, Mrs. Busybody Roselle, like a German spy and run afterwards and call you up, I'm out with another woman? She couldn't come over, like a person——?"

"Maybe she was embarrassed."

"Mrs. Roselle embarrassed! A barracuda is shy? Listen, I was in Longchamps for dinner with Miss Youssem, my designer, and if I'm going to hear from you another word on this subject——"

"Your designer?" she says, and it's already a different tone of voice.

"Yes, my designer. I'm getting out a line now. Maybe

258

after all these years you would realize there's problems. It's not enough I'm breaking my head in the place all day, working all night, till one o'clock, I got to come home and have an argument with you, suspicions, one of your psychology pals called up to make a little trouble."

"Stop yelling," she says, "you'll wake up Jenny."

"Never mind Jenny," I say. "You're only worried I'll give her a complex. It's time somebody should start worrying about *my* complexes in this house. Twenty-seven years I been checking in with you, like a night watchman——"

"Morris," she says, "stop acting like a child."

"Child shmild," I say, "I'm giving you fair warning, Sophie. Next time I'm coming home and I find you with the cold cream on your face and those irons in your head, you wouldn't have with me an argument. I'm going to turn right around and go to the club."

"What club?" she says.

"So I'll join a club," I say and I realize now it's ridiculous what's going on, I start to laugh, she starts to laugh and I'm wondering, why was I so excited, am I guilty, or what? I don't know. Anyway, Sophie is wiping the cold cream from her face, she says, "What did you have to eat at Longchamps? Gladys made such good chicken chockabelli tonight."

"You got some left?" I ask her. "I was so busy listening to Miss Youssem's problems, I forgot to eat altogether."

"She's also got problems, Miss Youssem?" my wife says.

And all of a sudden I got again a picture, like in front of the restaurant, and this time it's like a fist in my stomach. Has she got a problem, Miss Youssem! Maybe the worst problem in the whole world. Lonesome. A whole

259

evening she's talking, around and around, making herself drunk, and this is why, not the business, not the aggravation, not Rosenzweig, maybe not even Larry, she's got a crush on him. Don't ask me why she is alone. She is not a homely woman. Maybe there was a story, some kind, who knows, the war, something. Maybe even she likes it, to be alone. Or in the beginning she thought she would like it. You know, independent. Don't ask me. All I know, she is alone and for a woman thirty-two, this is a tragedy. I look at Sophie, with those things in the hair, they look like snails, shiny, and I suppose to her, after thirty years, I don't look like such a prize package neither, but all of a sudden I see her very beautiful, standing there. I know in this room, other rooms where we slept in a bed, together, there is something we got to be very thankful for. Not me, separate, not her, both of us together, and for this you pay a price also, you got always an extra worry, you're afraid something will happen to the other part of yourself. But one thing you're not afraid. You're not afraid of a door, you open it and there's only an empty apartment, with only a cat maybe, standing on the rug. You don't have to be afraid of closets which got only *your* clothes in them, of a window, you look out and there's nothing, only a city, a world, a universe in which you got to live alone. You know what I mean?

So I say to Sophie, "Listen, fix your hair up a little, it shouldn't look such a fright and come sit with me while I eat something. I'm starved."

Well, next morning I'm sitting at breakfast with Sophie, we're discussing family things, I don't remember exactly, bills or something, Jenny comes in, she looks me over very

260

good, like I would be a large interesting insect in her biology class, then her mother, the same thing, then she says, "Well, I guess you two have decided to be grown up about the whole thing."

"What are you talking about?" Sophie says.

"Oh, come on now, Mom," Jenny says. "I'm not a child. I know Pop had a date with another woman last night." She drinks down her orange juice and says, "Good morning, Gladys, I won't have anything this morning, just black coffee."

Gladys is standing there with a plate of toast, she's looking at me like I had all of a sudden horns on my head or something. "Well, let's not be square," Jenny says, looking from one to the other. "It happens in families. After all, father is an important man in his line of business and if a model wants to improve her station in life——"

"Now stop it," Sophie says. I'm surprised she is speaking so sharp. "If you say another word," she says, "I'll slap you. Your father and I are not television characters. I do not consider this a subject for humor."

So Jenny gives her a look, then she makes with the shoulders, who can understand parents, on or off television they're crazy. "Since you were listening——" Sophie says.

"I wasn't listening," Jenny says. "Pop was blasting."

"Your father," Sophie says, "was having a business conference at Longchamps with his designer last night."

"Oh," Jenny says. "Is that all? I thought the way you went on with Mrs. Roselle on the phone, it was a model or a showgirl or something."

"So now you're disappointed," I say.

261

"Well; it would have been interesting," she says, "to see if Mother is as emancipated as she thinks she is." And she bounces up now from the table and says, "I'm off to the grind."

"Wait a minute," I say, "you didn't eat anything. What's with an egg?"

"Oh, it's square to load yourself up with calories first thing in the morning. From now on I'm going to have nothing but black coffee. And a cigarette." She sees I'm going to say something so she says, quick, "When I'm eighteen, of course. Good-by, you two. I guess I'll be coming home to the same old ménage."

And she runs out of the house with her books.

"Thank God she's an extrovert," Sophie says.

"Thank God my mother couldn't hear this little conversation," I say. "She would turn over in her grave."

"You don't understand," Sophie says. "She's just relieved."

More psychology. I'm telling you, sometimes it's coming out of my ears. Well, I go down to the place, I go into Miss Youssem's office, she's working there already with her sketchbook, she's got on a flowered print dress, looks like she kept it in the icebox overnight, so crisp, and her face is smooth, the eyes clear. "How do you feel?" I say.

"Wonderful," she says. "I slept like a baby."

So, fine, one person, with seven stingers, would be up all night. Miss Youssem sleeps like a baby. I tell her about 816, what I did with the pattern, she's glad and I say, "So, next time you'll have a problem with Rosenzweig, don't take it so hard, come to me, we'll work it out. Yes?"

"Yes," she says, "I guess Mr. Rosenzweig has his problems with me too."

"Listen, we all got problems," I say. "The main thing, we should all have a little patience. A little humor. Right?"

"Right," she says. "By the way, Li Po says thanks for the chopped liver!"

"Lipo?"

"My cat," she says. "He could live on canapés." And she gives me now a big smile. So I'm feeling pretty good, not only I'm a diplomat but a Sherlock Holmes besides, I walk back to my office, I'm thinking how you could look at a woman every day, kind of blind, all of a sudden you see she is really a very fine-looking person, so much style —you know, Katharine Hepburn, a little, something like it. And I'm wondering, why didn't I do this before, get a little more on a personal basis, after all people got to work together, they shouldn't be like strangers. I go into my office, my friend Joe Wachtel is waiting for me there.

"You busy?" he says. "Come have a cup of coffee. I want to talk to you."

So I figure he's got something to tell me about his Maggie Dooley wife, he's always suffering, I heard the story a hundred times but he's a friend, you got to listen. I go down with him to Solowey's Dairy Restaurant, we order up some coffee and schnekens and he says to me, "Morris, I know you for a long time, twenty-eight years. I never stuck my nose in your business, right?"

"You got something on your mind, Joe?" I say. "Say it."

"I want to tell you something my analyst told me," he says.

"You're going again to the analyst?" I say. "I thought you were finished."

"I'm getting a couple booster shots," he says. "So let me tell you what he says. Men our age, he says, we got to be careful. You know, the youth is over, the struggle for a position in the world is behind us, marriage is an old habit, and we're getting a little worried, what is it all about, could we attract a woman now, could we hold a woman——"

Can you imagine? This poor *shnook*. Could he hold a woman. He should let go that prize of his for a minute, she would kill him.

"So what is your advice, Joe," I say. "I should get an analyst, a woman, or I should take hormones or what?"

"I ran into Harry Roselle this morning," he says. "It's true you were for dinner last night in Longchamps with a woman?"

"Yes, it's true," I say. "I confess."

"And you made the waiter dizzy, he was bringing so many stingers, he couldn't count them no more?"

"Don't worry, he counted them. It was all on the bill."

"Morris, this is no joke——"

"You're telling me it's no joke," I say. "If I will run into Harry Roselle myself, he wouldn't think it's a joke neither."

"Morris," he says, "it's not just Harry Roselle. You got to think of your family, your business, your reputation——"

"Joe," I ask him, "what does he charge, your analyst?"

"Fifty dollars an hour," he says. "For me, I'm an old patient, he makes it thirty-five."

264

Can you imagine? Thirty-five dollars. For a visit, mind you, not a season ticket.

"You want to take?" he says. "I'll see if I can get it for you for the same price."

"It's very tempting," I say, "looks like a real bargain. But I'll wait a little."

"It's a good investment, Morris," he says. "Men our age, there's always problems coming up."

"So far I managed all right with my problems," I say. "I'll try a little longer. Anyway, this woman I was out with last night, I'm not worried about holding her. I got a contract. She starts flirting with some other manufacturer, I'll take them both to court." He looks at me real funny and I say, "Joe, I had dinner with my designer, Miss Youssem, last night. We're getting out a new line now, she's tense, so I bought her a couple drinks, she should relax. So from this, Harry Roselle has got to make a whole *tsimmess*. Next time I will put up a sign, all the busybodies should know."

You think I'm maybe finished now with this nonsense? I'm not in my office five minutes, Rosenzweig comes in, he's holding a pattern.

"You figured out with 816," he says. "Three yards."

"Yes," I say, "and next time Miss Youssem tells you something, don't be so stubborn."

So I see he is giving me a peculiar look. "Morris," he says, "she's going to run the shop now, Miss Youssem?"

"What kind of a remark is that?" I ask him.

"All right, forget it," he says. "I made a remark. You're coming to the Turkish bath with me and Karp tonight? Or you got some other plans?"

"What other plans? It's Thursday, no?"

"Well, a person could change his mind," he says. "Fifteen years. Maybe you got tired. Maybe you want to do something else tonight."

"For instance?"

"For instance, a night club. A show. Maybe you want to take somebody to dinner."

So I'm getting a little mad but I'm holding myself in. It's kind of funny, too, you know.

"Who told you?" I say. "Harry Roselle, or it's on the radio, or what?"

"Morris," he says, "you know me a good many years——"

"Yeah," I say. "You're going to tell me now you never stuck your nose in my business?"

"I'm a broad-minded man, Morris," he says. "Miss Youssem is an attractive woman——"

"Oh, you noticed this," I say. "So why don't you act toward her a little human, instead of fighting all the time?"

"Who's fighting?" he says. "I got to discuss with her certain things, no? I got a shop to run, Morris. Doesn't run itself."

"I'm giving you all the credit," I say. "But the same time, you are dealing with a woman, a creative person, you could be a little diplomatic."

"Diplomatic," he says. "I'm talking to her, she looks at me like I was from isinglass. With you it's different. You could be a diplomat. She's got for you a high opinion. You could be the King of Siam——"

"Who told you?"

"Never mind," he says. "A little bird told me. Morris,

I'm pleading with you. Watch your step. You got a good business, a beautiful wife, devoted, two beautiful children——"

"And a production man," I say, "who is the biggest *noodnick* on Seventh Avenue. Rosenzweig, what do you want from my life?"

"Morris," he says, "even if you'll hate me, I got to tell you. Men are coming to our age, they got an idea they got to prove something——"

"Oh, for heaven's sake," I say. "From you too I'm going to get psychology? Send me in the shipping clerks already and let me get *their* opinion, I would like to get down to business sometime today."

You think I could? Rosenzweig goes back to the shop, five minutes later, a telephone call. My sister Bessie, from Flushing.

"Morris," she says, "you got somebody in your office? Or you're alone?"

"I got here a barber and a manicurist," I say, "and four dancing girls and a boy with a fan, he's keeping away the flies. You know how it is with your rich brother."

"I got to talk to you," she says. "Very important. Your door is closed? Somebody could listen in on the wire?"

"It's something for the FBI?"

"Morris, it's no joke. Myron just called me up. He heard on the street a rumor, you were out, dead drunk, with a woman last night."

"So?" I say.

"What do you mean, so? Who do you think you are, Mr. Secretary of State, no comment? I want to know what's going on. I'm entitled."

"Listen, Bessie," I say. "What should I tell you? A man my age, I figure it's getting pretty close to the end, I want to have yet a fling or two before they put me away in the cemetery."

"God in heaven," she says, "with my own ears I'm hearing this?"

"Why not?" I say. "They're not big enough?"

"Morris, tell me. Plain out. No fancy business. You're having an affair with another woman?"

"What then? With whom should I have an affair? Another man?"

"Morris," she says, "you are not talking to one of your Café Society bums. I'm your sister. Remember. I told you a long time ago. You are making too much money. This will be your ruination."

"What ruination? Caviar, champagne, women? This never hurt anybody."

"Oh, Morris, Morris, thank God Mama is not alive today, to hear you talk like this. What would she say, she should rest in peace?"

"I know what she would say," I say. "She would say you are a big blabbermouth and mind your own business. Go back to your television already, Bessie, you are spoiling the whole Nielsen rating there, in Long Island. And do me a favor. Give somebody else a chance with your telephone business. There's other members of the family. Good-by."

Well, you think *this* is the end, maybe? Comes in now Larry, he's got a telegram. "It's from Martin's in Toledo," he says. "They want to reorder 734. They'll take a run of sizes in all shades if they can have an exclusive for Toledo."

"No exclusives," I say. "They want to order like everybody else, all right. If not, not."

"That's what I figured," he says.

"So?" And I see he's still standing, I know I got to have another interview with the press. "What else is on your mind, Larry?"

"I hear you tied one on at Longchamps last night," he says.

"That was only the beginning," I say. "What a night. Fireworks. The rockets are still going off in my head."

So he looks at me like he's thinking, should he send for a doctor, the looney bin, the police, or what? I say, "What's the matter, Larry? What are you looking so stunned?"

"Well, I guess I'm a little shocked," he says.

"Shocked? Why are you shocked? You never got drunk in your life? You were never out with a woman?"

"Yes, but that's me," he says. "Doesn't seem to go with you, somehow."

"I see. For you it's all right. For me, you are becoming a moralist. Some philosophy."

"Morris," he says, "I'm a bachelor——"

"So who stops you from getting married?"

"That's not the point. But you *are* married. You've got a home, a family——"

"So what?" I say. "Listen, you said yourself, vanilla, vanilla—a man gets tired. He wants to try sometimes a little pistachio."

269

"Okay," he says. "But it shouldn't be flavored with cyanide. Tell me one thing. This was Miss Youssem you were out with?"

"Who told you?" I say.

"What's the difference? A little bird told me."

"That is some little bird," I say. "He's got a bicycle."

"Morris," he says, "you don't realize, you're older than I am but you're just a babe in the woods at this stuff. This could be dynamite. You want to have a little fling, okay. I'll fix you up with a couple of addresses——"

"Don't be a fool, Larry," I say. I'm tired of the nonsense. A joke's a joke. "Go down to Pinsky's Poolroom," I say, "and lecture there to the bookies. Maybe they are interested in your valuable opinions on sex."

Well, how do you like it? Once in twenty-seven years I went on a big escapade. For dinner with my designer. But you think this is the end yet? Wait.

All of a sudden, in the shop, it's like—what is the name of those two families in the South, they are always fighting? Yeah, the Hatfields and McCoys. We had in our neighborhood, in the old days on Delancey Street, something like it with the Ginsburgs and the Feitelbaums. But you wouldn't know. Anyway, suppose all of a sudden they should kiss and make up? Well, this is now Larry with Miss Youssem. He's got nothing but good things to say about her styles, she is the greatest designer in the world, when he goes into the designing room it's not to pick a fight, it's to tell her a little story, pay her compliments, bring her a coke from downstairs—a regular hon-and-dearie situation.

270

Well, Miss Youssem, I suppose, is in seventh heaven. But what is the big change with Larry? I'm curious. I call him in, I say, "How about going on the road, Larry?"

He gives me a quick look, suspicious—you know in the Bible, the story about David and Bathsheba? He sent away the husband to war, to get rid of him?

"What'll I go with?" he says. "We haven't got anything to show yet."

"So make a survey," I tell him.

"Of what?"

"Anything," I say. "Conditions. Everybody is making surveys; we could make one too."

"Come on, Morris," he says. "What's the gag?"

"No gag. But you got nothing to do here. No customers are coming in now——"

"Morris," he says, "why don't *you* go away for a while? Take your wife for a little vacation to Miami. You need a rest."

"You said it, I need a rest. But not what you think. All right, don't go on the road. But do me a favor. Go to Jamaica at least. Or Belmont. Or brush up a little on your pool. You're hanging around the shop all day, you make everybody nervous."

So he lights up a cigarette, he takes a big puff. "Morris," he says, "I like my job but I'm putting you on notice. You want to make a fool of yourself over Miss Youssem, you'll have to get past me. You can fire me. But I'm not going on the road." And he walks out.

How do you like this? A regular vaudeville show. I don't know whether to laugh or cry. Larry Kogen appoints

271

himself my guardian. Even if it costs him his job, he is
going to save me from myself. What do you say? Is this
loyalty, or not?

But then I'm starting to think. Maybe it's not just
loyalty. Like I told you, there is something about Miss
Youssem creeps into your skin. I don't know—class, something, this is a very unusual woman. Believe me, a man
knows a little the score, this type is more sexy a thousand
times than the new type girls, the cleavage starts at the
eyebrows. Maybe, with Larry, all the fighting, the teasing
before, it's like in the movies, it just shows he's really
attracted.

So I'm getting now a little worried. She's not a kid,
Miss Youssem, like that Italian model wanted to jump out
from a window, still and all, with the emotions, a woman,
you never know what could happen. Maybe the whole
thing will work out yet into a tragedy and I will be responsible. Or maybe, on the other hand, they will get so
lovey-dovey, they will decide what do they need me,
they'll make a partnership, go into business for themselves. Wouldn't be the first time it happened in our business, a salesman and a designer. A fine ending this would
be for a joke, no? I could be laughing out of the other
side of my face.

That evening, I come home for dinner, Sophie is on the
phone a half-hour with my daughter-in-law, Marie. She
comes to the table finally, I say, "What was the big discussion?"

"Nothing," she says. "She's lonesome for Harold. She's
getting new curtains for the bedroom. She saw a dress at

Bonwit's that looks like your style 706. And she's going to the doctor tomorrow."

"Is she pregnant?" Jenny says.

"Jenny, this is your business?" I say.

"Morris," my wife says, she gives Jenny a private look, I am not a member of this club. "This is every woman's business."

"Woman," I say. "Sixteen years old. She hasn't got time?"

Jenny gives me now also a look, what am I butting in this conversation, she says, "Are they trying?"

So I throw down my napkin. "Listen," I say, "if this discussion does not stop this minute I'm leaving the table."

"Oh, Pop," Jenny says. "Stop acting like Mr. Barrett of Wimpole Street."

"I am Mr. Seidman from Delancey Street and I still don't have to hear such discussions from a sixteen-year-old girl."

"For heaven's sake," Jenny says, "everybody in this house is so scared of sex."

"Is that so?" I say. "So what are you doing here, my fair lady? If I'm so scared?"

Our maid, Gladys, is serving the soup, she puts a hand to her head, she says, "What is this world coming to, talking like that in front of children." She's old-fashioned, Gladys, like me, she can't get used. So she goes back now to the kitchen, shaking the head, she's crossing herself there, I suppose. Jenny is laughing, she says, "You're cute, Pop. But oh, boy." And she makes with her fingers in the air, a big square.

"That's enough, Jenny," my wife says.

"Well, good grief, Mom. I asked a simple question about mating and reproduction——"

"Mating and reproduction," I say. "Beautiful words. For a horse doctor. Where is the mystery, the emotion——"

"You don't have to have a head full of lemon meringue," my Jenny says, "to feel emotion. If you're normal you have it. There's no point getting neurotic about it."

"I see. Falling in love is now a neurosis?"

"Morris," my wife says.

"It's chemistry," Jenny says. "Like everything else."

"Yeah? So tell me," I say. "This boy, Marvin Block, he's been around here lately. What is his formula? How much adrenalin and how much seltzer?"

So Jenny is blushing, finally, and she says, "Very droll," like a Broadway actress and Sophie says, "That's enough, there's too much hostility going on here," and finished, the discussion.

Hostility. Another word from the psychology book. This is now the whole story. Psychology and chemistry. I'll ask you a foolish question, you're a writer. What happened to sentiment in the world? The du Pont people are working on it maybe, they'll sell it soon in rolls like cellophane or Scotch tape? Seriously, what's going to be with the children growing up? From where is going to come the beauty in their life, the poetry? From nuclear fission? From Mr. Freud? Take with writing for instance. All right, on television I could understand. There's no time. Bing bang, the half-hour is over, they got to sell you beer, soap, cigarettes. For this they got to save a little, the emotion. Romeo should only have been holding in his arms a piece of soap instead of Juliet, you would have heard some real speeches!

And what's with the books? I'm only imagining it was different in my days? Dickens, Victor Hugo, Dumas—what happened to romance, altogether? Could you find somewheres a regular love story, should touch your heart a little? Like they called it in the old days, the Tender Passion? I should only say this to my Jenny, she would give me a look like she's ready to vomit. But what's wrong with it, a man meets a woman, he should make a nice speech, with a little emotion in his heart? No. Right away, wisecracks. Or first thing, the hero knocks the girl down, he says, "Let's understand each other, baby." Kiss Me Deadly. Kill Me Lovely. Love Me Dreadful. This is the kind of literature Larry and my models are improving their minds. And the movies? You shouldn't be insulted I'm saying this, but looks to me either they are making from sex a joke, it's embarrassing, or else, I don't know, some kind of war is going on between a man and a woman, when they come together finally for a kiss, the mouths are open, on the big screen it's half a block long, you could see the tongues, like from a cow, this is not love any more, this is delicatessen.

I don't know, it's like people would be afraid nowadays to admit they got inside them a little feeling, what we used to say, in my days, the Finer Things in Life. Why are they afraid? It's something to be ashamed?

Well, anyway, I'm wondering what's going to be the upshot between Miss Youssem and Larry, I haven't got long to wait. On Saturday she comes into my office, she's holding a dress she wants to show me but I see she don't really want to talk about the dress, there's something else on her mind. So I say, finally, "What is it, Miss Youssem? You got something you want to discuss?"

"Yes, I'd like to," she says. "It's personal. Do you mind?"

"We're friends, no?" I say. "Why should I mind?"

"You remember we talked about Larry Kogen?"

"Yes. You still want to teach him a lesson?"

She gives a smile, a little one, to the side, and she says, "He's become very attentive. I don't know what occasioned the change——"

"Could be spring is in the air," I say. "Could be he woke up, realized you are a very attractive woman. He's not entirely stupid."

So she doesn't say thank you, she doesn't smile now, nothing, she just stands there, there's a little pleat in her forehead. "He's made me an offer," she says.

I look at her, I can't believe it. Last week, a foolish little fantasy, all of a sudden it's a fact. "What kind of an offer?" I ask her. "He wants to go in business with you?"

She smiles. Kind of a smile. "No, he's not that far gone," she says. "He wants me to go to Atlantic City with him for the week end."

Nu, this is Larry all over. He starts a job, he really puts his heart in it. He's going to keep me pure, even if he's got to be a bum to do it. "So?" I say. "You want my congratulations?"

"You don't approve," she says.

"Miss Youssem," I say, "I'm your employer, not your

276

guardian. Who am I to approve or not approve? You got to figure out for yourself, what is best for you."

"Wouldn't it be a wonderful life," she says, "if we could always figure out what was best for us? No regrets, no hang-overs, no wasted years?"

"It's not such a big problem, Miss Youssem," I say. "You just got to stick to fundamentals. What's best is what's right. And a person is normal, he knows what is right, if he thinks about it a little."

"Well, I guess it's easier for some people than others," she says, and she turns around, she's going to the door.

"So you're going?" I say.

"No, I'm not," she says. She's not looking at me. "I find I have a previous engagement. I'm going home and feed my cat. And then I'm going to an Italian movie, down the street."

"Which Italian movie?" I say, I don't know what else to say.

"*La Traviata*," she says. "I like sad movies. I love to cry in Italian. It makes me feel educated."

She gives me again the crooked smile and she goes out and I'm sitting there, I'll tell you the truth, I'm a little stunned. Can you imagine, a person could start up such a thing, just from being sarcastic, he's annoyed, people are being such busybodies?

In the afternoon, Sophie calls up, she wants to know when I'm going to be home. There's a lecture by a famous lady psychologist who spent twenty-five years in Africa, she was studying there the sexual behavior of savages. She could have saved herself some carfare and settled

277

down on Seventh Avenue. She would also have got herself an earful. Anyway, the lecture is seven o'clock, Sophie wants to have an early dinner and go.

"I got a better idea," I say, "there's *La Traviata* playing at the Translux. Come down, we'll have a bite in Longchamps, we'll see the picture and afterwards I will buy you a soda. A great big chocolate soda."

"I want to hear this woman," she says. "She's supposed to be brilliant."

"Well, on this basis," I say, "I can't compete. What's with Jenny? Maybe she would like to go to the movie with me?"

So she asks her. No. Jenny doesn't want to go. *La Traviata* is corny, the story, the music is molasses and ipecac and besides she's got a meeting of her Saturday Afternoon Club.

I hang up and go out into the shop to see if Miss Youssem is still there. She's in her office, combing her hair. "You want company?" I say. She turns around, she don't understand. "*La Traviata,*" I say. "I got a chance to see it. My wife don't like foreign pictures and she's going to a lecture. Do you mind if I accompany you?"

"I'd love it," she says. "Will you have a bite with me first, at my place?"

"You want to bother?" I say. "We could eat somewhere."

"The last time we did that," she says, "it practically hit the front page of *Women's Wear.*"

"You heard?" I say.

"Indirectly."

"I know," I say. "A little bird told you. Flies to Atlantic City week ends."

So she laughs, like it would hurt her a little, and she says, "Anyway, I love to cook and I never have an occasion. Please let me. If you'll just stop with me while I pick up a few things."

She stops first in a liquor store. "Miss Youssem," I say, "we're going to *dine* again? Or this time we're going to eat something too?"

She gives me a comical look. "You have me down for a real lush," she says. "I just thought we'd have some wine, with dinner."

We go next to a fancy delicatessen, on the shelf there's a regular UN from cans, she picks up a couple things, truffles from France, lobster from Africa, cheese from Denmark, she won't let me pay, nothing, this is her party. We go to her apartment, it's very fine, fixed up modern, all the conveniences for a fine life, books, pictures, hi-fi, and there's her cat standing like a statue on the carpet, he looks me over very good, waits until I sit down, then he jumps on my lap, Miss Youssem puts a glass with whisky in my hand, turns on the phonograph and goes into the kitchen, and I'm sitting there like a Man of Distinction, with a Siamese cat yet on my lap. My sister Bessie should see this picture!

Well, what should I tell you, Miss Youssem fixed up a little snack with the lobster, Chambord couldn't do better. We had the wine, very tasty, and she gave me with it a little travelogue from wines, what kind goes with what, and where, I'm very glad to have the information, even

279

though in my circle, if you squeeze in a little seltzer with some Manischewitz you would never go wrong. But I remember I looked at the label, Val Polichella, and the light coming in slanty through the window, the way it matched the wine in the glass and inside of me such a strange feeling, how mysterious it is, life, how good it's been to me and how much I missed. Could you understand this, what I'm saying?

She brings in now a little machine, she got it in Italy, to make coffee, a special kind, *cappucino*, very strong but with some hot milk it's delicious. She's telling me meanwhile how she lived for a couple of years in Rome after the war and she met there a young man, Italian, an artist, she was very much in love with him. But something happened—they broke up. She doesn't make from it a sad story. "You know what I miss most about that whole wonderful time?" she says. "The talk. I've never really got used to living without it, since. Men don't talk to you here. They talk at you, or around you. They promote, or argue, or wisecrack." She gives me a smile. "You'd love Italy," she says. "You'd be right at home there."

"You mean I'm talking too much?" I say.

"I mean I'm having a wonderful time. Please don't stop." And she gives me some more coffee. So you know me by now, I don't need too much encouragement and it's such a sympathetic atmosphere, pretty soon I'm telling her things I haven't thought of them for years, the early days on Delancey Street, the struggles, the first time I wrote in night school a composition entirely in English: "An Immigrant Looks at America." My teacher, I remember her so well, Miss Farrell, a very fine woman, she read it to the

280

class and she told me afterwards she was proud of me, I had the soul of an artist. Made a big impression on my mind.

Well, we're talking like this, I'm drinking now a little brandy, I don't realize how the time is going by, the phone rings, I look at my watch. Nearly ten o'clock. Miss Youssem answers the phone, this is the conversation I hear: "Hello . . . Oh yes . . . Yes, I have . . . Quite sure, thank you . . . There isn't anything to discuss, and I'd rather not listen to one of your monologues . . . No, I'm sorry . . . No, please, I won't be here . . . Good-by."

She comes back. "That was Larry," she says. She sits down, I see she is a little pale. "He wanted to know if I had company."

"Poor boy," I say. "He must be very confused. When a boy like Larry wants to be in the first place a Casanova, and on top of this also a Boy Scout—"

She don't understand what I'm saying, of course, and maybe it's better she shouldn't. "You got any regrets?" I say.

She shakes her head. "He wanted to know what I was doing tomorrow," she says.

"So?" I say. "What are you doing tomorrow?"

"Well," she gives me the crooked little smile, her specialty, "I'll get up about ten, bathe, have a leisurely breakfast and then maybe do a few of the galleries."

"You want company?"

She looks at me. "You still feel you have to bolster my morale?"

"How do you know it's not *my* morale needs bolstering?" I say. She looks at me, I see there's tears in her eyes.

281

"What are you thinking?" I ask her.

"That you went to a very good night school. Too bad some people couldn't take the same course." She pokes with a handkerchief at her eyes. "The people in the shop should see me now," she says. "Rena Youssem, holder of the Cannes Festival Award for cockeyed design."

Well, I couldn't explain you exactly how, why, seemed very natural at the time, could be I was a little drunk, anyway I'm holding her in my arms.

"Still bothers you," I say, "what Larry thinks?"

She's got her head against my shoulder, like a child, and she turns her face up to me for a kiss. Long ago when she first came in the shop and the idea would come sometimes in my mind, you know the way a man is always wondering, not that he's going to do anything, just wondering, I would imagine to kiss her would be like a nice fresh lettuce from the icebox. Well, more wrong I couldn't be. Her lips are warm, sweet, smooth, and her figure also, it's so sweet, thin, but not too thin—well, what should I tell you, I'm not a writer but it's a pretty wonderful feeling I got, holding her in my arms. Like I would be twenty years old again and there's a whole new lifetime ahead of me, adventure, romance, I don't know what.

So I say, "Miss Youssem, darling, I think we still got time for the movie, and afterwards I would like to buy you a beautiful chocolate soda." And she doesn't say anything, she gets her coat and comes back, we go out, in the elevator she puts out her hand to me and I hold it, it's such a good feeling, so strong, I couldn't describe it. Like everything I missed in my life would be there. The shows I never saw when I wanted, the girls I didn't take for walks in the park when I was a young man working in a stationery store, the violinist I didn't become, I used to dream of it a little, long ago.

We come out of the building, a taxi is there, who gets out? Larry. He's wearing a dark coat and hat, he looks very fine. He is a very spiffy dresser, Larry.

"Well, Morris," he says. "Fancy meeting you here."

"What's with you?" I say. "You're back from Atlantic City?"

"Change of plans," he says. "Mind if I join you? All of a sudden my hotel is the loneliest place in town."

"What happened to the little black book?" I say.

"I mislaid it." He's looking at Miss Youssem and she's looking at him, I see she's got that pale look in her face again.

"We're just going to a movie," she says.

"Just what I feel like," he says. "A good movie."

"I don't think this would interest you," she says, "it's *Traviata*."

"Why don't you come down off your high horse?" he says.

"Why don't you stop being so beastly?" she says.

"Well, maybe if you'd give me a chance," he says.

All of a sudden I feel as if they don't even know I'm there any more. I could walk away, they wouldn't even miss me.

"Miss Youssem," I say, "I just realized. It's after ten. By the time I get home will be after eleven. Maybe I'll better skip the movie." I'm waiting to see will she give me an argument.

"That's a good idea, Morris," Larry says, "get yourself

a good night's sleep. I'll give you a synopsis on Monday."

"Thank you very much," I say. A synopsis I need. I got a pretty good synopsis of the whole situation. To Miss Youssem I say, "You want I should stay, I'll stay."

"No," she says. "It'll be long after midnight when we get out. I'm sure Mrs. Seidman would be concerned."

Well, I'm driving home, I got to laugh a little, but actually I'm feeling kind of depressed. Maybe if Joe Wachtel's analyst would be there I would take from him thirty-five dollars' worth. A woman gives me a kiss. She's lonely and I acted toward her a little human, so she's grateful. So right away I got to make from it a federal case. Sitting there in the apartment, with that funny light, seeing myself altogether different, Jascha Seidman with a fiddle under my chin, Filippo Seidman with a beret, in the Via Marguta, with an easel, drinking little cups of coffee the whole day. Such a fool. A fine production I made of my life altogether. From all the high ideas, An Immigrant Looks at America, what did I become? A tailor. All right, it's got a fancier name. Dress manufacturer. It's still a tailor.

I come into the house, Sophie is still up, reading. "How was the lecture?" I say.

"I didn't go," she says.

"No? Why not?"

"Just so. How was the movie?"

"It was a movie. *Traviata*."

"Did you go alone?"

"You're checking again, Sophie?"

"I'm just asking a question."

284

"You're asking? Or you got already a report from your FBI?"

"I don't need the FBI," she says. "You've got lipstick on your collar."

How do you like that? Once in thirty years. Is this justice?

"So what?" I say. "Maybe it's your lipstick."

"Morris," she says, "I want to know one thing. Are you going to make a career of solving Miss Youssem's problems?"

"Why not? We'll have two psychologists in the family instead of one."

"When I took up psychology," she says, "it was because I wanted to be a better mother, a better wife, a better person. I didn't know you resented it."

So all of a sudden I'm feeling like a dog but what can I do about it? I got nothing to say.

"You might have said something," she says. "After twenty-seven years there ought to be some communication at least."

"For heaven's sake, Sophie," I say, "don't make a *tsimmess*. Once in twenty-seven years I spend an evening away from the house, talking to my designer——"

So she starts to cry.

"Sophie," I say. "Please don't turn on the faucet."

"Things can happen to a relationship," she says, crying louder. "I'm not blaming you. If only it hadn't happened the night I find out I'm going to be——" and she puts her face in the pillow.

It's like I would get a clop on the head. I think, God

285

knows what happened, she got bad news from the doctor or something. I throw myself down by the bed, I say, "For God's sake, Sophie, what is it? Don't punish me. I didn't do anything. A woman was upset, she was grateful I showed her a little understanding, so she put her head on my shoulder a minute, like a child, and she got some lipstick on my collar. So you're going to make a regular East Lynne from this situation? Sophie, please, tell me what is it?"

So she turns around. "Marie is pregnant," she says.

"My goodness," I say. "When? When did this happen?"

"I couldn't tell you," she says. "You'll have to ask your son."

"I mean, when did you find out?"

"Tonight. Marie called up, dinnertime. The doctor just gave her the report."

"Well, we got to do something, Sophie. We got to have a drink at least." I get up, I'm dizzy, too much emotion or something, I got to hold onto the bedpost.

"Never mind the drink," she says. "You had enough already. I can tell. Fine thing. In your old age you've got to become a souse."

"Sophie," I say, "it's really true? Grandparents?"

I look at her face, I can't believe it. Couldn't be I'm nearly fifty years old. It's only yesterday my wife told me she was expecting. Now my son is going to be a father?

"What's the matter?" she says.

"You should see your face," I say. "You would think you are the one." So she blushes and I think, how wonderful. I'm going to be a grandpa and I got a wife who still blushes. And how beautiful she looks. A miracle, how a woman could keep the looks, so many years.

"You're going to be a very beautiful grandma," I say.

"Take off the shirt at least," she says. "I can't stand to look at the lipstick."

"This is the result of ten years studying psychology?" I say. "You're jealous of Miss Youssem?"

"Studying psychology is not supposed to turn you into a stick. Don't you think I've got reason to be jealous?"

"Sophie, I got a wonderful idea," I say. "How's about I should answer that question in Miami Beach?"

Well, so what do you think? I got to go to an analyst? What do you say—the analysts should come to me? Well, you are very kind but I think I'll stick to the dress business.

Larry? Oh, yes, I got to tell you. Next day, Monday, he comes into the shop, whistling, cheerful like a bird. He says to me, "Morris, did you see that picture? *Traviata?*"

"I saw the opera many times," I tell him. "You don't have to give me a synopsis."

"No, but how about that deathbed scene? When she's lying there, dying of consumption, and that guy comes in, I'm telling you, I thought they'd have to carry me out. I cried like a baby."

"Well, there is still hope for you, Larry," I say.

"Yeah, that's what Rena says." He gives me a big grin. "She's going to reform me. We're flying to Havana next week end."

"Well, this is certainly a step in the right direction," I say. "It's too bad they closed up the Barbary Coast. You could take there a Ph.D."

"You don't understand, Morris," he says. "We're getting married. Baby," he says, he claps me on the cheeks with both hands, "wait till you see the line you get out *next* season."

So I'm waiting. The baby? Please. Don't be in such a hurry. Takes time to produce a baby. Almost as much as a movie. Marie is only pregnant four months.

Yes, now Miss Youssem is going to be married, maybe there'll be less temperament, she'll relax and I'll have a little peace in the place. After all, Samson and me, we're getting to be pretty old dogs. And now that I'm going to be a grandfather, I would like to take it a little easy now. Save myself a little. I want to be around when my grandson is deciding which college to go to. Not that I'm going to mix in. No sir. I learned my lesson from my own boy. But tell me, you know something about Princeton? I understand they got there a wonderful school for science and, after all, these days, science is really the big thing. Don't you think so?